"A new g[...]ll tilt on the [...]nd poetic voic[...] of Barbados. [...]LL

"[An] imp[...]al, narrative voice. Mr. Lovell, who was born in Barbados in 1955, has a sharp eye for the extraordinary tropical land-scape and the eccentricities of his characters."
—*The New York Times Book Review*

"Lovell gives this history-within-a-history an authentic tone by keeping the plot moving and the writing simple."
—*Orlando Sentinel*

"Snuggle up in your most comfortable spot when you start reading *Fire in the Canes*. You soon will be swept away by the magic of Glenville Lovell's prose as he takes you on a journey to a fictional West Indian island at the turn of the century. The author tells his tale with power and elegance, enthralling readers in much the same way that his protagonist, Prince Johnson, mesmerizes the other characters in the book."
—*Emerge*

"A spirited tale of the post-slavery West Indies . . . an effective evocation of lush tropical nights . . . a promising debut."
—*Kirkus Reviews*

"A fascinating epic, full of lively characters, Caribbean history and African spiritualism."
—*IFA News*

"First novelist Lovell joins the ranks of such writers of magic realism as Alejo Carpentier with this novel . . . Lovell's story rushes onward at full speed, and it is difficult to separate magic from reality, which adds even more to the intrigue of this brilliantly crafted tale. Highly recommended."
—*Library Journal*

FIRE
in the
CANES

Glenville Lovell

𝓑

BERKLEY BOOKS, NEW YORK

FIRE IN THE CANES

A Berkley Book / published by arrangement with
Soho Press, Inc.

PRINTING HISTORY
Soho Press edition published 1995
Berkley edition / October 1997

The Putnam Berkley World Wide Web site address is
http://www.berkley.com

ISBN: 0-425-16040-8

BERKLEY®
Berkley Books are published by The Berkley Publishing Group,
a member of Penguin Putnam Inc.,
200 Madison Avenue, New York, New York 10016.
BERKLEY and the "B" design
are trademarks belonging to Berkley Publishing Corporation.

PRINTED IN THE UNITED STATES OF AMERICA

10 9 8 7 6 5 4 3 2 1

For my daughter, Courtney:
I cherish you.

ACKNOWLEDGMENTS

Many thanks to my mother, Ianthe, for sharing her memories, to my lovely wife, Karen, for her patience, love and support, to Etha for believing and to Leslie Garis for her words of encouragement, to Janet and Pamela for their valued critique; and to Laura Hruska and the great team at Soho for their tireless efforts.

FIRE
in the
CANES

Glenville Lovell

ONE

When Peata arrived in the village of Monkey Road with her daughter, Midra, in April of 1894 to take over the house of a sister who had left the island, she'd done so quietly. Moving into a small village without becoming a spectacle was not easy, but they managed to avoid gawkers by arriving in the night. They had been living in her sister's house almost a week before anyone realized they had come to stay. The reason for their secrecy was simple. It had been a long time since she'd lived in a small village, not since she was a girl, and before Peata let herself loose on the village she wanted to get a feel for the people, especially the men.

During that first week in Monkey Road—a week of no moonlight—she moved around the village after nightfall listening to the hope-glazed whispers of the men who gathered around smut-lamps to debate the latest village events and to send their dreams of a more prosperous and exciting life sailing heaven-bound on the thin smoke from their lamps. So the first time Peata skipped out of the house during daylight in one of her green satin dresses, she got the reception she expected. Walking with her head held

1

high, her eyes laughing, she seemed to be sending an invitation to every man she passed. An invitation to pleasure, to beauty; a chance to fulfill their deepest fantasies. It was as if the Pied Piper had swept into the village. Grown men and young boys alike began to follow her, not knowing or caring where she was leading them. When she reached her house and disappeared inside, they waited to see if she would come out again. As the sun began to set, the boys went home while the men returned to their benches under shack-shack trees to debate whether what they had witnessed was an apparition, still hoping the evanescent green spirit would pass their way again. They might have consulted Pa Daniel, the spiritual father and founder of the village, respected for his knowledge of spiritual and temporal matters, but nobody dared.

Monkey Road soon discovered that Peata and her daughter had not come there to add themselves to the toll of women shackled to the plantation nearby. The women in the village began to show their jealousy of Peata by warning their men that she was a whore from town come to steal their money. "A high yella woman with a young daughter, without a job, without a man in the house, wearing them kinda clothes could only be doing one thing to get by," they swore. "She must be some white man mistress," they'd say, rolling their eyes. But this kind of talk only made the men more curious about Peata.

Peata brushed aside the gossip; it did not change the way she paraded through the village. Her laughter still echoed her exuberant spirit, and she still wore clothes so rich in color and cloth that she seemed to have floated down from the dew-covered blossoms of the flamboyant tree. And the men still waited outside her house—sometimes singly, sometimes in groups—to catch her smile before going off to work the fields in the morning or, after work, before going home to vexed wives or the loneliness of an empty house.

Brandon Fields was only thirteen years old but whenever he saw her, he would stop and wait until she passed. In his dreams this gay woman was a butterfly on a hibiscus, floating down to kiss him until he turned into the sun. Brandon knew it wasn't just the clothes that made her different from the other women in Monkey Road, or her high-pitched laugh, like a bird singing. It was also the way she held her head: so high that it appeared to be suspended in the air. The other women all walked with their heads down, like duppies searching for the future.

Peata's love for black pudding allowed Brandon to get a better look at her; it brought her to his house every Saturday. That was when his mother made black pudding for an eager clientele, some of whom walked as far as three miles to buy what was considered to be the finest black pudding around. Even the white people sent their maids to buy Mabel Fields' black pudding.

When she came to his house, Brandon would sit and gaze at Peata's ample body. If she caught him staring, she would only smile and say something to make him laugh, such as "Boy, you like me or what?"

Peata was an immaculate combination of opposites, her smooth milky skin contrasting with her full lips, expansive nose, and square chin. Although she spent a lot of time in the sun, she always walked with a parasol. From the day Brandon saw her he yearned to touch her skin, to see if it was as soft as it looked. But to Brandon the most incredible thing about Peata was her timing. Even his mother marveled at how she always seemed to arrive at their house just as the first thin serpents of pig's belly filled with grated sweet potato, blood, and spices came coiling out of the pots. Never a second before, nor a second after, no matter what time Mabel finished her black pudding, whether early in the morning or late in the evening.

One day while she was sitting in his mother's yard eating black pudding, she called him over.

GLENVILLE LOVELL

"Touch me," she said. "Go ahead."

Surprised, he stepped back.

"You's a man, ain't ya?" she said with a laugh. "I ain't meet a man who didn't want to touch me. You not go disappoint me, eh?"

Ignoring his mother, who frowned from the other end of the yard, he put his hand on Peata's face, letting it linger for what felt like an eternity before he escaped from the yard to brag to his friends Pudge and Kanga that he had touched the skin of the white woman. Pudge, who had this theory that white people smelled different, did not believe him even after he let them smell his hand. "She ain't really no white woman, anyway," Pudge said. "She yella. Besides, I like her daughter better." And Kanga agreed.

On the surface Midra was the opposite of her mother. As fair as Peata was, Midra was dark, a dark incipient version of her mother. Her hair was short, and she did not braid it in cornrows like the other girls her age, but left it unruly and uncombed to frame her warm, large eyes and solid, sculptured nose. In the evening, when the sky still burned, her skin seemed to glow under the mauve-sprinkled sky. By the time she was thirteen, Midra's body already hinted at the ampleness of her mother's, and her smile had taken on a haunting quality. Now that she was fifteen, men were thinking of ways to seduce her.

For all her luxuriant appearance the Midra who came to Monkey Road was a lonely girl. She did not make friends easily with the other girls in the village, most of whom worked on the plantation. Midra lived in a world of her own making. A dreamworld where she spoke to her father "across the sea." He was so black that his skin glowed, her mother had told her, and one day he'd disappeared across the sea. "I don't have nothin' more to say 'bout that man," she had told Midra, "so don't ask." But in Midra's dreamworld her father returned, bringing her gifts of perfume and beautiful clothes. He was a giant with tree branches for arms, so large that they could cover her completely. There was one thing about this father she did not like: he could not speak. But he listened.

Except for the occasional trip to Mabel's to pick up black pudding for Peata and an equally rare visit to the butcher to collect bull's testicles—another one of her mother's favorite dishes—Midra hardly left the house. On the rare occasions when she did so, her movements were as carefully anticipated and watched as her mother's by the men-in-waiting of Monkey Road.

Midra did not dress in gaudy colors like her mother. Her dresses, made of plain but well-pressed cotton, flowed to her ankles in the same unruly way she wore her hair. When a high wind sneaked under the material, filling it like a balloon, attempting to lift her off the ground, she never seemed concerned with the gravity-defying desires of the dress as it flew above her head revealing white cotton bloomers. In one smooth motion she'd haul the thing in, but if it battled back, she'd leave the dress swimming above her head until the wind released it. Those moments, moments of ephemeral delight to men waiting under trees on broken benches serving up their daydreams to a blistering sun, rendered Midra a yielding firefly in their night dreams. And to none more so than to Brandon Fields.

Brandon had heard of Midra long before he met her. His friends—Kanga, who like him was an apprentice blacksmith, and Pudge, an apprentice tinsmith—had chanced to see her drawing water from the well and had described her beauty to him. By the time he first saw her as she came to buy black pudding for her mother, he was already caught in her spell. After setting eyes on Midra, he no longer found her mother so bewitching. The next day as they were taking the sheep to graze, he declared his love for Midra to Kanga. But over a year passed before he uttered a word to her— partly because of his own awe, partly because the mother and daughter disappeared from the village after only six months there. Then when he had almost gotten Midra out of his mind, they came back, with a baby.

He spoke to her for the first time one evening when he went to Small Paul's next door with some scraps for his neighbor's pigs. After feeding them, Brandon went into the house hoping to catch Small Paul in the mood to tell a story. He found Midra there patiently curled up in the polished chair in the front house, breast-feeding her baby. Wearing a pale gray dress, her unbridled hair flying free as always, she did not flinch when she saw him staring at her exposed breast. The baby took his mouth away for a moment, and her nipple dazzled Brandon. Feeling a sudden intense stirring in his crotch, he shifted his gaze to her feet, observing her even toes and thickly muscled ankles. In all his young life he'd never been so excited—even more than the time Gunny's girlfriend had let him feel the rubbery wetness between her legs. In the musty room the luster of Midra's skin shone, and she seemed even more beautiful than before. He asked her if she knew where Small Paul was, but she took no notice of him, seeming to be lost in a world of her own.

He went into the next room, where he found Small Paul asleep. On a chair next to the hammock was a bowl of eddoes and steamed dumplings, half-eaten. He eased himself out of the room, not wanting to wake the slender, bushy-headed old man, whose silvery white hair grew like rope down his back and over his forehead, hanging over the edge of the hammock like the tendrils of the bearded-fig tree. When he returned, Midra had not moved. Hoping she would glance up and notice him, Brandon hovered over her like a hummingbird. But she continued to ignore him, so he finally perched on the arm of the chair opposite her and spoke again.

"Smalley's asleep," he muttered timidly.

Her eyes rested on his dark face. Brandon stretched his neck, hoping he could make his head touch the low ceiling. She didn't seem to notice how long and smooth his neck was, however, as her eyes clouded with a look of extreme boredom.

"Smalley's asleep," he repeated.

"So?"

Her abrupt tone did not discourage him.

Brandon looked at the infant in her arms.

"What's his name?"

The baby had finished his feeding. She wiped her nipple clean of spittle before returning it to her bodice. She sat the baby upright in her lap and began to rub his back somewhere between his tiny shoulder blades. The baby belched.

"What the baby name?" he said again.

"He ain't got no name."

"He ain't got no name?" Brandon paused. "So what you call him?"

"I don't have to call him nothin'. He mine."

"What your mother call him?"

"Ask my mother."

He could not think of anything else to say. She began to rock the baby. Brandon rose from the chair. As he left the room, he noticed her thin, seraphic fingers clutching the baby tightly.

He was pleased with himself. At least she'd said something to him. That's more than his friends Pudge and Kanga had gotten. He did not ask the question he had wanted to ask: What was she doing there? For now, he was glad she had spoken. There was hope.

TWO

At six that Friday morning the fowlcock sounded his trumpet only four times, and Mabel Fields nearly jumped out of her skin. She sprang from the bed, ran to the kitchen window, and pushed it open, her roving eyes searching the yard for the gold and black rooster that announced a fresh day to the village of Monkey Road. It stood in the middle of the yard, its black plume poised. But silent. Mabel waited. The hush continued. The fifth and sixth notes she was waiting for did not come. She padded back to the bedroom where her husband, Darnlee, was still asleep.

"The cock only crow four this morning," she said, shaking him.

He opened one eye for a second, rolled over onto his stomach, and went back to sleep. Getting up in the morning was never easy for Darnlee. But his wife had developed a strategy to get him out of bed in time for work whenever he threatened to sleep past six o'clock. She poked him hard in the tender spot between his ribs. This tactic had never failed her, and it worked again to perfection. He opened both eyes this time and bolted upright.

"The cock only crow four," Mabel said again.

"Good for the cock," he muttered.

He closed his eyes but Mabel jabbed him, this time harder. So hard, in fact, it made him squeal.

This particular fowlcock, a gift from their next-door neighbor, Small Paul, would always crow three times, then after a minute's pause it would crow three more times, for a total of six. Six times at six o'clock. That was its ritual. Only once before had it deviated in all the years she had owned it: it had crowed four times, and at midday her mother had collapsed and died. So now she felt the least her husband could do was wake up and reassure her that he was all right.

She jabbed him again.

"Get up, Darnlee. Get up, man! Get up!"

Darnlee sucked his teeth and opened his eyes, trying to focus. He pulled himself up from the newly filled grass bed, which made a rustling noise, and scratched his head.

"What time it is?" he asked, hoping it was no later than five o'clock, which would give him time for some early morning fooling around with his wife or, failing that, at least another hour of sleep before he had to leave for work. Mabel was her most passionate early in the morning, and from the look of things the fowlcock had already stirred her up. He smiled. After fifteen years together, waking up to Mabel in the morning was still the best part of his life.

"It's six o'clock," Mabel said.

"Six? You sure?"

"Of course I sure. That's why I wake you. The cock only crow four, and that ain't right."

"The cock got a right to crow how much he want. He's a man, ain't he? Maybe he vex 'cause he got to get up to crow for people like you and me who can't afford a clock."

Darnlee laughed and tried to pull Mabel onto the bed. She slapped his hands away. She was not in the mood for fooling around.

Darnlee opened the bedroom window and spat his disappointment onto the leaves of the olive tree, barely missing a baby monkey who seemed to have been eavesdropping on the windowsill outside. It jumped to the ground and scrambled up the coconut tree.

"I don't like it, Darnlee," came Mabel's voice. "You listenin' to me?"

"Maybe you miss the first two," he said irritably. He stuck his head through the window.

"I ain't miss none. He only crow four. I hear every one," Mabel said.

"You mean to tell me you ain't got nothing better to do than study that fowlcock this blessed morning? Look, go make me a cup of cocoa-tea, let me get outta here, if you can't find nothing better to do!"

"It's a sign, Darnlee. You remember what happen the last time this happen?"

"You want to watch signs? Go right ahead. But while you watching signs, make sure you don't forget to put sugar in me tea."

With that, he dismissed her with a loud sucking of his teeth and took his khaki trousers from the foot of the bed. Darnlee was a lean, muscular man, and quite tall. He wore a thick beard that hid a scar on his lower jaw—the result of a butchering accident. His small tired-looking eyes were set underneath a proud and prominent forehead, a feature he had passed on to his only child, Brandon, who was asleep in the next room.

Monday through Friday he worked at the plantation. On weekends he teamed up with Malcolm Barnes as the roving butchers of Monkey Road, slaughtering anything from turkeys to cows, killing the animals on the spot and transforming the house of the owner into an abattoir for the day. Darnlee bragged that he was the strongest and most fearless butcher to ever walk the streets of Monkey Road. To back up his claim he would tell the story of the five-hundred-pound bull he had wrestled to the ground by the horns single-handedly while simultaneously plunging a sixteen-inch blade through its neck and into its heart. Later, after the animal had died, when its innards were taken out, the heart displayed one precise six-inch slit. Darnlee would then issue an open challenge to any man in the village to duplicate this feat. No one ever took up the challenge. But then no one except Darnlee and his partner knew if that story wasn't just that—a story.

Darnlee thrust his right leg into the trousers. Why was she bothering him about a fowlcock, he thought angrily as he thrust his left leg through. Especially since she didn't want to fool around. He didn't know a blasted thing about lazy fowlcocks who didn't crow right. And he resented being brought into her superstitions. So what if the same thing had happened when her mother died? That didn't prove anything.

"Something bad go happen," Mabel was saying. "You know I right. Something bad go happen."

"I thought you gone to make my tea, woman."

Mabel stood her ground.

Darnlee buttoned his fly and slipped a knotted piece of string around his waist. He looked around for his khaki shirt.

"All this time you here confusing me with this foolishness, we coulda been doin' something worthwhile, ya know," he chided, making one last effort to pull her into his arms.

Mabel slipped from his grasp and went to make the cocoa.

Darnlee poked his head through the blinds and looked at his son curled up on the floor in the corner of the other room. He smacked the boy on his behind. Brandon woke with a startled cry.

"Brandon! Get up and carry out the sheep, boy. Get up before them people from Calvary Hill come and get all the good grazing spots. Get up!"

Every morning he had to say the same thing to his son, who seemed to forget that the grass in the pasture where everyone grazed their stock was so sought after that it drew farmers from other villages, creating a tremendous rush early in the morning to get the best grazing spots.

The half-acre pasture, once part of the plantation, was now owned by Ezra Jessup, a mulatto whose passion for girls half his age had destroyed him, but not before he had sired more than fifteen children—all sons. Jessup had spent his first thirty-five years in Monkey Road, where he had been born to a village woman and the then plantation manager. It had taken his father that long—thirty-five years—to acknowledge Jessup as his son, in a deathbed confession to a Roman Catholic priest administering last rites. In his will his father left him the land, a house three miles away from Monkey Road, the sum of one hundred pounds, and a rickety buggy. Jessup moved into the house but refused to work the land, leaving it fallow, forbidding anyone to trespass on it and never visiting the pasture. The villagers took advantage of Jessup's absence to graze their livestock on his land.

Two years after his father's death Jessup began making periodic sweeps through the village in his red buggy, with his growing population of sons straggling behind him. He would seize any livestock grazing on his land and at the same time survey the stock of young girls running wild in the village. The animals were held for sale to the butcher or for ransom: the pleasure of the livestock owner's daughter for a day.

Because of the stream flowing underneath it from the gully, the grass in Jessup's pasture was always sweet and bounteous even in the dry months of March and April. The villagers were unwilling to give up the riches of Jessup's land even when threatened by his raids. So to protect themselves they developed a warning system. Every Sunday morning a boy or girl was selected to be the lookout for that week. Every day, from the time the livestock was taken to graze in the morning until it was time for them to return to their pens in the evening, the lookout would stand on a hill where he or she could see both the pasture and the road where Jessup's buggy would enter the village. When food was brought to the hill at midday, the lookout would eat with one eye trained on the road and the other on the pasture. If the crimson buggy with E.J. & SONS painted in orange on both sides was spotted, the lookout would run through the village screaming "Red Ezra coming! Red Ezra coming!" This alarm would bring the villagers scrambling out of their houses, and in two-twos the pasture would be empty of all animals except for grasshoppers or a strident dog or cat belonging to no one in particular and quite oblivious to Ezra Jessup's menace.

It all came to an end the day Jessup caught Marcus Gaye's two white goats. Marcus was a laborer with one daughter, Carmen, a fifteen-year-old beauty. Everyone in the village marveled at Marcus's goats—at their sparkling ivory coats, which Marcus washed every morning before leaving for the plantation, and at their thick legs, which would someday make great goat stew. The day Jessup took her father's goats, Carmen was too busy to hear the lookout's warning. She was rapturously entertaining the carpenter from next door behind closed windows and drawn blinds. The cry of "Red Ezra coming!" went up, and the villagers scrambled to gather in their stock, all except Carmen, whose own cries of passion were smothered by the mid-morning heat in the buttoned-down one-room house. Jessup and his boys tied the two goats to the back of their buggy and drove off. By the time the poor girl found out what had happened and ran out, wearing nothing but the carpenter's shirt, the goats were already bleating their way to Jessup's holding pen.

Marcus knew that to get his goats back he would have to offer Jessup his daughter for a day. The mulatto, who'd had his eyes on Carmen for a long time, was beside himself with joy. But she refused to go though her father beat her. Instead she ran away with the carpenter.

Jessup assembled the goats for auction. Marcus pleaded with him to give back his goats, but his tears brought only laughter from Jessup and his sons. In a fit of rage, Marcus grabbed a knife from the waistband of one of the butchers waiting to bid and stabbed Jessup and three of his sons before he was subdued. Jessup survived but his sons died. The shock sent Jessup to the madhouse.

Carmen never returned to Monkey Road. She stayed with the carpenter for two years in the village of All Saints. During those two years the carpenter never saw Carmen naked again. Each time they made love, she kept her clothing on. One day the carpenter came home and Carmen was gone. She had run off with a sailor to South America.

The village people were sorry for Marcus, who was hanged for killing Jessup's sons, but happy that the raids ceased, leaving them free to fatten their stock in the pasture.

The cocoa ready, Mabel removed the flavoring bay leaf before filling a shiny tin cup to the brim for her husband. Darnlee was very particular about having his cup filled to the brim. A man's portion, he called it. She set the cup in a bowl of water to cool and watched the thin curls of steam rise. The smell of fresh cocoa and bay leaf reminded her of the sunny Sunday mornings when her mother and grandmother would sit around an open fire in the backyard, roasting corn and telling stories while their hot cocoa cooled on a rock beside them.

A sleepy-eyed Brandon stumbled into the kitchen still wearing a dress of his mother's that he'd slept in. He passed through the kitchen door and was halfway across the yard before his mother stopped him.

"Where you goin', Brandon?" she asked, standing in the kitchen door.

"To carry out the big man sheep before he break me neck."

"Boy go wash the yampi out ya eye. And when you go stop runnin' 'round the village in me dress like you's still ten years old?"

"Them flour-bag shirts you make for me to wear look like dresses, anyway," Brandon shot back. He showed his authority over the ram by slamming the back of his hand against the animal's neck.

Darnlee entered the kitchen and stood behind his wife. His khaki uniform had a faint whiff of stale sweat and manure.

"You want anything else with the cocoa?" asked Mabel, leaning away from him. "Some cornmeal bakes?"

"Me don't want to get to work late. Just gimme the cocoa, let me go."

Darnlee put the steaming cocoa to his lips. He sipped tentatively, testing its temperature. Finding it to his liking, he swallowed the rich beverage in one continuous gulp and then threw the grounds out the open door. He belched.

"Be careful going down that hill, ya hear," Mabel cautioned as he stepped through the kitchen door. "Besides the fact that he only crow four when he shoulda crow six, I didn't like the way he crow neither. He ain't crow like he accustom. He ain't crow strong at all this morning."

"You still concernin' yourself with that stupid fowl-cock?" her husband scoffed.

"Ya never know. That hill very dangerous when it wet. You may slip and fall down and break you' neck or something. And what I go do if something happen to you? Who go gimme sugar in the mornin'?"

She whispered the last statement, her eyes lowered. Darnlee laughed.

It had rained heavily most of the night. The early morning sunlight spun sparkling rainbows over the tiny pools of clear water that had settled in the yard. Mabel leaned against the kitchen door as she watched her husband bathe his feet in one of the puddles. She liked his feet. They were big, flat, steady feet. Just like him. The thought made her smile.

Darnlee finished washing his feet. He noticed that his son was lollygagging in the sheep pen.

"Boy, what ya waitin' for, eh? For ya grandmother to come back from she grave? Hurry up and carry out the sheep!"

"Yes, Pa."

"And don't forget to carry the scraps for Small Paul's pigs when you get back. He want to kill one a them sows next week. The fatter she is the better for we."

"Yes, Pa."

"Yes, Pa, and you still playing the fool? Is only two sheep you have to carry out!"

Brandon grabbed the ropes attached to the necks of the sheep and fished two stakes out of a pool of water.

"Watch out for them monkeys, Brandon. Them does get very fresh with their ugly self when the rain fall," Mabel said as her son slid warily past his father and out the yard.

"What the rain got to do with the monkeys gettin' fresh?" asked Darnlee, amused.

"I don't know. But this morning already one come right up to the kitchen door and then jump up on the table, look me full in the face before shooting right back through the door."

"You sure that ain't a sign too? If them monkeys is spirits like some idiots in this village believe, them mighta come with a message from ya mother," Darnlee laughed. "Ya sure them ain't whisper something in ya ear?"

"I don't know how you could be laughing, Darnlee. These ain't things to laugh at, ya hear. As for them monkeys, I believe them go make bad for this village if somebody don't stop them from destroyin' the plantation crops."

"You got proof is the monkey doin' it?"

"That's what everybody say."

"Who's everybody? I ain't sayin' it."

"Who else it could be then? The watchmen claim them never see a soul yet every year the plantation say half the crops does disappear."

"Any of them watchmen would close his eyes for the right price. A few months back, on me way to work I pass and see Gunny draggin' a big bag of potatoes into his yard. Now you know Gunny ain't got no ground to grow no potatoes. I make it me business to ask him where he get them from. Ya know what he tell me? He find the bag at the side of the road. He didn't even shame. And he ain't the only one I see with bags of potatoes dragging home early in the morning. I see Juke-Juke and that worthless girl Raven and she friend Myna. All them claim them find the bags by the road. Now tell me, how comes you and me don't find no bags by the road? I ain't sayin' Gunny and them so is who stealin' the plantation crops but nobody ain't convince me yet is the monkeys doin' it. Spirits or no spirits, I believe them monkeys gettin' blame wrongfully."

Darnlee slid over to his wife and squeezed her buttocks through her dress, skipping away before she could slap him. He left the yard laughing.

Mabel went to the window and watched her husband disappear into the dancing mile trees that lined the narrow road until all she could see were the monkeys waving wildly in the branches. She closed the jalousies and bent down to pick her son's bedding from the floor. A tarnished shilling dropped from the bedclothes. She picked it up and put it on the shelf above her head. She looked around for the broom and caught her reflection in the tiny mirror on the wall. She was a sinewy woman with bold eyes and high arching cheekbones. She kept her thick black hair, with its thin streak of gray in the center, in two shoulder-length braids.

She had done all right by Darnlee. He wasn't much of a drinker and he didn't run behind other women. In this village that was a man to cherish. But she was surprised at his touchiness this morning. He, of all people, should understand her sensitivity to the spirits. Even if he was in a bad mood because she didn't want to make love, how could he ignore the obvious signs? After all, they'd seen it happen before. Not only with this fowlcock but the one before too. That one had been stolen, so now she never let this one out of the yard. Fifteen years ago, pregnant with their first child, she woke up with a bad feeling one morning. When she mentioned to him that she didn't feel right because the fowlcock hadn't crowed, Darnlee had simply laughed. The next day, before the sun rose, their daughter was stillborn. The only reason she had mentioned it to him at all was because the same thing had happened a year earlier. That particular morning the cock didn't murmur a sound either, causing her mother to warn all her children to be careful of the bad spirits in the air. Later that day her brother's wife gave birth to a dead baby boy.

The fowlcock was alerting them to something. Somewhere. But where? She didn't know anyone who was pregnant.

She would never admit to being a superstitious woman. There was nothing *superstitious* about the things she felt in her blood. She came from a long line of women who were highly sensitive to the supernatural. Her mother and grandmother were that way, and she thought of herself as being that way too. Darnlee's laughter could not change that.

To this day she could remember the dream her mother had a week before the great hurricane of 1881. In the dream her mother was standing in the middle of a huge field of bananas so ripe that they had turned the color of the midday sun. Yet nobody came to cut them. And when they fell to the ground, not even the ever-hungry monkeys came to feast. The bananas stayed on the ground until they rotted and dissolved into the soil. The morning after the dream, her mother began packing clothes and food into boxes, along with the few pieces of silver she had gotten as gifts from suitors when she was a young girl. Everyone thought she was crazy. Only Mabel, eight months with child, hobbling on swollen feet, bothered to help her. Four other children, all boys, laughed at them.

"Ma gettin' crazy in she old age," one son said.

"Every year she does prophesy some calamity and none of them ain't happen yet," laughed another one.

"I dream all the animals run away," she warned her five children. "That means something bad on the way. A earthquake, a storm, I ain't know what but something coming."

"You crazy, Ma. We don't get earthquakes in the West Indies," taunted the eldest son.

"It go destroy this whole place. Mark my word," replied their mother.

Their mother finished her packing and went to borrow a donkey and cart from a neighbor. When the neighbor told her the donkey was lame, she came back to the house and put as many of her belongings as she could carry on her head and ordered Mabel to follow her.

"Don't mind them," she said to her pregnant daughter as they set out. "You' first child born dead but this one go be healthy and live long. Come, follow me."

"Where we goin'?" Mabel asked.

"We goin' to the plantation," her mother replied. "We go stay in the sugar mill 'til this thing pass."

"What 'bout me man, Darnlee?"

"Darnlee go find you. Come."

When they arrived at the mill Bra' Pile, long considered by many in the village to be an idiot, was already there with his two sheep, his two fowlcocks, and four hens. He'd had the same dream, he told them, but had to leave behind his pig, which was too lazy to walk and too big for him to drag.

Also in the mill was Ma Parker, a poor old woman who complained of every ailment known to man and some she invented. On Monday and Tuesday she suffered asthma attacks and Wednesday through Friday a combination of arthritis, bronchial fever, and temporary deafness. She was known to make her misery dramatic with sudden delirious collapses in the street and miraculous recoveries once she was transported home on the broad back of some helpful young man. She, too, had dreamed of ripe bananas rotting and brought along her pig and her ten-year-old great-grandson, Edgar.

These five slept in the mill for two days. When the word circulated around the village of their gathering, the gamblers began to make bets as to who would be the first to succumb to Ma Parker's niggling and groaning and flee the mill.

The morning of the third day, Mabel's mother came out of the mill intending to return to the village to try for the last time to persuade her sons to join her. Heavy clouds approaching chased her back. She ducked her head under the low arch of the mill door and bolted it shut. "It coming," she said to the group.

At midday the hurricane hit with such ferocity that people ran screaming into the streets as the roofs of their homes were ripped away by high winds. Women racing to find shelter had to use their bodies to shield their babies from flying pieces of metal and tree limbs. Arms and feet were severed, animals decapitated, and trees uprooted. Houses were piled on top each other. The wind and rain lashed the village for hours, bringing it within a glance of obliteration. Indeed, the carnage was spread across the island.

Inside the mill the wise five heard the commotion outside

and prayed. A hail of men, women, and children, drenched and frightened, descended on them, wailing and banging at the door. Soon the mill was overflowing with weeping families, some of whom had seen loved ones sliced in half by flying galvanized iron. It rained for four days and nights. Mabel lost two of her brothers during the first day, and on the second, huddled in a corner of the mill, she gave birth to Brandon.

Brandon passed the monkeys chattering noisily in the branches. He was used to their antics in the morning; their presence was what made his village unique. In Calvary Hill, the village where he was an apprentice blacksmith, people made fun of him for living in what they called "a patch of monkeys," but he didn't mind their laughter. He didn't tell them what Small Paul had told him: that the monkeys were really spirits. He just laughed along with them. He loved his village, monkeys and all.

It was a tenantry village situated on land owned by the plantation, with tiny houses knitted together in a tight circle by a series of narrow dirt roads. The mile trees that lined the main road rose more than thirty feet in the air, and this road running through the village from one end to the other was loosely paved with stones and marl that had to be repaired after each heavy rainfall. The road sloped sharply as it left the cluster of houses, branching off into the gully on one side and Jessup's pasture on the other. Beyond the gully were the plantation fields and beyond that the plantation compound made up of a great house, overseer and servants' quarters, stables, and a sugar mill.

Brandon arrived at Jessup's pasture and looked around for the best grazing available. Already the pasture was almost full of sheep and goats. He found a spot and hastily drove the stakes into the soft soil with a large stone, testing them to make sure they were secure enough to hold the sheep until evening. He hitched the sheep to the spikes and gave the ram one last slap before racing home.

His mother was waiting at the kitchen door with scraps for Small Paul's pigs.

"Let me get a cup of cocoa-tea to break the air out me stomach first, nuh Ma," he pleaded.

"Take the scraps first. And listen, I ain't hear Small Paul voice hollering at them pigs this mornin'. Normally I woulda hear him by now. Check and see if he alright. I just don't like the way the fowlcock crow, Brandon."

Brandon picked up the bucket filled with breadfruit skins, leftover sweet potatoes and rice, and set off for Small Paul's yellow house next door, one of the few in the village that was painted, though it was all chipped and cracked. Brandon walked through the patch of pigeon pea trees growing near the front of the house and stripped a few chips of paint off the side of the house on his way to the back entrance. He let himself through the gate, as he always did, patted Small Paul's three-legged dog, Sprats, on the head, and dropped the bucket next to the pigpen. The hungry pigs were squealing and biting each other. But the house was quiet.

Brandon was surprised that Small Paul was not in the yard. Since he'd retired from his job as watchman at the plantation a year earlier, Small Paul, who lived alone, had always fed his pigs before the sun came up. His wife had left him many years past, too long ago for Brandon to remember. What he did know was that Small Paul had not gotten over it, because he was always cursing his wife "back where she came from" and made a point of telling Brandon he would never live with another woman "not even if God bring she and drop she in me lap and tell me she's a angel." When Small Paul got drunk he became very talkative, spinning tales from his prodigious collection of stories that Brandon never tired of listening to. But drunk or not, Small Paul was an early riser.

When Brandon knocked on the kitchen door, Sprats began to bark. The boy found a stick and jimmied the latch, then stepped into the kitchen. The house had a damp, musty aroma.

He called out Small Paul's name. No answer. A plate of unfinished pork balanced on the edge of the knobby wooden table. A steady stream of ants danced along the rim of the plate, down the legs of the table, and through a tiny crack in the floor. Brandon crushed a handful of ants and tasted the pork. Not bad. He called Small Paul's name again and walked to the front of the house, where Small Paul slept.

He caught a glimpse of a white dress going out the front door. Could that be Midra? Yes, it was her. He could tell by the ankles and the hair. Nobody had ankles like Midra. He rushed to the window to catch another glimpse of the most beautiful ankles in the village but all he saw were the pea-tree leaves closing behind the fleeing figure. He went to the bedroom, where Small Paul was lying on his back in the hammock. In his left hand he clutched a pair of women's white underpants. The smile on his face was stiff, the hand cold to Brandon's touch. His mother's premonition had found a victim. Small Paul was dead. Instinctively he squeezed the underpants through Small Paul's stiff fingers and drew them to his face. A wonderful, living smell.

THREE

That night Brandon could not fall asleep. He lay on the floor on his bedding, twisting and turning like a fly in a spider's web. Small Paul's smile was floating in his head; he didn't have the look of death like his grandmother when they'd found her. He'd had no trouble believing she was dead, her face wrapped in a bitter, twisted look of anger, like someone disappointed, someone not yet ready to become a duppy. Small Paul seemed to be sleeping, his thick locks resting on the side of his sad, serene face.

Around eleven Brandon got up and went to the window. He drew the blinds and pushed the squeaky window open. He stared into the darkness searching for the moon. He found it sailing at half mast across a blank and silent sky. There were no stars. This solitary half-moon peeking at night's black skin was all he could find. Monkey Road, earlier astounded by Brandon's news, now lay dreaming.

Brandon cocked his ears, listening for the crickets or some other indication that something out there was alive, but the night sent him only silence. No crickets singing, no dogs barking, no frogs croaking. Everything was dead. Except the Lady-in-the-Night flowers whose fragrance stole into the room on a lazy breeze. Throughout Monkey Road the only Lady-in-the-Night trees that blossomed year-round were the two in Ben Payne's garden. Considered to be natural wonders, they were envied by garden lovers all over the island, whose own plants bloomed only four times a year.

Brandon decided to go for a walk. He checked to make sure his parents were asleep, then quietly let himself out through the back door. Not sure where he was going, he found himself walking in the direction of the gully. He stopped in front of Ben Payne's garden to break a branch of aromatic white blossoms from one of the two Lady-in-the-Night trees. They had drawn him like a magnet. When the branch broke with a loud crack, he crouched nervously under the tree, hoping the noise had not awakened Ben. He waited a few moments. Nothing moved except a firefly dancing above his head. He caught the firefly in his hand and made his retreat with the branch of flowers.

When he got to the edge of the gully, Brandon set the firefly free and watched it flash quickly into the darkness. He sat down on the grass. He had never gone into the gully at night. The duppies that lived there were angry spirits: that is what he had been told since he was a little boy. Only men dared walk through the gully at night, and brave men at that. He was almost a man, he thought. He wasn't afraid of the dead. He had seen his second dead person today and would walk through the gully tonight to prove his courage.

He had never seen a duppy. Small Paul had told him that to most people they were invisible; only people who were sensitive to the spirits could see them. According to Small Paul, who was one of the privileged few who could see duppies, they looked like normal people except that they walked with their heads down. If you saw one you had to sidestep because they never took their eyes off the ground, and it was bad luck to walk into them. The reason they walked with their heads down, Small Paul said, was because they were looking for the future they had lost. Brandon had wanted to ask Small Paul why the women in Monkey Road walked with their heads down like duppies. What were these women searching for? But he never did. Now Small Paul was dead and, from tonight, would be a duppy roaming the gully at night with his head down searching for his lost future.

The mile trees were singing. Tonight their song was mournful. The gully was full of mile trees, and their plaintive wailing seemed louder than he had ever heard it. He peered at the wall of darkness blocking the mouth of the gully, hoping his eyes could penetrate the blackness. Small Paul had told him a story about Africans who were burned to death there in slave times. When he mentioned the story to his mother, she ordered him not to talk about it again, declaring that it was one of Small Paul's 'nansi stories to scare him. It had scared him all right, especially when Small Paul had told him that the spirits of those burned-up Africans were as angry now as when they'd died almost a hundred years ago.

The darkness at the mouth of the gully remained impenetrable. If he wanted to see behind the wall of blackness, he realized, he would have to walk through it. He hesitated. He remembered that Prince Johnson had been found dead at the mouth of the gully about a year ago, just before Midra and her mother disappeared from the village. Before it became clear what had happened, there was talk that he had become a victim of the angry African spirits.

Brandon remembered the morning of Prince's death clearly. He had followed the crowd to see the dead body laid out on the grass, but he'd gotten there too late. When he arrived, it had already been taken away. His friend Pudge, who saw the body, told him that Prince had more than a hundred bullet holes in him, yet there was no blood on the grass near his body. What had happened to Prince's blood? Had the spirits stolen it? And could Prince talk to the spirits in the gully like people were saying?

Fear seized him as he realized that he was standing near the spot where the body had been found. For all he knew he might be standing in the exact spot where Prince had died and his blood was stolen from his body. That thought changed his mind about going into the gully. Not tonight. He was not man enough yet.

He was about to leave when he saw something move at the mouth of the gully. Crouching, he instinctively held up the flowers in front of him. He hoped it wasn't one of those angry, burnt-up Africans. A firefly flickered brightly, and then he saw Midra coming out of the gully.

She was carrying the baby. The firefly leading them burned as bright as the moon, illuminating her face. He could see her smiling at the baby. He got up and walked toward her. When she saw him, she stopped and stared, first at him, then at the fragile flowers he held. Not knowing what else to do, he offered them to her. The look in her eyes was one of annoyance. She tried to step around him on the narrow path.

"Them smell sweet," he said, trying to stall her. "Just pick them off Ben Payne tree."

She stopped. "You in me way," she said.

"What you doin' down there? You wasn't frighten?"

He reached to touch the baby and she slapped him.

"What you think you doing?" she snapped.

The slap stung his face, and he stepped onto the grass to let her edge past him. The darkness swallowed her up. The firefly remained behind, performing a mocking fire-dance in front of his face. He angrily snatched it from the air and was about to crush it. Then with a nervous laugh, he tore a petal from the Lady-in-the-Night, folded it around the firefly, and slipped them into his mouth. He swallowed hard and then followed her into the darkness.

• • •

When Midra woke up the next morning, it was already past eleven. The room was bathed in sunlight, and the yellow curtains swirled under a slight breeze. She was sweating. The sun was shining directly into her eyes, but she made no attempt to move. She felt the warmth deep in her nostrils and followed her urge to breathe the sun into her. Her baby was asleep beside her.

A yellowbreast fluttered onto the windowsill clutching a gooseberry in its beak. It dropped the yellow fruit and flew back to the tree. The berry rolled to a stop next to the bed. She picked it up and bit into it. The tangy fruit splashed onto her tongue as saliva sprang from all corners of her mouth to embrace the thousand thrills bombarding her taste buds.

She felt dirty. Inside and out. She eased herself up from the bed trying not to wake the sleeping child. This morning she would take a clove bath.

Midra bathed in clove at least once a week. By crushing the cloves with a mortar and pestle and then putting them in a piece of burlap to be immersed in the bathtub, she had found a cheap and easy way to perfume her body. Bathing in clove reminded her of Rose, a prostitute who rented the room next door to them in the boardinghouse they had occupied in the city. Rose would come to their room every morning after working the night before to entrust her mother with money for safekeeping from her boyfriend, who beat her and took her earnings to go drinking with his friends and other women. And she would stick around until midday talking to Midra about things that happened to her during the night. Rose explained how she put cloves in her bathwater to get rid of that unwashed smell left on her body by men who had not bathed in weeks. Listening to Rose talk about the men who left their wives at home to seek her out taught Midra a lot about the things men would do to get a woman and prepared her for the hungry looks thrown in her path.

As she lay in the tub outside wishing Rose were still alive, Midra could hear her mother singing in the kitchen. Life in the village was a little better than what they'd had in the city, but she was surprised her mother had the patience to put up with the treatment they got from other women. The shock her mother had given this tiny village when they arrived almost two years earlier had not yet worn off.

When they'd first arrived in Monkey Road, it had been the height of the crop season, and apart from its quietness, the thing that had caught Midra's attention about the village was its perfumed verdure. Monkey Road was surrounded by green sugarcane and all kinds of blossoming plants, many of which she had never seen before. At night the smell of boiling cane juice from the plantation, mixed with the essence of the Lady-in-the-Night, floated over the village like a thin perfumed veil. She found these new fragrances intoxicating.

Midra had been happy to escape the cramp of city dwelling. The thin cardboard partition that separated the tiny square room they lived in from others of equally meager dimensions made the idea of privacy an absurdity. She heard every fight, quarrel, bout of lovemaking, birth, and death that happened in the boardinghouse. Their room was always filled with cloth. Her mother was a dressmaker but made little money, since she spent more time making dresses for herself than her customers.

Peata found other ways to make money, though. Apart from being a sharp dresser she was also an electrifying dancer, and once she discovered that people were willing to pay to see her dance, she took full advantage of it. When she hit the dance halls she would put on an unforgettable show for those who were fortunate enough to see it. Despite her size, Peata could wiggle and squirm with the tiniest worm, and when time came for her ampleness to be the center of attention, she would take her skirt by the hem and raise it halfway up her thighs, drawing cries of approval from the men in the hall. As she began the slow circular undulation of her hips, the walls would shake from her sheer sensual power. However, it was when Peata speeded up her hip-thrusting gyrations and began to work her hips with abandon that even the most frigid of dance halls lost its inhibitions and joined her in an impetuous display of sensuality. By the time she left the dance hall Peata's bosom would be loaded down with money slipped to her by admirers who paid as much for the joy of seeing her dance as for the opportunity to experience the lavishness of her breasts while they dropped their money into the pouch of her bosom. No doubt about it, Peata had found a way to control men. A way to get what she wanted without always giving them what they wanted. Her promise of fulfillment could be put off for as long as she could dance or leave her laughter lingering in the air, filling their heads with thoughts of intoxicating nights in her bed.

By the time they moved to Monkey Road, Midra had seen her mother work her magic on all kinds of men. Sailors, fishermen, laborers, they all came hoping for more than they would receive. Peata would get them to buy her clothes and perfumes, food and liquor. Sometimes they would slip as much as a shilling or five pence into Midra's hand, hoping that their generosity to the daughter would find favor with the mother.

But Midra had come to understand her mother's magic. This would be the closest many of these men would ever come to touching a white woman, and often that was all they wanted. A chance to touch Peata's close-to-white skin. One day a man came looking for her mother, who was not at home. On hearing this, the man turned his attention to

Midra. "How come you' mother skin so pretty and you so black?" he asked her. Midra did not know what to say but Rose, who was with her, threatened to throw some stale pee on the man if he did not leave.

The house in Monkey Road was a mansion compared to their tiny room in the city. A tidy chattel house of shingles, it was only two rooms with a small kitchen but Midra loved it. There was a yard and a tiny front garden with a goose-berry tree and a luxuriant Lady-in-the-Night outside her window. Midra could not remember ever inhaling such an elegant scent; not even the most delicate of perfumes her mother wore could compare to it, and to indulge her senses she would leave the windows open all night.

Midra got out of the tub and turned it over, disposing of the dirty water on the grass. She stood in the sun relishing its warmth as the water trickled off her body. When she was sufficiently dry she went into the house.

Peata was in the kitchen holding the baby.

"You went out last night," Peata spoke softly so she would not wake the child. "Where you went so late?"

"Nowhere," said Midra. "Why you holding him? He still sleeping."

"He don't usually sleep this late."

"He ain't got nowhere to go. He can sleep as long as he want."

"Where you went last night?"

"For a walk."

"Why you take the baby?"

"He's mine. I can take him anywhere."

"He's only six months. You shouldn't be taking him out in the dew so late."

"He like the night air," Midra said, taking the baby from her mother. The baby woke up as soon as he smelled his

31

mother. Hungrily, he opened his mouth to receive her nipple.

"Anytime I say something to you 'bout that child, you tell me is yours. I know is yours," her mother was saying, but Midra wasn't really listening. She was wrapping herself in the broad leaves of a father-tree, which would hide her from the world.

"I know the baby is yours," Peata repeated. "I don't need you to keep tellin' me he's yours."

"You wish he was yours."

"That is foolishness, Midra."

"You could as well admit, Ma. You know is true."

"What make you think I would want to have that manchild?"

"I ain't blind, Ma. I got eyes."

"And why ya didn't use them to see what Prince was goin' to do to you?"

"You don't know nothin' 'bout what Prince do to me."

Midra left her mother in the kitchen and went into her room where Peata found her a few minutes later, crying.

"What you cryin' for?"

"Every day, every day you keep quarreling with me. I don't understand it. Why, if it ain't 'cause I got Prince child and not you?"

"Is because I went through what you goin' through. Is because I can see how confused you is and want you to wake up and realize this Prince ain't worth loving. Not only because he dead and can't help you, but 'cause it would probably be the same if he was living."

"How you know that?"

"Because I know his kind."

"I don't want to hear no more of this, Ma. My head hurting me."

"All right." Pause. "You goin' to the funeral?"

"Who funeral?"

"What ya mean who funeral? Small Paul."

Midra paused. "No."

"No?"

"I say no."

"Why?"

" 'Cause I don't want to."

"He used to give you all them things from his ground, and you ain't goin' to his funeral?"

"No."

"What wrong with you, Midra?"

"Nothin'."

"You been actin' so funny lately, I don't know. What am I sayin', you been actin' funny ever since that night you let Prince Johnson drop his seed inside you. It seem like he exchange you' mind for that baby."

"Don't start on Prince again, Ma. Don't start. Is time you leave me be. Whatever Prince do to me, it done. I have the baby. Prince dead. You fret me enough. Don't fret me no more."

Her mother left the room, and Midra hugged her baby and cried.

What Peata had found on their arrival in Monkey Road was a village of young men and women too bored to resist the seduction of a good-looking, pretty-skinned woman who knew how to entertain. Before long her new home had become a gathering place, a party house, a place for flirtation and teasing for the most frolicsome men and women.

They gathered on Friday or Saturday nights. The men brought pork and fish, which they paid Peata to cook, consuming copious amounts of rum and molasses while they ate. Then, with their stomachs full, their heads light, and their tongues loose, someone would produce a banjo, someone else a drum, and they would sing and dance through the night as they coaxed and sweet-talked each other to unleash their passion under the stars in Peata's backyard.

Sometimes they got rowdy, but Peata never let things get out of hand. The men all openly desired Peata but none of them knew how to win her. Even when she got tipsy she still had enough presence to dissuade a hand wandering up her thighs or a mouth chasing the jewels of her bosom. If she was in the mood, Peata would allow the wandering hand to linger, to trail the outline of the fine hair that grew sparsely on the inside of her thighs, to loiter just long enough for a probing finger to slip past the threshold of her sex, and then she would pull away laughing. Peata knew she was teasing them, but they were all like little children. And like little children, capricious and flighty, they would quickly find other amusement if she gave into their impulses. She preferred to keep them waiting. That was until Prince Johnson came along.

Prince Johnson came once a month, on some rare occasions twice, for an evening of eating and drinking and the ribald behavior that went along with intoxicated young men and women. He was a seaman, working on a freighter that took supplies between the islands and as far south as Brazil. At twenty-five he was tall with a light brown complexion and the alert eyes of a mongoose. A crown of sun-bleached reddish curls framed his thin, lively face. He always brought with him a bottle of Spanish wine, a bottle of Cuban rum, and a bag of nuts. He gave the nuts to Midra, the rum to Gunny, the banjo player, and shared the wine with Peata, sitting on the floor of the kitchen while the men and women got drunk around them. No one suspected why Prince came. Not even Peata, who thought he came to dance with her. No one realized it was Midra's beauty, not the wine, that made him drunk.

Peata kept waiting for Prince to make his move. Spurred on by the wine, they laughed and danced together until the first cock crowed and it seemed as though an understanding had developed between them. An understanding of what Peata wasn't yet sure, but she liked this man—his quiet intelligence, his big hands, and the heat that flowed from his body when they danced. Being close to him was like being next to a burning coal-pot. But despite the warm feeling she got from Prince, he was elusive and told her little about himself. Even that did not dim her hopes. Elusiveness was all right for now. It was better than forwardness when the result was sure to be disappointing. On that elusiveness she could erect a poised, passionate lover, something she had not seen in these parts as yet. The village of Monkey Road seemed to be inhabited by men who made love as though they were in a house on fire. She wanted this man and was willing to wait.

One time she caught him staring at Midra. This made her so jealous that she sent Midra to her room. After that she made sure Midra was already in bed by the time Prince arrived.

By nine o'clock Peata's tiny kitchen would be overflowing with the aroma of fried fish and fire-blackened pork that had been roasted in the backyard. Gunny was always a little ahead of everyone else. Wiggling his slender frame like a spider, he came straight from his job at the sugarcane factory with his bottle of rum and his banjo, smelling of smoke and molasses. Most of the men would go home to wash up first and change their clothes. But not Gunny. Gunny's girlfriend would not see him until the next morning because he'd get so drunk that Peata would have to put him to sleep on the floor of her kitchen. Following closely behind Gunny would be Bussa, Juke-Juke, and the fiery twins, Ranny and Randy. Ranny and Randy, well known for their generosity and admired for their good looks, would always have two or three young girls tagging along with them. Next came Spoony-Leg Carl, Myna, Raven, and the rest of the crowd. And, just before midnight, if it was the third Friday of the month, Prince Johnson would show up,

dressed in brown. Peata met him at the door where she
would make sure he kissed her before leading him into the
kitchen to feed him. After eating, they would open the bottle of wine he brought.

"Why you come here?" she asked him one night, hoping
to accelerate the chase.

"Same reason everybody come."

"That ain't true."

"Tell me why I come then."

"I don't know."

"I come here for the same thing as everybody else."

"What's that?"

"Energy."

"Energy?"

"Yes. Energy."

"What you talkin' 'bout?"

"You can't feel it? It in you' own house."

"You want to know what I feel?" Peata smiled.

"I know what you feel."

"What I feel?"

"You feel the energy too."

"I feel love."

"That's energy."

"That the energy you feel?" she asked.

"Yes."

"So what's the problem?"

"Problem?"

Peata began to feel like he was laughing at her.

"Yes, what you frighten for?" she said.

"Nothin'."

When he left that night without making any attempt to
touch her, Peata was so overcome with frustration that she
could not help crying. Midra, who had stayed up listening
to the ribald jokes and laughter from the next room, heard
Peata crying. She came out to see what was wrong, but her
mother shouted her back to bed.

Later, Peata counted the money. Half a pound. Half a pound in her pocket and a ton weight on her heart. The money was more than enough to take care of their needs for the week. But what she wanted most was Prince Johnson. She was not prepared to wait any longer. Next time he came, she would seduce him.

FOUR

The speed with which Peata captured the hearts, spirits, and pockets of the young men in Monkey Road alarmed a lot of the women hopeful of catching a stable, hardworking man to settle down with. Jealousy turned into violence one day as Midra was drawing water from the water cart that came through the village once a week. Her challenger was Gunny's girlfriend, who bumped into Midra as she was about to raise the bucket of water onto her head. The force of the blow knocked the bucket off Midra's head, and the water spilled all over her. Midra could feel the water trickling down her back as she stared angrily at the wide leathery-skinned woman.

"Why ya don't watch where ya goin', girl?" snapped the woman, whose jaws opened and closed like a dog waiting for a meal.

"You bump into me first," Midra replied indignantly.

"You like you's a bumba, eh!" the woman shot back, bracing for a long tussle. This young girl with unruly hair and eyes ablaze was obviously not afraid of her. "Who you think you is, eh? Where you come from with ya frowsy self? I never did like town people, ya know. You an' you mad-ass mother come 'bout here with all ya nasty ways and think we frighten for all ya?''

Midra said nothing. She turned around to refill her bucket.

"Ya have to wait ya turn now," the woman snapped. "You ain't see I here before you?"

Midra stepped back as the woman pushed her bucket away. She noticed that the woman's face was puffy as if she had been beaten, and her hands trembled.

"What does go on in that house on Friday night?" the woman asked. "What my man does be doing in there?"

Midra shifted her stance, waiting for the woman's bucket to fill.

"I talkin' to you, ya little pig. What you' worthless mother does be doin' with all them men inside she house? She better not be messing with my man 'cause I would lick in she tail! She ain't even shame, with a young girl in the house? But all the same she drop you and the sap can't be no different to the seed so you's probably the same worthless thing as she."

Midra swung the metal bucket as hard as she could. It connected with the woman's head and toppled her into the gutter. Midra saw the blood spurt and dropped her bucket and ran off. The woman, covered with bloody, wet, green dirt, scrambled to her feet cursing. Midra did not run home. She ran into the gully where no one would look for her.

Midra planned to wait until darkness approached before going home. The woman would go directly to her house to complain to her mother. If she went home now, the situation would only get worse. By tomorrow it would blow over. Until the next time somebody called her mother worthless to her face. They could say what they liked behind her back but anyone insulting her mother in her presence would pay dearly.

She stretched out under a guava tree. The wind fussed with the whistle-thin needles of the mile trees, which moaned from the stimulation. Midra closed her eyes and went to sleep.

She woke up to the smell of ripe guava. One had dropped from the tree and lay exposed next to her. Darkness filled the gully. She had been asleep a long time. Midra picked up the ripe guava and bit into the tender shell, sucking out the pink pulp and seeds. A shadow shifted high in the mile trees above her. She dismissed it as a monkey and stuffed the remaining guava in her mouth as she got up to go home. She was hungry. The shadow dropped from the tree, and she spat out the guava in fright. Prince Johnson stood before her.

He was wearing a brown shirt and brown pants, the same clothes he wore to their house on Friday nights.

"You frighten me, ya know!" she said angrily.

"I frighten you?" He laughed.

"Yes, man!"

"Sorry." He chuckled. She noticed that his palms were black.

"What you doin' down here so like you's a monkey?" she said.

"Only monkeys does come down in here?" He rubbed his black palms together as the monkeys suddenly started to chatter noisily above them. "What you doin' here if is only a place for monkeys?"

He took a step toward her. She stood her ground.

"I hidin'," she confided.

"Hidin'? Or searching?"

"Searching for what?"

"Who knows. We all searching for something."

Midra noticed his eyes and thought how oddly transparent they seemed. His arms were long with thin, bony fingers. He smelled of the earth.

"You hungry?" he asked. She nodded and he gave her a handful of groundnuts. The dirt that covered them was damp.

"You just dig these?" she asked.

"Uh-huh."

"From where?"

"Want to see?"

"Yes."

"Ya sure?"

"Why? You steal them?"

"Steal?" He laughed.

His laughter ricocheted off the leaves, and the monkeys sang out in rhapsody. He took her hand.

"Come."

"I gotta get home. My mother must be looking for me."

"It ain't go take long."

"Where we going?"

He held her firmly. She was surprised by the heat that flowed from his hand. It was like holding fire. His step was light and he walked quickly, skipping over the rocks and pools of water along the way with the agility of a monkey. A little stream ran alongside them. He ducked under the tendrils of a bearded-fig tree, then changed direction, crossing the stream. They emerged into a clearing where the path became wider and the chattering of the monkeys became faint. Soon the chatter disappeared altogether.

They walked on in silence for a while along this path. There was nothing but sourgrass on each side of them now. Midra knew they must have left the confines of Monkey Road.

"Where we is?" she asked.

Without answering, he gripped her hand tighter and walked on. Soon they came to a wide unpaved marl road, its whiteness stark and serene in the darkness. They crossed it and dropped into a trench separating the marl road from an open field. Scrambling out of the trench, they stood in a large field of young canes. A white house loomed in the distance. It was about three or four hundred yards away but the house stood out clearly against the muted background.

"You know what that is up there?" Prince Johnson said. He stopped and rubbed his hands over his face. The black mud from his hands painted his features. He rubbed his hands across her face. The soft mud felt like silk.

"What this for?" she asked.

"That's the plantation house," Prince Johnson said, "the people who own the gully and all the land around it. And, except for a few spots, they own all the land in Monkey Road too."

"Nobody in Monkey Road ain't own no land, then?"

"No. Them renting."

"I want to see that house," she said. "I want to see it close."

"You want to go inside?"

"Inside?"

"Inside the bedrooms?"

"You can get inside?" She didn't know much about plantations, but she knew that white people owned them and that black people couldn't just walk up and expect to get invited inside. "You know them people?" she asked.

"I know a lotta people." He laughed softly and cocked his head to one side as if listening to something. A delicate breeze flicked the tiny cane blades.

"Come on," he said quickly.

"What?"

"I smell the dogs."

"What dogs?"

"Come on!" He grabbed her hand again and they raced across the cane field, her feet flying across the ground. She felt as though she was not traveling under her own power, she was moving so fast. And she felt light, like air itself. They crossed the cane field quickly and came to another field some hundred yards away from where they had started out. It was a blanket of green.

"I never run so fast in me life," Midra laughed, "and I ain't even outta breath."

He kneeled down and pulled some of the green plants from the ground. He shook the dirt from the roots and gave them to her. Midra dropped to her knees in the green bed and began to pull up the groundnuts alongside him. She stopped.

"What we doin' is wrong."

"Wrong?"

"Yes."

"Who say it wrong?"

"This belong to the plantation."

She noticed that he had a bag tied around his waist. The bag was brown like the rest of him. He had dug up enough groundnuts to fill the bag. As he pulled them from the ground, he would shake the loose dirt from around the tiny bulbs and put them in a heap behind him. The heap was now very large. The full moon had dropped low over them, illuminating their work. Her head was spinning, and the green field seemed to be swimming under her. Prince stopped and cocked his head. She cocked hers too, but heard nothing.

"The dogs getting close! Come!" In a blur he stuffed the groundnuts into the bag and grabbed her hand. They flew across the field the same way they had come and jumped the trench. In no time they had crossed the marl road and were walking along the wide path back to the gully. Prince stopped.

"You tired?" he asked her.

"No."

They walked on. When they came to the stream, Prince opened the bag, letting half the nuts fall into the water.

"Why only half?" she asked.

"The other half for the monkeys."

She knelt to help him wash the dirt off the nuts.

"Them have the dogs to catch the monkeys. But them go only catch shadows," he said with a mocking laugh.

"What the monkeys do them?"

43

"Is what them do the monkeys."

"And what's that?"

"You will find out."

He reclined on the grass under a tree with broad leaves. The moon lit up his red hair. Standing behind him, she reached out to touch the tree and was greeted by its sharp needles. She cried out.

"Careful. That tree got pimplers."

"I just find out!" she cried.

"You get juck?"

"Yes."

"Let me see. It bleeding."

He drew her finger to his mouth sucking hard. She felt the blood ooze from her finger onto his lips.

"Feel better?"

"Sorta."

"You know this tree?"

"No."

"This tree is the kill-tree. The leaves, the roots, the bark. Every part of it is poisonous. It does kill."

"You mean I go die?"

"No, you have to eat it." He laughed. "Nothin's gonna happen to you."

He began to crack the nuts, popping them into his mouth, chewing rapidly as he did so, eating noisily with his mouth open and chuckling to himself every now and then.

Midra followed suit. The nuts were tender and sweet, the sweetest nuts she'd ever tasted, even sweeter than the ones he brought for her on Friday nights. The thought of eating such sweet nuts under a tree full of poison made them taste even sweeter. She moved closer to him and began to chew as noisily as he did. She felt giddy. The sweetness of the nuts brought with it a feeling of freedom and abandon. Prince began to whistle softly. The moon, his red hair, the kill-tree, the sensation of liquidity, of wanting to flow like water—everything in the gully seemed to be filtering out of a dream. She felt the softness of the grass under her and stretched herself out on the thick carpet. She closed her eyes and quietly slipped deeper under the spell of this night. The song he was whistling became a dizzying echo as the moon's brilliance made her feel like she was glowing from inside. The sensation of flying swept her up. She smiled. She had never felt so untrammeled, so buoyant. Now she was entering a cave filled with nuts and guavas and animals. And she was the only light. She dazzled. The walls glowed. A beautiful baby monkey sat on a mask of a woman with one breast, her arms holding air. She ate more nuts from the floor of the cave and danced with the monkey. She put the mask on her face and saw a woman searching for her son. The monkey became a snake, sucking the heart from the guavas before it disappeared under her dress with the seeds. She was thrilled. She screamed at the unbearable ecstasy. The seeds escaped and began to grow. The snake withdrew and became a bird. They flew off near the moon.

FIVE

Midra woke up in her bed and saw her mother standing over her. It was morning.

"How you get in here?" Peata demanded.

Midra could not remember coming home. The sun was shining directly on her face, scattering its warmth across the room. Her fingers and her clothes were covered with dirt.

"You smell like a animal," said Peata angrily. "I bolt every door and window in this house last night. How you get in?"

"I don't know."

"How you mean you don't know? I want to know what happen to you last night. Where you was since evening when that foolish woman come here complaining you nearly kill she with you' bucket? You know how much search I search for you, eh?"

Midra tried to recall how she got home but couldn't. Her body felt tired. She did not want to get out of bed. There was a dull aching sensation between her legs. She touched the spot and scraped the caked blood.

"Get up out that bed!" her mother was shouting. "I

want you to go to the butcher. When you come back, I will deal with you.''

It was Sunday, the day Peata got her bull's testicles fresh from the butcher. Midra hated going to pick them up because of the looks she got from the men liming there: drunk, with hungry eyes, like scavenger dogs that smelled fresh meat for the first time. They sniffed at her and cackled when she took the bull's testicles, still hot with blood. Why did her mother have to send her to get them today? Why did she have to wake up from the beautiful dream she was having?

Peata sat on the bed after Midra left. She was exhausted from being up all night. How did Midra get into the house without her knowing? Her nerves were crawling, and the only thing that would calm them right now was a plate of bull's testicles.

On a whim she had begun eating bull's testicles when she was pregnant with Midra. One of those whims you get when the baby you are carrying seems to demand that you eat everything in sight and anything that comes to mind. And she had continued eating them, not only because she liked the taste and the calming effect they seemed to have on her, but also because each time she ate bull's testicles she renewed a promise she had made to herself the very morning she first yearned for this delicacy: never to let herself fall under the spell of a man again, a spell disguised as love.

She had loved Midra's father with all the passion he could wring from her body, mind, and soul, and he had left her pregnant and heartbroken. She had not been able to think of the man without breaking into tears or the cold sweat of anger; sometimes she got into such a frenzy, she'd find herself wheezing and gasping for air. Thinking about him always left her feeling weak, humiliated, and afraid, like a child wandering into a dark room only to find there was no way out. Every time she'd thought about Dove, it was like poison being released into her blood, and she struggled to keep him locked away, out of her thoughts. But that was the past. Now, when she looked back on the experience, she laughed at herself for being so simple and lovesick.

Dove had been a fisherman who spent more time thinking of ways to get to Africa than he did fishing. She was fifteen when she met him. He didn't know for sure how old he was, he said, because the old woman who found him in the canes when he was a baby and raised him until she died didn't know when he was born, and she never bothered to count the years that went by. Dove's dark, serious eyes never left her face whenever he talked to her, and she often wished she could crawl out of her skin and into his, to see what he saw when he looked at her with such intensity. Whatever it was, it was something other people didn't see or were too busy fawning over her to notice. By the time she met Dove, Peata had grown accustomed to men and women who seemed to lose their senses over her almost white skin and black curly hair. She was often given money by old women, friends of her grandmother, simply because "she was so sweet-lookin'." Many years later, when she was struggling to raise Midra in the city, Peata allowed herself to be seduced by a rich merchant who convinced her that she was the most beautiful woman he'd ever seen. He set her up in a house and promised to marry her. But she found out at a party she attended—where every other woman there seemed to be a mistress of a wealthy merchant—that her suitor was already married to a white woman and had two other mistresses who, like her, were also of light complexion. He took good care of them, he told her confidently when she confronted him, as good as if he had married them. And he had given her what he gave the other two: a house, a maid, and fine clothes. All he asked in return was her faithfulness and her readiness when he came to her. She spat in his face and returned to her one room in the city.

Dove never once said anything about her looks, maybe that was what made him so appealing. He saw beyond her almost white skin, into her heart, felt her love for him, and loved her back. She did not take his talk of going to Africa seriously even after he told her he had made it as far as Brazil once, having heard that many ships left Brazil bound for Africa. But after spending two months there, he was unable to find a ship going to Africa and returned home on the schooner that had taken him to Brazil. That was when he decided to build his own boat. At the same time he began training his body to swim to Africa just in case his boat proved unworthy of the high sea.

"I think you crazy, Dove," she said to him.

"Why?"

"You go take me with you?"

"I will come back for you."

"Why you want to go to Africa so bad?" she asked him.

"You ain't know? That is where we come from."

"I don't know 'bout you, but I know I come from out me mother belly," she laughed.

He got angry and didn't speak to her for a week. But she sat every day and watched him chisel away at the trunk of a mahogany tree he had cut down to make his boat. At the end of each day's work he would swim four or five miles out to sea as part of his training, then fish. He never returned without catching one or two big barracudas or albacores, which he brought to shore strung together on a string around his waist.

"People say you does catch fish with you' hand," she said to him one day.

"That is true."

"How you does do that?"

"When I see them I does go limp like I dead. When them come close, I does grab them tail and stick me knife right here.'' He grabbed her neck to demonstrate where he stuck his knife. ''Right in them gills. Fish can't live long without them gills.''

He pushed her to the ground, and they rolled around laughing on the grass.

He had almost finished his boat when she realized she was pregnant, but it did not change his mind about going to Africa.

''How you could leave me when I go have your child?'' she protested. ''What so important 'bout goin' to Africa?''

''It just is,'' he replied.

''What 'bout the baby?''

''The baby go be fine.''

''How you know?''

''I don't.''

''Then why you say so?''

''Me don't know what else to tell you.''

The seriousness in his eyes that often seemed to penetrate her had woven a net of passion around her, a net she mistook for love. Now she was trapped. Nothing was going to stop him from leaving, and it was too late now to let go of him.

He left two weeks later. He pushed his little boat into the sea and paddled his way into the sun without her. She felt as though the waves had smashed her heart against the side of the boat, squeezing the last drops of blood from it and tearing it asunder until, like salt, it dissolved. The pain was excruciating, and Peata thought it would never leave her. One day, lying in bed, after a night of ceaseless crying, her belly spreading with child, she felt a sudden craving for bull's testicles. She did not know where it came from, but no sooner had she experienced this sudden craving than her grandmother returned from the butcher bearing two huge bull's testicles. Her grandmother had begged the butcher for them, thinking that Peata might like them. From that day until now Peata had never missed a Sunday without a dish of delicately prepared bull's testicles. Her way of cooking them was quite simple: after putting them in lime and salt for half an hour, she boiled them in slightly salted water, crushed clove, and pepper until they were tender. Then she ate them while they were still warm. From the beginning she found their distinctive taste and aroma not only appealing but soothing, and it seemed to help her put Midra's father out of her mind.

But those same serious, elusive eyes that had entrapped her before had reentered her life in the person of Prince Johnson, and she had to make an effort to escape them before they caused her pain again. It was becoming clear to her that Prince was another man in whose heart dwelled a thousand dreams, all of which were more important to him than love. No matter how much you loved a man like that he would never understand what a woman is giving him when she offers her heart. The next time Prince came she would tell him not to return.

Maybe she would seduce him first and then tell him not to return.

No. She did not want to see him in her house again.

Yes, bull's testicles were the only things that would calm her nerves this Sunday morning. Between Prince's insensitivity to her feelings for him and her daughter foolishly filling her with fright, she was surprised she could still think. Luckily she had not held a party last night. She had spent the night walking the length and breadth of the village looking for Midra. When she became exhausted, she had broken off a fat tamarind branch and returned home, locked all the doors and windows, determined to give Midra the beating of her life whenever she came home. She was not angry because Midra had struck the fat woman with her bucket and run. She had all but ignored the incoherent complaint of that woman, who had a habit of dropping low remarks to her when she passed her on the street. It served her right. She only wished she had been there to knock her back into the gutter. No, she was angry with Midra for filling her with a panic that she had never experienced before, the panic of a mother losing her child.

When Dove had told her how the old woman had found him in a cane field, her first thought was that he had been abandoned by his mother, and she tried to offer him sympathy by saying that she couldn't understand how a mother could do that. But Dove was forever unsentimental about that part of his life. "Maybe she didn't abandon me," he used to say. "Maybe somebody steal me and to this day she still lookin' for me."

The confrontation between Midra and her mother did not occur that night because shortly before dawn Peata had fallen asleep in the kitchen, not hearing Prince Johnson stepping nimbly through the window he had opened with the deftness of a cat. And after delicately depositing his sleeping load onto the bed, he left as quietly as he'd come.

Midra returned with the bull's testicles.

"You still ain't tell me where you was," Peata said as she put them in lime and salt.

"I not sure where I went," Midra said.

She didn't know what to tell her mother. There was so much about last night she did not understand herself. How much of what she was remembering was real and how much of it was a dream?

"Midra, you like you gone out ya mind!" Peata cried. She was trying desperately to hold back the fury of motherly justice that was about to sweep over her like a wave. She clutched the tamarind branch tightly. "You want me to beat you 'til you remember?"

"Beating me ain't go do nothin'," Midra replied. She was surprised at her own calm. How could her mother understand the liberating sensation of flying and the feeling of excruciating pleasure she had experienced? It must have

been a dream, she thought to herself. But she had seen
Prince Johnson. She was sure of that. There was the dirt
on her hands and feet. Memory and dream may be alike
but you do not bring evidence back from the voyage into
a dream. Or do you? She was not sure.

The sensation of pain brought her back to the present.
Her mother was beating her. Peata struck her again with
the fury of a mother who felt that somehow she had been
betrayed. She had expected Midra to perhaps lie about
where she had gone, but what she did not expect was
Midra's reticence. Midra felt the impact of the tamarind
rod, but she absorbed each lash like the sea taking in rain.
Not crying. Not cringing. She stayed curled up like a baby,
as Peata rained blow after blow on her until she became
exhausted and slumped to the bed crying beside Midra.

"How you could do this to me?" Peata cried. "You
think I make outta stone? I's your mother, you ungrateful
thing! You don't care a damn 'bout me. You leave me here
to worry 'bout you all night and look how you come in
here. Like some animal from the gutter. Ya hands and
clothes dutty, dutty like you come from digging cane hole,
and you tellin' me you don't remember where you went.
You think I's a jackass or what? Girl, I feel like killin' you,
ya don't know?"

Midra reached out her left hand and touched her mother.
It was the only thing she could think of doing, to let her
mother know that she was telling the truth, that she was
not sure about anything that had happened last night. She
wanted it to be clear more than anything, not because she
was afraid of another beating but because deep down inside
she felt awe at the forces that had possessed her last night
and was afraid. She wanted her mother to hug her.

Midra's hand rested on her mother's lips. Peata did not
move. Neither woman moved. Peata smelled the dirt on
Midra's fingers, and without understanding why she was
doing it, slowly began to lick the dirt from them. It had the

strange taste of blood and guava seeds. Of bull's testicles. Midra remained motionless until her mother had licked off all the dirt, then the two women held each other as though they were holding onto the last breath of life. And then the news came in the person of Gunny. Prince Johnson was dead.

SIX

It was Small Paul who actually brought the news to the village because he had been there and seen the whole thing. The news he passed to Gunny was that Prince had been caught in the field of nuts by the owner of the plantation and shot. The body was found at the mouth of the gully where Prince had collapsed after running from the field. Never mind that no blood was found in the field of nuts, and no trail of blood led to the gully, that was the news Small Paul gave Gunny and it was the news he passed on. It was not his story, so he could not vouch for its truthfulness; he was just the news-carrier. It was this news he gave to a half-naked Peata, whose tongue was black with dirt and whose scream when she heard it sent chills racing down his spine.

Word of Prince Johnson's death spread through Monkey Road faster than a cane fire in a high wind. That Sunday morning, under flamboyant trees, under shack-shack trees, and anywhere that people gathered in the village, men and women alike could be seen with tears running down their cheeks. These people were not concerned with what Prince Johnson was doing in the white man's field of nuts; if he went there to steal, as the owner and the police claimed, that was not their business. The Prince Johnson they knew was not a thief but a young man of conscience. He had a seriousness about him that won the confidence of the elders in the village like Pa John and his wife, with whom he ate dinner every Sunday he was in the village. In return, whenever Prince came back from a trip, he would bring something special for them; a piece of sculpture, an animal figurine, always something beautiful. And he often gave them money. In fact, he gave money to anyone who asked. That was the Prince that Monkey Road cried for.

Prince Johnson had lived alone in a one-room house left to him by his grandfather. Both his parents had died when he was a child, leaving his grandfather to raise him. Because everyone knew him to be a seaman, no one thought it strange that he was seldom seen in the village. No one saw when he left to go to sea and no one saw when he returned. He was either there or not there. When he wasn't there, everyone assumed he was at sea. When he was there, they enjoyed the vitality of his presence. Men, women, and children.

His popularity was enhanced by the things he brought back to Monkey Road from his trips. Sweet-smelling soaps and oils, perfumes, fancy-looking hairbrushes with silver handles, sculptures and paintings, and silver and gold jewelry. Most of these objects he would give away, and his generosity was never questioned. That was the Prince Johnson the village wept for.

Vida Ducamp heard the news in the village of Calvary Hill and wept. Vida knew another Prince.

For almost seven years Vida had lived in Monkey Road with a man who took very good care of her. He never hit her and she enjoyed his respect, something most women in Monkey Road did not get from their men. They had three

children together, and her husband did his best to provide
for them so that she would not have to work. But his job
as a driver at the plantation was not really sufficient to keep
the family well fed and clothed. After six years with this
man she had developed a restlessness she could not control
no matter what she did. She hated cooking and cleaning.
Her three children, aged two to six, were adorable, but there
were times when she wished she could leave them all and
go off somewhere by herself for a long time. She found
herself leaving home and walking to the beach, where she'd
spend the whole day watching the flirtation of waves with
cliffs. Many times she did not come back until after dark,
forcing her husband to go to his mother's house—where
she would have left the children—to eat. Other times, she
would walk to the capital to observe the men and women
sauntering about the wharf. One night her husband threatened to beat her for not having his food ready when he
came home, and she stopped her wanderings.

A few days later the children accepted some little trinkets
from Prince Johnson, tiny wood sculptures of horses and
birds. When she went to thank him for the gifts, she found
herself talking to him freely and realized that there was
something about him that made her feel infinitely warm and
soft inside. Before long she was laughing with him and
telling him her innermost secrets. Like her desire to travel
the world by sea.

"You mean become a seaman?" he asked her.

"A seawoman," she laughed.

"Oh, yeah. What about the man you live with?"

"He could become a seaman and follow me if he like."
Prince laughed.

Her deep, intense eyes, her cheery smile, and the ample
flesh on very large bones created an aura of power that
captivated Prince. The way people moved was important to
him; he liked the effortlessness with which she moved, as
if walking on her toes. Unusual for such a large woman,

he thought. When she told Prince she craved nuts late at night and sometimes the craving would be so bad that she would stay awake, unable to go back to sleep, unless her husband made love to her, he laughed again.

Vida pretended to be offended by his laughter but was quickly recompensed with an offer of a large bag of nuts, which he would deliver to her that night. She did not want to make her husband jealous or suspicious, so she agreed to meet Prince near the gully away from meddling eyes.

That night after the children had gone to sleep she told her husband she wanted to take a walk and left the house. The night was very dark. No moon. No stars. Black clouds, bloated with rain, skimmed the sky. A feathery breeze made the bamboos sing. Prince was waiting for her at the edge of the gully. He took her hand. She hesitated for a moment. Then the boundless feeling of warmth came over her again, and she followed him into the gully. He stopped on the grass near the stream and sat down. She went to him instinctively.

Their first kiss seemed to have no end. The clouds exploded in a heavy downpour but that only seemed to fuel their desire. Clothes melted in the warm rain. The lovers rolled around in the downpour, groping and grabbing for anything to keep from falling into the abyss of pleasure they each knew was coming. His tongue zoned in on her desire. At once hard, stubborn, and swift in the small of her back, flicking at her like a fire; and then pliant, delicate, languishing on her nipples, her calves, between her upturned thighs. It seemed to burrow into her like an animal searching for a home. Her frenzy became too much to bear, and her screams brought the monkeys alive. When she got on top of him, rocking back and forth on his hardness, the night became filled with shrieking monkeys urging the lovers on.

Later as they lay in a bed of water they laughed together. Vida was the first to speak.

"I ain't never been in here before. Not at night."

"You scared them vexed African spirits go get you, eh?"

"Funny how you does be scared to do something 'til you do it the first time and realize it wasn't nothin' to be scared of."

"That's true."

"Where them nuts you offer me?" she asked.

He got up and walked a few feet over to a burlap bag hidden behind a large rock near the brook. He opened it and poured half of its contents on the ground. Vida, still naked, sat on the rock making waves with her toes in the brook.

"Where you get all them nuts from?"

"Take what you want," he said.

"You thief them?"

"I don't thief."

She stooped to grab a handful of nuts. He was standing next to the bag a few inches away from her. She looked at his feet and noticed how long his toes were. They were like fingers. Long and slender. She had never seen toes that long.

"What you lookin' at?" He smiled.

"Your toes."

"They run in the family," he joked.

"All your family have toes like that?"

"Yes," he replied.

She stood up.

"I can't go back. My man will know," she said.

"How?"

"I smell like you."

"How I smell?"

"I not sure. You just smell different."

"You have anywhere you could go?"

She paused for a moment, thinking. "I got a sister in Calvary Hill, I could go there."

"What about your children?"

"I don't know yet."

"Let me walk you."

They got dressed. The rain had stopped. He took her hand as they left the gully on the other side of the village and began to walk along the quiet road between two fields of sugarcane.

"I think you make me pregnant tonight," she said, breaking the silence.

"How you know that?" he asked.

She squeezed his hand as if to tell him it was something that only women knew, something that a man could not understand, but he persisted.

"That was my first time," he said sheepishly.

"No wonder." She giggled.

"No wonder what?"

"No wonder you give me so much. You full me up with you' stuff. I don't think it go ever come out."

They laughed together. Prince wanted to turn around and take her back to his little house so they could laugh together all night, but he knew if he did that, her husband would come looking for her. They arrived in Calvary Hill and she led him to a brown house.

"My sister live here."

Prince held her hand tighter, not wanting to let her go. The street was quiet. The house was dark. The rain was coming down again softly.

"I have to get my children," she said.

"Don't worry 'bout them," he said.

"I can't face him. Not after what I do."

"Don't worry. You go have your children tonight."

"How?"

"Don't worry." He let go of her hand. "Go inside and don't worry."

She did not move.

"Don't worry, I tell ya. Go on inside."

Someone lit a lamp in the house and a window opened. Prince turned and walked off into the night.

Later Prince knocked on the house in Calvary Hill and delivered Vida's children. He left before she could ask him how he'd gotten them out of the house.

In the days following Prince Johnson's death, the police found in his house silver cups, knives, spoons, and gold ornaments, which they said he had stolen from plantation houses throughout the island. This proved that the plantation was justified in killing him, they said. The man was a thief.

The police also found an abundance of elegant wood sculptures of smooth, long-necked Africans, and unusual-looking animals and birds. They speculated that he might have stolen those too but had no idea where they came from.

No matter what the police said, the villagers would not accept the plantation's right to kill Prince. They kept up their anger at the plantation until the start of the crop season. Then they refused to harvest the crop. The standoff lasted two weeks. The plantation threatened to bring in workers from other villages and to turn out the tenants in Monkey Road. The next week the strikers were back cutting cane. But during that crop season mysterious fires destroyed more cane than was reaped.

Three weeks after Prince Johnson was buried, Midra woke up one morning and vomited in the bed. Peata knew immediately that her daughter was pregnant and almost as instinctively knew who the father was. Feelings of betrayal swept over Peata, and she wanted to beat her daughter again, this time for sleeping with the man she'd wanted. She thought of those restless glances that had passed between Prince and Midra on Friday nights. And it made her angry that she had not figured out the reason Prince never touched her. He'd wanted Midra, not her. She should have seen it. If she had seduced him, she might be feeling what her daughter was feeling now. All the same, how could she allow Midra to have that baby? The man was a thief.

After the third straight morning of vomiting, Midra fell back into bed too sick to move. Peata got up to make her a cup of lemongrass tea.

"You with child, you know that."

Midra could only nod her head.

"You still go tell me you don't remember what happened to you?"

Midra remained silent.

"This baby belong to Prince, ain't it?"

Midra nodded again.

"You know it belong to Prince but you don't know how it happen? Midra, I think you ready for the madhouse. You go have to get rid of that child," Peata said bluntly as she handed the cup of tea to Midra. A silence fell on the room. Peata moved from beside the bed to sit in a chair against the opposite wall. Midra appeared to be impervious to what her mother had said. She sipped the hot tea cautiously.

"You hear what I say?"

An odd glint shadowed Midra's eyes as she slowly fixed her gaze on her mother, a look that made her seem older than her fifteen years. The queasiness in her stomach was beginning to pass.

"You mean kill it?" she said finally. She looked at her mother as though she could not see her properly. Like someone trying to focus against a harsh light. Peata, trying to appear firm and resolute, looked away.

"Yes," Peata said calmly. "There's a herb you can drink."

Deep inside she wanted Midra to fight back, for she knew that if Midra protested, she would give in. She did not really want Midra to get rid of the baby. But she had to punish the girl for what she had done. Midra got up from the bed and went into the backyard to the outhouse. Peata followed her, thinking that she was going to be sick again, but Midra was fine. She disappeared into the outhouse, leaving her mother to stare at the tiny green lizards lounging on the door. Peata waited in the doorway of the kitchen until her daughter came out, but Midra walked silently past her into the house and back to bed. All day Peata waited for Midra to say something, but she kept her silence. Peata made a big fuss of preparing fried cassava and a spicy cook-up of pork, rice, and beans.

Midra ate the food in silence. Overcome by frustration and guilt, Peata repented and told Midra she could do as she wanted with her baby. Still Midra said nothing. Peata then began to talk about her longing for bull's testicles during her own pregnancy. When she asked her daughter if there was anything she felt like eating, Midra said, "Nuts and guavas."

Midra and her mother disappeared from the village for nine months. Peata wanted Midra to be away from the meddlesome eyes of Monkey Road, at least until the mess about Prince Johnson and the police died down. Faced with Midra's reluctance to leave, Peata insisted that if the police found out she was carrying Prince's child, they would accuse her of having something to do with his clandestine activities.

Tensions between the police and the villagers escalated. The police started making regular sweeps through the village, searching people's houses and backyards based on speculation coming from the plantation that Prince had been the leader of a gang and now the gang was stealing their crops in retaliation for his death. The watchmen who reported the thefts said they did not see the thieves so the monkeys became the logical culprits. A few people were hauled before the magistrate, but the watchmen continued to report the disappearance of potatoes and the destruction of young canes. After six weeks of constant police presence in the village, the watchmen reported that the stealing had come to a halt, and the police suspended their raids.

Peata and Midra went to stay with Peata's grandmother in the city. When Midra went to look for her friend Rose, she found out that Rose had been killed by her boyfriend. She took flowers and some clove to Rose's grave. When he was born, she named her son Hartseed. But he was Baby Prince to her.

SEVEN

When Midra returned to Monkey Road, she had become even more withdrawn. Her mother took the baby for walks while she stayed in the house, passing the time sleeping or trying to retrace the sequence of events of that now fateful night with Prince, hoping to find the key to unlock the riddle of her confusion. But it was like trying to catch rain in a bucket with holes. Repeatedly she would get the sensation of entering a bright, cool place and of looking at the world through the eyes of a mask, but just when she thought she was about to comprehend the feeling, it would slip away from her. A cave. A mask. A woman looking for her son who could fly. And sometimes in that cool place she felt her father was there waiting to speak to her if only she could see through those eyes.

Now sixteen, she had fully developed the voluptuousness of her mother. Occasionally, when she went to Mabel's house to buy black pudding for Peata, she would catch Brandon staring at her. His smile and inquiring look would be answered with a blank stare, the same blank stare she would fix on Small Paul's house whenever she passed it. But sometimes she would stand and stare at the house for a long time before continuing on her way.

One evening, Small Paul looked out of his window and saw Midra in the street. She was standing there with the baby slumped on her hip, that blank expression on her face. Small Paul called to her from the window, but she ran off.

Two days later, in the noonday sun, Small Paul saw her—sweat glistening on her forehead, the baby slumped on her hip crying, with the same expression on her face, staring at his house again. This time Small Paul opened his front door and went to sit by the window, waiting to see what would happen. Midra came and sat in the doorway. A short time later, a quick gust of rain drove her into the house to avoid getting wet. The wind was blowing the rain all over the house so Small Paul closed the door. He watched the tiny raindrops splatter the green leaves of the pea trees outside his window.

The rain did not last long. When it stopped he opened the door again, but Midra did not move from her seat on the floor. She stayed in his house until twilight. During that time she fed the baby twice but did not speak.

Though he had seen her walking the streets and had encountered her several times at Mabel's house, Small Paul knew very little about her and was beginning to get the feeling that she was not right in her head. But there was something about her that attracted him, that tugged him like an undertow in the ocean.

The next day she came to his house and found the door open. Small Paul told her he had just dug some potatoes and eddoes from his small plot of land and she could make some soup for the baby if she wanted to. She did. And left some for Small Paul. Before she went home he gave her potatoes and eddoes to take with her. She did not return that week. The next week, however, she came every day, and by the end of the week Small Paul was holding the baby and talking to her about his life as though he had known her forever.

Since witnessing Prince Johnson's death, Small Paul had

kept himself away from people. He'd sold his donkey and cart and spent his time feeding his pigs and weeding the tiny plot of land behind his house. Besides going to Ben Payne's house to have a drink once a week, this had become his only activity. He still went to Ben Payne's house because he felt a kindred spirit in Ben. Ben knew that love could drive a man to hide inside the darkest closet of his mind, that a certain kind of woman could make a man hurt so much after she was gone that he would rather live in darkness than show himself to the bright light of life. That was how he had felt when his woman ran away with another man. And he knew Ben had felt the same way when his wife died, a loss that sent him to the madhouse for two years. But there was a sweetness to that pain, making Small Paul cling to the memory of that lost love, even as the love turned to hate.

Eager for anything to take his mind off Prince's death, which still haunted him, he was delighted that this young girl chose to spend time with him. She did not talk much but she listened well and she was beautiful. To encourage her continued presence he gave her anything she wanted from the plot of land he worked. Her fluid eyes sucked him in like a stormy sea.

Her beauty began to filter through the web of his dreams, and the moistness that seeped through that web onto the fabric of his hammock he would let linger for hours the next day. For the first time since his woman had left him, he felt himself looking forward to the crowing of the cock because it meant a new day had arrived. And that meant another chance to hear her voice. Another chance to hold her baby. No vision was sweeter than the sight of her nursing the baby in the chair in the front house. The sight of Midra's nipples in the boy's mouth stirred Small Paul in areas he thought had died a premature death.

Midra pretended not to notice him sniffing around her like a lost puppy when she fed her son. Once, after she had fallen asleep in the chair with her son still at her bosom, the little boy also fell asleep, leaving his mother's unattended nipple for Small Paul's impertinent gaze. For a while Small Paul could not believe his good luck. He fell to his knees before the sleeping girl and began to suck on her nipple, drawing the hot life from her breast. When Midra began to stir, he jumped up and left the room, returning a few minutes later to catch her placing her exposed breast back inside her blouse.

From that day, he tried to think of ways to keep her at his house long after twilight—when she usually went home—and could do nothing unless she was there. To keep her he talked on and on. He told her about his love for the woman who'd run away with two of their sons, leaving the eldest with him, how he had not seen them for twenty years and would do anything to see them again before he died. Midra listened, without showing any emotion, to his tale of suffering.

Then he began to talk of his experiences as the watchman for the plantation. He told her of the night he was beaten by a group of thieves and left for dead in a field of potatoes. He did not know how he survived that beating. It was Prince Johnson who found him and brought him home. Midra's ears perked up. She asked him if the stories about Prince stealing from the plantation were true.

He had always known that Prince Johnson was stealing from the plantations, he told her. ''It wasn't just the one 'round here. He hit every plantation in the island. He steal everything he could from them plantations. The potatoes and corn he would steal and then leave them on the doorstep of people in the village who didn't have nothin' to eat. Them didn't know it was Prince who put the food at them door. Prince wasn't out for glory. He just do it because, well, he was Prince. That's the way he was. The silver and gold and valuable things he would take by boat to the other islands, where he exchanged them for wood carvings from

68

Africa. He used to go as far as Brazil for them African sculptures and masks. Is the masks that he was really interested in.''

His talking about masks suddenly cracked a shard of memory of that night in the gully with Prince. The mask was coming into focus: a woman and a monkey. A very odd feeling came over her as she conjured up the mask in her mind and saw clearly the deep crack in the woman's chest. One of the woman's breasts had been ripped away. She remembered the mask over her own face. The eyes of that mask were also the eyes of the past but what she had seen was hidden from her now by a fog. A woman searching for her son? A woman giving birth on a mountaintop?

"Midra?" Small Paul's voice entered the fog.

"Yes."

"You all right?"

"Uh-huh."

"What you studyin' so?"

"Nothin'. Why he was so interested in them masks?"

"Who? Prince? He just love them things. I believe Prince loved them masks more than he love woman. I mean, Prince coulda had any woman 'bout this village. Any woman. He was a generous man. Would give a woman anything. But he used to ignore them. Didn't seem to have interest in no woman. Had his mind on other things. On one thing in particular, to tell the truth. He was obsessed with finding a piece that was broken off from a mask he had.''

Midra's eyes widened. So Small Paul knew about that mask too.

"What it look like?"

Small Paul paused.

"How good did you know Prince?" he asked her.

"He used to come to our house. To the parties. He drank wine with my mother. But I didn't know him too good."

When he looked at her this time the softness had gone

from her eyes. She was lying. The truth suddenly dawned on him. He looked at the baby and laughed to himself. How could he have missed it? Hartseed was Prince's child.

"Let me tell you something 'bout Prince. Something that only one person in this village know beside me. And that body is Pa Daniel, the father of this village, who know everything there is. Prince was not the person everybody in the village think he was. Prince come from a line of shape-shifters." He paused, waiting to see her response. "You know what that is?"

"No."

"Somebody who could change themselves into anything. Prince favorite animal was the monkey. Because he was a trickster. He like playing tricks on them plantation people. He liked to taunt them. Creep in them house like a cat and sleep under the mistress bed, and when the poor woman wake up next morning she would see a monkey sitting on her pillow. Frighten the poor woman near to death before he become a bird and fly through the window."

"Stop making sport!"

"I not making no sport, girl. That is why I don't talk 'bout these things. Most people don't understand them. Prince was different. His grandfather that raise him was like that. It come down through them family. And when them change shape, nobody don't know is a human in that animal shape. I's one of the few people could tell it is a human in that animal body. Pa Daniel is another one. And my son could tell too."

"How Prince could do that?"

"How? I don't really know. How birds does fly?"

"What about the mask? The one Prince had that was broke?"

He did not answer her question. Instead he asked, sheepishly, "You think your mother would let you live here?"

She was caught off guard. She remained silent.

"I have a empty bedroom. We could sit up all night

talking 'bout these things. You seem to like these stories. I know enough stories to keep you listening forever. I could use the good company.'' He paused. ''I don't know why, but as long as it is that she gone I never get over that woman. Love is a funny thing. Is the worst pain in the world. I thought she was happy with me. I really thought she was happy. We had the house, we had the children, I had the job at the plantation and I was making extra money with the donkey and cart, drawing things for people. I thought the woman was happy. I still don't understand how she could up and run off with another man like that. I was nice to the woman. You could ask anybody in the village. I search up and down, and I couldn't find where she went to. After five years pass and I ain't hear nothin', I begin to think maybe I blaming myself for nothin'. Maybe she dead. Maybe she didn't run away. She dead and just nobody ain't find the body. And then out of the blue, twenty years later, I get to know the whole story. Where she is and who she run away with.''

Midra felt sorry for him but she wanted to hear about Prince.

''You ever see the mask?'' she asked.

''The mask?''

''Yes, Prince mask that broke.''

''Oh, yes. I believe it come down through Prince family, you see. It hold the spirits of Prince ancestors in it. That is why he went to all that trouble tryin' to find that piece that get break off.''

''What you mean by hold his ancestors' spirits?''

''From his people all the way back to Africa. Pa Daniel who get bring to this island as a slave from Africa tell me that the minute them Africans step off the slave boat them used to start looking for ways to escape. Some try to swim back. Some take poison hoping that them spirits would go back. And some of them believe the best way was to call on them ancestor spirits, who would give them the power

71

to get back to Africa. So is my belief that one of Prince slave ancestors make the mask to call up the power of his ancestors. And Prince promise his grandfather he would find it and put it back together.''

"You say you see the mask then?" asked Midra.

"I see it, yes."

"What it look like?"

He paused.

"Please, tell me," she begged.

"Why you so interested in these things? You had something with Prince?"

"Prince? No. I don't know. I just curious."

He accepted the lie, not really knowing why, and got up to close all the windows and lock the doors before sitting back down. When he sat down he took a deep breath and uttered a long sigh before he spoke.

"It very big, this mask. About thirty-six inches high. Make out of wood. Dark wood. Like mahogany but I not sure. He wouldn't let me touch it. It have two parts to it. The bottom part is the face of a monkey. The monkey had two lines running down each side from the eyes to the chin. On top the monkey head a figure of a woman with a long neck with her legs open, and the way she sitting with her legs open is like she inviting you to enter her. She have two lines running down her face and a child latch onto her back. Now the thing 'bout this mask is that this woman only have one breast. The other one missing. And the breast is long and pointy like a knife. Prince explain to me why the woman only have one breast. The other one is in the mouth of her little baby who was nursing. But that is the part that Prince didn't have. The baby and the other breast is the part that get break off.''

There was a long pause. The mask he had described was the same mask she had seen or had dreamed. She still wasn't sure.

"How you manage to see it?"

"One day I was walking through the gully and I butt up on him with the mask in his hand. I believe he did waitin' for me."

"Why?"

"He say he had a feelin' the piece he was lookin' for was somewhere in the village. He thought I mighta know where it was."

"Did you?"

"No."

"I hear you was there," Midra said.

"Where? You mean . . . You mean when he get shoot?"

"Yes."

Midra unbuttoned her blouse and began to feed the baby.

So this was what she wanted, he thought. He would tell her the truth. He had never told anyone what really happened. Not even Ben.

"Well, yes, I was there. In fact I help them catch him."

The baby pulled himself away from his mother's breast and began to cry. Small Paul moved closer and patted the baby's head.

"Come on, little fella, ain't nothin' like you mammy's milk. Drink up," he cooed.

The baby cried harder. Midra got up and paced the room, rocking the baby to her bosom. She pressed the nipple to his lips and he began to suck again. Midra sat down facing Small Paul. She kept her eyes focused on the baby's mouth as he tugged ravenously at her breast. She felt a quick stab of pain at her nipple as if the baby had bitten her. She wanted Small Paul to continue his story but was afraid to look him in the face.

"How they catch him?" she asked.

Small Paul waited a long time. He watched the baby's little mouth moving rhythmically. Every once in a while the nipple would slip out of his mouth and the baby would retrieve it again without opening his eyes. He pulled the bench closer.

"I see Prince many times goin' into the plantation house and he know I see he too," he started. "And he know I woulda never say nothin'. But as I tell you before, I did recently get to find out where my wife disappear to. A friend of Prince who used to work on them boats like he used to, entice her to one of them French islands and she never come back. And the hurtful thing is he didn't even stay with her too long. He leave her there and went to live somewhere in the jungle of South America. But I suppose she did just too shame to come back. This friend come back here a few years ago and was livin' in town before he dead recently. And Prince know it, but he never let on to me. When I find this out I could only think of one thing to do. But Prince friend already dead. I wanted to get back at him so I went to the plantation owner and tell him what I know 'bout Prince. And we set the trap. Like I say I know Prince does change his shape but ain't no way that white man at the plantation was goin' to believe me if I tell him that. So I tell him we could wait at the edge of the gully because Prince does change back to a human when he get into the monkey patch. 'Cause you see, the monkeys is his guard. So said, so done. Prince come through the cane field into the gully with a bunch of silver spoons and a gold watch. The plantation owner shoot him on the spot. Right there at the edge of the gully where them find the body. I was never so frighten in my life. Afterwards I was shame. I was sorry I tell them. Really sorry. But it too late for that now. I know the plantation owner had a gun but I was thinkin' he just go stop Prince and call the police. I didn't realize he would shoot him just so."

The tears rolled silently down Midra's smooth cheeks. Forcing back the urge to scream, she gripped the baby too tightly. He began to cry. Midra got up and walked to the window. She opened it, her back to Small Paul. Stifling air rushed out of the room and a cool wind took its place. She wiped away her tears. From the window she could see the monkeys gamboling atop the mile trees in the gully. On the breeze drifting through the window came the smell of Prince. The fecund smell of nuts and earth. The mollifying smell of leaves and rain.

Small Paul kept talking to her back.

"Them shoot him and leave him there but I couldn't move. I stay there all night. The rain come and wash his blood down into the gully 'til the place was clean. Clean as a whistle. Like if his blood was too precious to leave on the grass. I stay there all night just looking at his body." He paused. "I know that baby is Prince own," he began again. "And I sorry for what I do. I know that can't bring Prince back and I would like to make it up to you and the baby. Come and live with me. You and the baby. I would do anything for you. I would take care of the two of you. 'Til I dead. Anything you want."

She turned away from the window and opened the door and went out.

Midra hugged Baby Prince close. She walked briskly to the edge of the village until she came to Pa Daniel's crumbling house. She knocked and a big man with long silver locks opened the door. He smiled and invited her in. Midra entered the cool dark room and stood amidst a jungle of plants. The plants, of different sizes, filled the entire room, blocking the sunlight. Pa Daniel beckoned her to sit in a large wooden chair with a carved headrest of a monkey's face.

Pa Daniel was a fixture in Monkey Road. He had been there as long as the village had been inhabited. No one really knew how old he was. To the villagers he was time itself. His face was smooth, completely hairless. His hair had always been silver and his house had always seemed to be on the brink of collapse. Midra looked at him without feeling any apprehension, only a determined curiosity. She had heard that Pa Daniel was the person to see to make wrong things right. His massive body rose above her as he took the baby from her arms. "This is a beautiful boy," he said. "He got powerful blood in him."

He tossed the baby in the air and caught him. The baby laughed. Pa Daniel tossed him into the air again and again, each time catching him in one hand as the baby bubbled and laughed. He returned the baby to his mother's arms and sat down on the floor under an oil-leaf bush.

"What can I do for you, Midra?" he said.

Somehow she was not surprised that he knew her name. Maybe he already knew why she had come. She began to relate the story of her baby's father and his death. He stopped her.

"I know all that. Tell my why you come to me."

Midra took a deep breath. She could smell the damp earth in the pots that held the plants. The dark room suddenly seemed very bright.

"I want to make it right," she said in a voice so soft that she thought he would not hear.

"How you go do that?" he asked.

"Give me something to put Small Paul to sleep," she said.

"To sleep? For how long?"

"For as long as Prince is asleep."

"You young, girl. And full of passion. When you do things like this in a passion you does often live to regret it," he said.

"Prince dead. And I ain't go never know what happen to me that night," Midra cried.

"This ain't go bring Prince back."

"Why he should live if Prince dead? He kill Prince. Prince ain't do him nothin'! I ain't go have no peace if I have to walk 'bout this village knowing he livin' and Prince dead."

"What make you think his life is peaceful?"

"Give me, let me go," Midra said determinedly.

"I don't have nothin' to give you. Go home! Go home, girl. Go home and forget 'bout this. Go home and raise your baby to be strong and healthy, that's what you should do. Don't do something you go regret."

He opened the door and sunlight gushed in.

She stepped into the street, and the door closed behind her. As she walked away her anger only swelled more. She bit her lips hard, drawing blood. She suddenly remembered the kill-tree. She turned around and headed for the gully.

The kill-tree was not nearly as big as she thought, its pinnate leaves, without the shadow of night to magnify them, not nearly as broad. In fact, the kill-tree was no more than a bunch of large shrubs growing together in such a tight bond that they could easily be mistaken for one tree in the night. Needles over two inches long covered the tree, and Midra remembered the painful prick of its thorns. Careful not to impale herself again, she broke leaves from the tree one by one. When she felt she had enough, seven in all, she wrapped them tightly together and tucked them in her bosom.

Leaving the gully she could feel the leaves against her nipples. When she got home she wrapped the leaves in cloth and hid them under her bed. Then she stripped naked and took a bath before lying down with her baby.

When Midra and Baby Prince came over that evening, Small Paul managed to persuade Midra to drink rum out of a cup. The first drink made her light-headed. After the second drink she was so giddy that she felt she was floating. When Small Paul tickled her on the bottom of her feet, she began to laugh. When he began to suck on her big toe, her laughter erupted into shrieks of pleasure.

Small Paul surrendered all pretense. Sucking with fervor and abandon, he worked himself into position to get his

hands under her dress and pulled her underpants over her
ankles. But she slipped out of his grasp and ran laughing
into the backyard. He chased her: around the yard, back
into the house, into the yard again, until he was exhausted.
She ran back to the house, leaving him in the yard gasping.
When he finally made it back inside, he found her slumped
in a chair in the front house. Still breathing heavily, he
collapsed on the floor at her feet.

Midra got up, went to the kitchen, and filled a pot with
water from the clay monkey-jar. She lit the stove and put
the water to boil.

While Midra waited, she washed the cup and put some
lemongrass into it. Then she took the leaves from her
bosom and weighed them in her hands. The remnants of
Small Paul's supper, pork stew, lay on the table. His three-
legged dog was barking in the backyard. Mosquitoes
buzzed around her head, and a group of moths played at
death on the hot glass shade of the kerosene lamp. Steam
began to rise from the pot. She added the leaves, letting
them steep in the boiling water for a few minutes before
turning off the stove. After Midra poured the brown-tinted
tea into the cup, the lemongrass floated to the top and then
settled to the bottom. She sweetened it and then poured the
rest of the water with the leaves out the window. Then
Midra grasped the cup by its broken handle and slowly
returned to the front house.

She found Small Paul in the hammock with her underwear clutched to his face. She placed the tea on the night
table beside the hammock and sat in the chair. When he
took the first sip he smiled; the slightly bitter taste told him
his torment would be over soon and he was happy.

Small Paul remained inert, a foolish grin frozen on his
face. The moths continued to challenge death, beating their
wings against the hot glass shade, and the dog continued
to bark outside. A long time passed. Midra fell asleep in
the chair.

When she woke, it was morning. The kerosene lamp had gone out. Small Paul was still. The cup was empty. The moths had all disappeared. The dog still barked.

She heard someone coming and ran from the house, forgetting her drawers clasped in Small Paul's hands. When she got home she washed up to nurse Baby Prince.

Her milk was blood and she wept.

EIGHT

It was a hot cloudy day. Midra hoped the rain would fall to cool everything down. Sweat was trickling from her armpits. She hated days like this. It wasn't so much the sweating, it was that sticky feeling like she had swallowed the berries of the clammy-cherry tree and the viscous juice was now oozing from her pores, pasting her clothes to her body. Especially between her legs. She was sure that men could smell a woman's sweat between her legs. That was why they hunted women down, to devour that smell.

She was walking along one of the narrow cart-roads when she heard someone call her name. Looking back, she saw Brandon waving but kept walking. He ran and caught up with her and settled in beside her, walking on the grassy verge since the road was only wide enough for one person. The sweat was a waterfall down her thighs.

Brandon smiled at her.

"Why you always skinning your mouth so, like you eat bad meat?" she said, hoping to discourage his attention. She did not want his company. What did he want? Why did he pursue her? He didn't look old enough to smell a woman's sweat. She did not like anything about him. His spindly legs and prominent forehead over those delicate watery eyes made him look like a spider.

"This belong to you?" he asked, withdrawing the white underpants from his pocket.

Midra was startled. They were hers. Where did he get them? A quick flash of Small Paul taking off her drawers suddenly came back to her.

"Them not mine," she said calmly.

"You sure?"

"You deaf, or you's a idiot?"

"You lie. These is yours," he challenged.

"Who the hell you calling a liar!" She slapped him.

He slapped her back. The pain stunned her temporarily and she cried out. Her teeth found his forearm. She snapped her jaws tightly together and heard him howl before she let go and took off. He chased after her. She could feel him gaining on her and she changed direction, cutting through a backyard where a woman was bathing a little baby. A dog barked. Running between two houses, she sped into a cane field, hoping to lose him in the maze of ripe canes. She paused to catch her breath, listening. Hunched over, breathing heavily, she saw his shadow out of the corner of her eye, but too late. Like a snake he had managed to wiggle his way between the canes without making any noise. His grip on her dress was firm, and she struggled to get free in vain.

"I go scream if you don't let me go," she threatened. She tried to bite him again, but this time he seized her neck with his other hand, squeezing her so hard that she was the one who howled in pain. He gripped her the way he gripped the ram when he wanted it to stay still. But Midra was not the ram and she kept struggling to get free. She kicked at him and they fell to the ground, with her on top of him. Still he held her firm. He pulled her to his chest and locked both arms around her back, making it impossible for her to move. She stopped fighting.

"Ya done now?" He laughed.

"Let me go!"

"Ya done?"

"Let me go, I said!"

"I ain't holding you," he taunted.

She tried to get up but he held her down.

"You think I making sport with you, you idiot!"

His fingers burrowed into her neck.

"You hurting me!"

He let her go. She was too exhausted to move. Sweat dripped from her brow onto his blue shirt. As she lay there she could feel his heart pounding beneath her. The dank earth around the sugarcane roots piqued her nose. A sudden, insouciant surge under her made her jump up. She saw the erection straining at the front of his pants. He covered it in embarrassment as she ran from the cane field laughing.

She expected him to follow her. After walking about fifty yards she stopped and looked back. Except for a dog urinating in the grass, the road was empty. Why was he not following her? She felt a twinge of disappointment. She dallied under a sugar-apple tree, hoping to see him emerge from the cane field. Maybe his legs weren't so skinny, she thought. And his grip was strong, like a man's. And maybe he was old enough to smell the sweat between a woman's legs. Finally, she gave up and walked on home.

When she got there, Peata and the baby were nowhere to be found. She took off her clothes and filled the tub with water. She took her time bathing, relishing the cooling sensation of the water on her sore neck. Afterwards she powdered her body and went to sleep.

It was almost dark when Peata and Baby Prince returned. The baby was asleep, and Midra took him from her mother and placed him facedown on the bed. Then the two women sat next to him and ate the coconut bread and black pudding Peata had brought.

"What you go tell Hartseed 'bout his father when he get big?" Peata asked.

"I don't know."

"You might be better off not tellin' him who his father was."

"Why?"

"What you go be able to tell him beside his father was a thief?"

"Why you botherin' me, Ma?"

"Nobody don't want a thief for a father."

"Better a thief than no father at all."

"Who needs a father like that? A no good thief!"

"Was my father a thief?"

"Worse than that. He was a heart-eater. Thief my heart and eat it. And then went 'long licking his lips."

"And you expect me to eat Prince heart 'fore his child get a chance to see it?"

"What make you so sure Prince had a heart?"

"There's things 'bout Prince you don't know. Things Baby Prince should know."

"Like what? What you know 'bout that man? Nobody don't know nothin' 'bout that man. He was the most secret man I ever meet. When ya think he here, he there. When he suppose to be there, he turn up here. Who the hell was he? Nobody don't know. All you know 'bout Prince is that one night he take you and stick a child in you' ass and gone 'long happy to his grave leaving you with the headache of raising his child."

"There're things, Ma, you don't know. It go surprise you but I know in me heart, Ma, one day this boy go be proud of his father. Just you wait."

The two women quarreled on into the night. Midra was tired of having this fight with her mother. Baby Prince was now nine months old, and the fights with her mother over Prince had not abated since the day Prince was killed. She knew her mother was jealous. But what was she supposed to do?

Sometimes she wished that night had not happened at all. What had Prince really done to her that night? Where had he taken her? If all he'd done was let loose his seed in her womb her life would be a lot easier. But there was more. He had left her with these sensations, half memories, which burned her like a cold fire: the mask; that cool, bright place, which she realized was a cave; that woman on the mountain giving birth. The euphoria of flying. The more she thought about it, the more confused she became. She had returned to the gully, searching for the cave, but could not find it.

She wondered how many women he had done this to, made to feel this way. Maybe there are plenty of women like me, taken on that nocturnal journey, she thought. It did not matter. She remembered Pa Daniel's words. What mattered was raising Baby Prince.

She opened the window to let in the Lady-in-the-Night to soothe her senses. Ah, how simple it was to be soothed by gentleness. Ah, sleep.

He stayed on the ground, waiting for his embarrassment to subside. Her laughter echoed in his head. Brandon could still smell her. She had laughed at him but he would die for her if she asked. She had laughed but in her eyes he saw love.

The bed he lay on was made of trampled cane blades: a mixture of fresh green stalks broken off in their struggle and dried brown stalks that had been on the ground for so long that the sweat of the earth had seeped through to the top. Brandon was conscious of the dampness beneath him. And that smell! Clove. An intoxicant, like fermented sugarcane, that flowed quickly to his brain, making him giddy and perplexed at the same time. He wanted to laugh and he wanted to dream.

Brandon sat up. He broke a piece of sugarcane from the bunch nearest to him and began to rip the skin apart with his teeth. The sweet juice flowed onto his tongue. Leaving the cane field, he emerged onto the path to the full effect of the sun and saw his father approaching. He tried to duck back into the cane field, but his father had already seen him.

Darnlee walked slowly toward his son. The bag of butcher knives sagged heavily from his weary shoulders. He had been up since four o'clock in the morning. His blood-stained pants were torn at the knees, his knees bruised from a prolonged struggle to restrain the pig he had killed. His partner, Malcolm, had stayed at home sick after a drinking binge, forcing him to slaughter the pig by himself. He had thought of taking his son but Brandon didn't have the stomach for blood.

The pig he killed had been a courageous sow determined not to die. Trying to tie its four legs together was like trying to tie a ship's sails in a storm. His knees hurt. His right shoulder hurt from being thrown against the side of the pigpen too many times. His pride hurt from embarrassment. Six people had watched and laughed as he struggled for more than half an hour to subdue one sow. The two sisters who owned the house and their children had all laughed at him. How could they laugh? He was the most accomplished butcher in Monkey Road. This would never have happened to him in the old days. Then he'd been a king. In the old days he would've wrestled that sow to the ground with one hand tied behind his back. But times had changed. Maybe his days as a butcher were over.

He reached the embankment where his son stood waiting.

"What you doin' in them canes, boy?"

"I just went to break off a piece of cane, Pa."

His father eyed him suspiciously.

"What that you got in your pocket?"

Brandon had completely forgotten about the undergarment.

"What?" Brandon asked innocently.

Darnlee pulled the white drawers from his son's pocket.

"Where you get this, boy? This belong to you' mother?"

"Oh, that!"

"Yes, this! Who this belong to?"

"Oh, that? That . . . I just find that in the canes."

Darnlee laughed. The undergarment was too small to be his wife's. He wondered what young girl his son had been fooling around with. He patted the boy on his shoulder to reassure him. The boy was almost as tall as him, and obviously he was beginning to feel his oats. From the look of things, he'd just fed some of those oats to a young girl in this field of canes. He remembered that he had also started at about this age in a cane field, the girl an adventurous older cousin who'd seduced him.

Darnlee stuffed the undergarment back into his son's pocket. Remnants of dried pig blood from his hand rubbed off onto the white garment and his son's pants.

"So you just find them in the canes, eh?"

"Well, what really happen is this," Brandon began.

"Look, son. You getting to be a man, now. I can see that. You learnin' a trade and you probably beginnin' to see ya pee foaming in front of you. I know what that feel like, believe me. I just hope that 'cause some young girl let you take off her underthings you don't begin to feel that it make you a man. Especially when you in my house. You understand that?"

"I understand, Pa."

"And you better not let your mother see that thing."

"Yes, Pa."

"Who she is?"

"Who?"

"The girl."

"Ah . . ."

"Is that crazy-eye girl that does come for black pudding for her mother?"

"She ain't got no crazy-eye, Pa."

Darnlee smiled. The boy was defending the girl. That was a good sign. It showed character. The girl was a good-looking, healthy young thing. The boy was lucky. Hard to find girls looking that healthy. Most of them had to work too hard from early on, and by the time they reached fifteen years they looked like old women. This girl looked like she didn't do anything but sleep. If his son could keep her, he would be the envy of all his friends. Never mind she had a way of looking at people that made you think she was crazy. She was healthy-looking. That was the most important thing.

Brandon stuffed the undergarment out of sight and walked home savoring the new bond—equality as men— that had just sprung up between him and his father. Brandon broke the piece of cane he was eating in two and offered the smallest piece to his father, who accepted it in silence. Darnlee gave his son his bag of knives and Brandon smiled.

When they got home, Mabel was in the backyard cooking. Brandon raised the lid of the buckpot and saw the black pudding simmering in its brown stew. Mabel, hand on hips, cursed at her son. "Get away from there, you thin scally-wag!"

Darnlee went into the house and fell on the bed like a sack of yams. He was dreaming before his head touched the lumpy pillow. In his dream he could hear pigs laughing. Every pig he had slaughtered swam before him, spouting jets of blood. His wife and his son sat on a rock laughing.

It was about two o'clock before Mabel's black pudding was finished and people began arriving to collect their orders. Brandon was sitting on a rock near the sheep-pen, watching the fowlcock attempt to mount a hen without

much success. Gunny's girlfriend came and rubbed her
blubbery thigh against his face. He ignored her and she left
with Gunny's dish of black pudding. She always did that
to him even with Gunny present. This time she also whispered something in his ear, which he ignored. He certainly
would not meet her behind the church.

Peata arrived late for the first time he could remember.
The black pudding had been ready almost half an hour. She
was carrying the baby, who seemed to be asleep. Without
a word she came over and put the baby in his lap and
returned to the center of the yard where his mother was
slicing the black pudding. The baby opened his eyes wide
and began to bawl.

A few minutes later Ben came into the yard with a tall
woman and introduced her as his mother, who had come
to visit him from her village near the sea. He had brought
her to taste Mabel's black pudding. Mabel beamed with
pride.

"But you' mother don't look no older than you, Ben,"
Peata said.

"I's eighty years, girl. Been around a long time," the
tall woman laughed. Her sand-sprinkled hair was neatly
braided in cornrows and smelled of coconut oil. Mabel
commented that the tall woman reminded her of her own
mother, who looked a lot younger than she really was. The
tall woman asked Mabel if her mother was in the house
and Mabel explained that her mother had died.

"Me own mother dead the day slavery abolish," the tall
woman said. "The said very day. She didn't live a free
day."

The tall woman scrutinized Mabel for a long time. "That
you son over there?" she said, glancing in Brandon's direction. "I hope you pass on to him what you' mother tell
you 'bout them slave times. Make sure you tell him them
things. I make sure I tell my Ben everything me see in them
days. The things we pass through is things I hope our chil-

dren never have to see. The mistreatment. The unfairness. I hope you tell him them things.''

Mabel was silent. The tall woman thanked her for the black pudding and left the yard with Ben.

Peata stayed behind.

''Wonder why she tell you that,'' Peata said.

''What?''

'' 'Bout you' mother.''

''Who knows,'' Mabel replied.

''Maybe them was born on the same plantation,'' Peata said.

''My mother wasn't born no slave,'' replied Mabel.

''I know my grandmother was born in slave times,'' said Peata, ''and my mother barely escape it. My grandmother say that even then some plantations still try to act as though the law that abolish slavery never come through. Like, in fact, them was still slaves. Ain't that something, nuh?''

''I never hear 'bout nothin' so.''

''I wouldn't put it past them wicked people that own the plantations. The way them does treat we people is still a shame. That is why I would chop off me two foot first and poison meself before I step on a plantation say me go work for them. Not me, soulie-gal! Not after what I see happen to me mother.''

Peata took the baby from Brandon and left the yard. Brandon watched his mother remove all of the black pudding from the two pots into a large basket on a table. A bowl with souse decorated the other end of the table. The wood fire, which he thought he had tamed, flared up again.

''I thought I tell you to out that fire, boy!'' his mother shouted.

Brandon removed the smoldering embers from beneath the pot, leaving the ashes. A steady stream of thin smoke wafted above the empty pot.

Mabel sat on a rickety bench near the entrance to the yard and leaned against the kitchen wall. Bending all day to fan the fire now had her back and neck feeling like a two-by-four that had been left in the rain for a week, and her eyes were still running from the smoke. She closed them. Fanning the fire was Brandon's job, but he had run off as soon as he finished grating the potatoes and didn't return until she saw him tramping in behind his father. She didn't know where he'd disappeared to, but if someone paid her to, she would guess it had something to do with that girl belonging to Peata. Weeks ago she had noticed how he would sneak out of the house every time the girl passed by and how his eager eyes would light up anytime she came to pick up black pudding for her mother. She knew there wasn't much she could do to prevent him running after girls. He was reaching that age. And men weren't much different from dogs when they smelled a woman they liked. They would offend Heaven and defend Hell to get to her. But she had an uneasy feeling about that girl. Something wasn't right about her. There was a recklessness about the way she walked, an abandon that bordered on being disrespectful. The girl and her mother didn't really belong. Monkey Road was a quiet village, didn't need those kinds of people. The way they had quickly pulled the mask of modesty off the village, displaying its naked lustfulness threatened to change Monkey Road forever. Look at what had happened to Prince Johnson—a decent, quiet man until he got caught up in that house, went stealing to impress them, and ended up dead. She didn't want that to happen to her Brandon.

She would be the first to admit that most men in the village took advantage of vulnerable young girls. So many girls became pregnant by the time they were thirteen or fourteen, it was a shame. Some men tried to keep one family, but still too many of them had children from different women at the same time. That wasn't right. But that was the nature of the beast women were given to ride, it seemed. Her mother had said it was worse during slavery times. The plantation owned the children a woman bore, so most men didn't look back at them and some women did anything to avoid childbirth, including not sleeping with any man at all. For years. It is hard enough when the child you carry for nine months is born dead. How would a woman feel if someone had the power to just come and take away her child? Like it wasn't really hers. Her mother had told her that when some women got pregnant they used to shed tears of joy if the baby was born dead. Others would drink salts when they missed a monthly. Sometimes they drank too much and died.

Yes, some of the men in the village were betrayers and lustful womanizers. Some of the women, come to think of it, were as lascivious and unfaithful as the men, but their behavior was often left to imagination and gossip. It had never been wantonly displayed in public until Peata came to the village. Stories coming back from that house of revelry were of men and women coupling in the open view of others—coupling that left nothing to the imagination, she had been told. So it was no surprise to her when the daughter got pregnant. That girl made her uneasy. Simple as that. And she didn't want her son mixed up with her.

Mabel stretched and yawned, then leaned back and closed her eyes again. She would like nothing more than to go lie down across the bed with her husband, but half the black pudding was still unsold. She thought of leaving Brandon to take care of the customers when they came, but the last time she did that he ate half of the black pudding himself. She hadn't had it in her to beat him that day and ended up laughing.

"Ya know, Ma." Brandon's voice shook her out of her dreams.

She did not answer him and kept her eyes closed, hoping he would think she was asleep and leave her alone.

"I was thinking, Ma." He touched her head and she opened her eyes.

" 'Bout what?"

"Small Paul."

Small Paul had been dead and buried about two weeks. Try as she might, she could not convince her husband that the fowlcock had alerted them to Small Paul's death. "That fowlcock want work!" was all he had said, but she was relieved that her fowlcock had returned to normal.

"Ma," Brandon interrupted again.

"Stop aggravating me, boy."

"You ever see a duppy?"

"Boy, what foolishness you askin' me?"

Mabel opened her eyes and saw the flies hovering over her basket of black pudding.

"You ain't see the flies tryin' to carry 'way the basket?" she said angrily. With one swoop of her hand she chased the flies over the top of the paling.

"Small Paul say he could see duppies."

"So what that got to do with the flies boring a hole in my black pudding? Boy, how many times I have to tell you. Small Paul was nice but he was crazy. Ever since that woman run 'way and leave him, he was never the same. All them things he tell you he make up. The only duppy Small Paul ever see is himself."

"Before Grandmother dead I ask her if Small Paul make up that story 'bout them slaves that get burn up down in the gully? She say you lie. That it true. Small Paul ain't make it up."

"You ain't too big for me to break you' neck with a slap, hear boy! Who the hell you calling a liar?"

"It ain't me that say you lie. Is Grandmother!" he protested, backing away.

"Not one more word 'bout slaves and spirits and foolishness," Mabel snapped.

He ducked under the slap aimed at his head.

"All this talk 'bout slaves! I don't know what Ben bring that old woman in me yard for! Stirring up this talk 'bout slaves. You ain't no slave and I wasn't no slave and that is all you got to concern you'self with! Ya hear me? You don't know nothin' 'bout slavery. Small Paul dead. If slaves get burn up in that gully, that's their business. Ain't nothin' we can do for them now. If you know what good for you, boy, you would forget all these stories Small Paul tell you, and you would stop runnin' down behind that wild girl and learn you' trade. That is the best thing for you."

She had him cornered against the sheep pen.

"I love Midra and she ain't wild."

He stared her boldly in the face, and the hand she had raised to strike him got stuck in midair. If she struck him, she knew she would beat him dead for talking back to her like that.

Mabel dropped her hand, spun around, and went into the house, forgetting about black pudding, customers, flies, and the smoke that still made her eyes run. She fell so heavily onto the bed that the force broke several bed boards. The bed fell to the floor with such a tremendous noise that it brought Brandon rushing into the house.

Later that night, Darnlee attempted to drive away the choir of laughing pigs from his memory when he made love to his wife. Their lovemaking was the most violent and noisy it had ever been. Mabel was most surprised by the sudden attack in thé middle of the night. She urged him on, however, not sure where his energy came from, but accepting the windfall of passion with glee.

Spent and sucking at the air like a dying fire, Darnlee could still hear the jeers of bleeding pigs. Mabel rubbed his heaving chest, lovingly tangling and untangling the stunted bristles that dotted his chest. She felt twenty years younger.

"You alright, Darnlee?" She giggled.

Above her girlish giggles Darnlee still heard the chorus of bleeding pigs getting louder. "What you laughin' at?"

"You! What get into you tonight?"

"I don't see what you laughing at."

Mabel decided to keep quiet. She knew when her man was not up to skylarking. But she wondered why. Surely he must have felt her giving more than she had given in a long time. She began to wonder if Darnlee had been tantalized by some young girl and, failing to get her, had come home with the pent-up lust.

Darnlee, still breathing heavily, spoke to her in a raspy voice.

"I been thinkin'." He paused to take a breath. "I been thinkin', it might be time to stop butcherin'."

"What you talkin' 'bout, Darnlee?"

"I gettin' tired of it."

"You? I don't believe that."

"Why?"

"Just don't sound like you, that's all."

"What don't sound like me?" he challenged.

"You alright?"

"What you mean by that?"

"You ain't butt up no young girl that turn you' head, eh?"

"A man can't change nothin' beout it involve something to do with another woman?"

"Just askin'."

"It ain't got nothin' to do with that."

"With what?"

"Another woman. It just somethin' come into my head while I was sleepin'."

"If you stop butcherin' what I go do?"

"I don't know."

"You can't stop. What I go do if you stop? You know the sun don't 'gree with me. That plantation work would kill me 'fore me time. What you expect me to do if you stop killin'?"

"Just a thought."

With his chest now safely gathered into a smooth rhythm, Darnlee closed his eyes, feeling his wife licking the salt from his nipples, and smiled as he drifted off to sleep.

In the next room Brandon heard his parents making love, and he dreamed of Midra. They were in the cane field again, and this time she did not laugh. The dampness underneath him, saturating his bedding, was not earth-sweat but his own life-milk. The dampness spread under him and over the world like a warm wave.

NINE

Despite his mother's objections, Brandon pursued Midra unrelentingly. Once or twice a week, on his way to Calvary Hill, he would stop by her house carrying something from his mother's garden. Sometimes he brought spinach, sometimes eddoe hearts, which Midra loved cooked with eddoe flowers and saltfish. She began to look forward to the days when he would knock on their front door with a smile on his face and the green leaves tucked away in his bag. She started to take walks with him. He would carry Hartseed as they walked together along the dung-covered roads, smiling and waving to old men and women sitting on their front steps.

She was glad he did not work at the plantation. Men who worked at the plantation seemed to have their ambition sucked out of them. Their only desire seemed to be to make it to the end of the week so they could have a good time with any woman they could find. Maybe in some part of their minds they thought of getting out from under the plantation, of being their own men; but seeing no way to do it, they resigned themselves to their fate. Prince knew how to do it. He never worked a day on the plantation. She was glad Brandon was like that.

He showed her places where he'd played as a little boy: the pond behind Ma Parker's house where he used to catch cockles and tadpoles; the plum tree in front of the Methodist Church he'd fallen out of when he was eight, after which his mother beat him with a tamarind branch and then put him to soak in salts. He revealed to her his boyhood fears, which made her laugh. Like the time when, at age ten, his mother sent him to get some broomweed bush to make tea for his ailing grandmother. The only place the bush grew was behind Pa Daniel's house. When he got there he saw Pa Daniel and three women he did not know gathered around a crucifix in the middle of the yard. The women were singing and clapping. He watched Pa Daniel cut off the heads of three fowlcocks and let the blood drain into a pan near the crucifix. When Pa Daniel looked up and stared at him as if he were to be next, he ran away in terror. From that day he would never go near Pa Daniel's house for anything. Not even his mother's threats to beat him all around the village could get him to change his mind.

They had been taking walks together for more than two years before they made love for the first time. She would have resisted any attempt before that time, unable to separate herself from the memory of that one night with Prince.

It happened one rainy afternoon. The rain had started the night before and continued unabated all morning and into the afternoon. Peeking out through the window, Midra saw the low-hanging gray clouds and knew it would rain the rest of the day. When it rained like that, steady and unrelenting, there was nothing one could do but sleep or listen to the drops pelt the shingled roof. Hartseed was tripping over himself on the floor and crying to get her attention. But Midra was in a world of her own. Hartseed got tired and fell asleep. She stretched out next to him on the floor and slept too.

An insistent knocking at the back door woke her up. She got up to see who it was. She unlatched the top part of the door and looked out. It was Brandon. She opened the door hurriedly.

"What you doin' in the rain, you idiot?" she laughed.

"I come to see you."

"You couldn't wait 'til it stop rainin'?"

"What if it don't stop?"

"It have to."

"What make you so sure? It don't look like it go stop rainin' to me. I think it go rain forever. I think it go rain 'til it flood and everybody go get wash into the sea, so I decide if I go get wash into the sea, it better be with you."

She laughed. With a piece of cloth she began to wipe the water from his chest. His flesh was warm under her sensitive fingers, and she could feel his heart beating fast. "And why you ain't wearin' no shirt?"

"So it could get wet?"

She finished drying his chest. He held her hand and she moved to him. His eyes shifted nervously.

"Where you' mother?" he asked.

"Sleepin'."

He held her there in the kitchen, afraid to move or to let her go. "Leh we go in my bedroom," she said finally.

He hesitated. She had never allowed him into her bedroom before. "Come, huh!" she insisted.

She left him standing in the kitchen and went to the bedroom. Hartseed was still asleep on the floor. She lifted him onto the bed trying not to wake him. Brandon appeared at the doorway. She noticed for the first time that he had mud on his feet.

"Brandon! You ain't even wipe your feet!"

He turned around and went back to the kitchen. The rain was falling harder. When he appeared at the doorway again, his feet were dry and clean. She looked at them. He stared at her. She was naked. His toes were thick and swollen-looking, and his broad feet settled and expanded on the floor like roots. She stood still, waiting for the tree to come to her.

He stared at her for a long time. The humidity in the room made her feel moist all over, and tiny beads of sweat trickled down her inner thighs. He must be able to smell her sweat by now, she thought. She took his hand and drew him into the room. Unhooking the green and red mat from the nail on the wall, she let it drop to the floor.

Later they lay there holding each other, their sweat blending, listening to the sound of each other's breathing. The rain continued to beat down on the roof. Their love-making had not woken Hartseed. In the tranquility of the room she felt comfortable in his arms, pleased though not satisfied. He had been quick and furious. She had hoped he would linger some more, but the disappointment soon passed as she drank the salty liquid from his chest and he began to do the same to her.

He dressed and went home in the rain. She remained on the floor wishing he had stayed. The feeling of his slender athletic legs wrapped around hers and his bony fingers playing with her ears still teased her senses.

Her mother came to the bedroom door and saw her sprawled on the floor. She noticed the sweat on her daughter's belly and knew it was not hers alone. The couple had been very quiet, but Peata knew when a woman had just made love. Mother and daughter looked at each other, and Peata's eyes showed her awareness of what had happened in the room not long ago. There was nothing to be said. Two women lived in the house now. That was understood.

Peata left the room. Midra got up lazily and looked on the placid face of her sleeping child. Prince's child. Maybe he will come back in the spirit of his child, she thought. And as she watched her baby sleep ever so quietly, Brandon was supplanted by the memory of Prince.

Would she ever be free of the torment of that one night with Prince? Would she ever be able to stop trying to remember what had happened? When does dream stop and memory begin?

While she dressed she looked outside. The water ran swiftly across the rocks under her window, forming puddles where the earth had been washed away. Maybe Brandon was right. There was going to be a flood. If only a flood would come and wash away the cloud from her dream. She tingled with the memory of Brandon's love. Or was it Prince's? She wasn't sure. Brandon was a lot like Prince, she thought. Or was he? She really wasn't sure of that either. She hadn't known Prince, except as a sensation. But a sensation that would not go away.

The rain was coming down even harder. The puddles outside grew larger and the angry rain tried to break through her window by smashing against it with such a terrible noise that it woke Baby Prince and he began to cry.

Brandon completed his apprenticeship and got a job working in Calvary Hill. His pay was two shillings a week, which he gave to his mother. One evening, walking home from work, he met a woman on the road selling cloth and hats. She had walked all the way from town, she complained, and had sold only one hat and not one piece of cloth. Brandon took a casual look at her wares, not really expecting to buy anything. But he saw something that he liked. A piece of cream-colored fabric that was so soft, it felt like water. He had never felt anything like it before and he asked the woman what kind of cloth it was.

"That is silk, boy."

"Silk?"

"You never see no silk before, eh?"

"No."

"Rich people does buy that. You can't afford that."

"How much it cost?" He had gotten paid that evening.

"That is too much for you, boy. Look at this piece right here. Beautiful cotton."

"How much for the silk?"

"That is three shillings."

"Three? That's too much."

"How much you have?"

"I only got one shilling," he lied.

"It's a nice piece, boy. You don't see this kind of cloth 'bout here. It come from Europe. Want to make your mother or your girlfriend look special? This is it. But it don't come cheap. Only rich people does get to wear this kind of cloth. Tell you what. See this hat here? I could let you have the piece of silk and the hat for two."

"One and a half."

"You got you'self a deal."

He stopped at Midra's to give her the hat and cloth and ate there. It was dark when he got home. His mother had a bowl of rice, okra, and saltfish waiting for him.

"Me not hungry, Ma."

"You not hungry? What you mean you not hungry? I had the food waiting for you a hour ago."

"I'll eat it in the morning," he said, as he went into the yard to wash up.

His mother was sitting in the kitchen when he returned to the house feeling clean and enthusiastic about going to see Midra later.

"You ain't get pay today, Branny?" she asked.

"Sort of."

"Sort of? What that mean?"

"I sort of did but I sort of spend the money."

"On what?"

"On somebody."

His mother did not say another word. She got up and quietly walked into her bedroom.

He dressed and left the house, passing his father sitting on the front stoop.

"How Midra doin', boy?"

"She fine, Pa."

"Listen, boy. I got to kill a pig in the mornin'. You want to help me?"

"What wrong with Malcolm?"

"Malcolm go kill me dead if I not careful. The last two times we kill he was so drunk that he nearly stick me instead of the pig."

"You should find somebody that could hold his likker, Pa. The next time a knife slip out Malcolm hand, it go stick in you' neck instead of your jaw."

"That's what I frighten for. You don't want to help me, boy?"

"I don't like being round no blood. You know that, Pa. Talk to Pudge. He like that sorta thing."

When he got to Midra's house, the front door was wide open. He walked in and said "Good evening" to Peata, who was on the floor playing with Hartseed, and walked into the bedroom looking for Midra. She was not there.

"She ain't here," Peata informed him. "She should be back any minute now."

"Where she gone?"

"She went to get two eggs from Bra' Pile."

"Why you didn't tell me you want eggs when I was here before? We got eggs at home."

"I thought we had. The hen lay two eggs just this mornin'. The mongoose musta find the nest. Sit down and relax yaself. Midra should be walking through that door right now."

But he sat for more than half an hour watching Hartseed climb onto Peata's back, giddy-her-up like a donkey, and ride around the room. The little boy's happy face would break out into giggles whenever Peata stopped and brayed and bucked as if to throw him off.

"I goin' by Bra' Pile see if I find she," Brandon announced impatiently.

"I don't know what keeping her," Peata said, not looking at him as he slipped out the door.

Bra' Pile's house was only about five minutes away. He knocked on the window, and Bra' Pile peeped out through a hole in the side of the house to tell him that Midra had left an hour ago. He thanked Bra' Pile and left.

He returned to Midra's house. She had not come back. He decided to wait outside under the gooseberry tree. By the time Midra arrived half an hour later, anger was boiling in his chest.

"Evening, Branny! You waiting for me?"

"Don't 'evening' me. Where you been?"

"To get some eggs."

"Where you went for these eggs? You was laying them?"

"What wrong with you?"

"Where you been all this time, Midra?"

"I just tell you."

"I went to Bra' Pile looking for you."

"Come and go inside the house. Come!"

"No! I want to know where you went!"

"Don't holler at me like that, Brandon Fields. I ain't no fowl."

"Where you went?"

"Nowhere."

"How far that is from here?"

She laughed.

"I serious, Midra. I want to know where you been."

"It ain't nothin' to fuss over. Come, let we go in the house and lay down."

"I ain't going nowhere 'til you tell me where you been."

"Look, I tell you it ain't nothin' to fuss over but if you want to stay out here and fuss-fuss all night, go right ahead. I going in me mother house and lay down."

She left him under the gooseberry tree and went into the house. At the door she looked back to see if he was following her, and when it became clear that he wasn't, she closed the door.

He stood staring at the house, unsure of why he was so angry. Was it because he expected her to be more subservient after he had just spent his whole week's pay on her? Was it simply a matter of jealousy? He sat down under an olive tree to contemplate his next move. He was too embarrassed to go begging back. And he was too hurt to go home.

After what seemed like an eternity of repeating the ritual of plucking strands of grass, chewing them, and spitting them out, the door opened and Midra emerged. She came to him, drew him to his feet, linked his arm in hers and began to walk away from the house.

"Where we goin'?" he asked.

"You want to know how far nowhere is from here, I go show you."

She led him to the edge of the gully.

"This is where you went?"

"Yes. Come."

Holding back the many questions he was burning to ask, he followed her into the gully. She sat down on the grass. He remained standing, leaning against a guava tree, his hands folded across his chest.

He did not let on that this was his first time down in the gully at night. He looked around, expecting to see duppies appear from behind the bulky shadows or spirit monkeys alighting from the treetops. But nothing happened. He began to relax. The gully at night was as ordinary as it was in the day.

"So why you come down here?" he asked.

"This is where I meet Prince that night."

"Which night?"

"The night he get kill. Today is five years now."

She was right. The five years had sped by so quickly.

"Prince's spirit down here," Midra continued.

Brandon was suddenly filled with jealousy.

"You make love to Prince down here?" It was half question, half accusation.

"Yes," she replied quietly.

His anger boiled over. He was upon her quickly, tearing at her clothes in a jealous passion. She did not stop him, aiding him in fact. Then she broke free and jumped into the stream. He waded in after her. As he lunged at her, he tripped and fell with a splash. She laughed. He lunged at her again, once more missing and falling. The more he tried and failed to catch her, the more she laughed, and the angrier he became. Onto the bank, into the water, back onto the bank, he chased after her but she eluded him with ease. Exhausted and embarrassed, he retreated to the grass. On his back, gasping for air, he realized for the first time that the moon had woken up. Though it was not quite full yet, he could taste its liquid brightness on his tongue. When Midra crouched naked over his face, blocking out the moon, his tongue was introduced to a flavor just as sweet. A magical taste he had never experienced before. He stayed in that position until it was time to leave. He had never made her so happy and he knew it.

A month after Hartseed's sixth birthday, a shiny hot day in 1902, Brandon and Midra got married. Reluctantly, Mabel agreed to accept the union. Actually, she had no choice. Darnlee had made it clear he was in Midra's corner the first time Brandon told them he had invited Midra to eat with them. When Mabel began to voice her displeasure, Darnlee announced that Midra was welcome not only that Sunday, but any other day of the week. As Midra sat eating with them, Mabel could not resist the urge to make snide comments about Prince. "You ain't frighten you' son grow up to be a thief like his father?" Mabel mocked. But before Midra could respond, Brandon jumped to his feet. "Ma, if you don't have nothin' nice to say,'' he shouted, ''don't say nothin'!'' Mabel was surprised at the way her son leapt so quickly to the girl's defense and even more surprised that Darnlee did not chastise him for speaking to her that way.

Later that night Darnlee administered his own tongue-lashing to his wife: ''If you don't stop dropping low remarks to Midra, you go find you'self without a son,'' he told her. ''If you think you could stop that boy from liking the girl by saying nasty things to her, you making a big mistake.''

''She too wild for Brandon,'' Mabel tried to explain.

''Too wild. What that suppose to mean?''

''You know what I mean. Look at the things people say does go on in that house she live in. All the slackness. And she right in the middle of it. She after Brandon 'cause he got a trade.''

''Is that what got you so frighten?''

''What?''

''You ain't go be able to control Brandon's money if he get a girlfriend?''

''You's a man and all ya men does only care 'bout one thing, that's the problem. If Brandon get use by that girl, it go be your fault.''

After that, Midra ate with them every Sunday until the marriage. Mabel still believed Midra would one day break her boy's heart, but without her husband's support she knew there was nothing she could do.

Everyone was surprised when they announced the wedding. A marriage was an unusual event in the village despite the efforts of the missionaries lodged in the Methodist Church.

The church, sitting on a little ridge at the head of the village where the main road began, was the solitary stone structure in the village. It also supported an adjoining school, which was used as bait to get the villagers to join the Methodist Church. Most of the villagers who knew how to read and write were taught these skills by the missionaries. It was this promise of education for their children that proved most persuasive in getting the villagers to accept the teaching of the church.

But some slave habits die hard. While the missionaries had managed to convert about half the village, they had not been as successful in getting young couples to marry. Fresh from the legacy of being denied paternal rights to their own children during slavery, most men opted to live with women outside the sanctity of the church, usually waiting until they were so old before considering marriage that no other woman would have them but the one they lived with. And sometimes even that woman would refuse to marry them.

Life in the village had taken a turn for the worse. Because of a depressed market for sugar in England and elsewhere, plantations throughout the island that provided most of the employment were in decline. The sharing of food among the villagers did not keep everyone from going hungry.

So Brandon and Midra's wedding day was a day of celebration for the entire village. Not only was it a rare event, but it gave the villagers an opportunity to forget the problems that beset them—a day to dance and sing. Small gifts of food came from every corner of the village: two yams here; two potatoes there; a couple of eddoes from Bra' Pile; half a pig from Ben Payne; a leg of pork from Gunny (without his girlfriend's knowledge), and lots of molasses; a hand of figs from Ranny. Little by little the food trickled in, and by the day of the wedding there was enough for a small party.

On the morning of the wedding Brandon took Hartseed with him to the shoemaker in Calvary Hill to collect a pair of black and brown patent leather shoes given to him by his father, who had begged for them at the plantation. When his father brought them, there was a small hole in the sole of the left one but with a new sole and a spit of polish, they would look brand-new. It would be the first time he had worn shoes, and he looked forward to putting them on almost as much as getting married to Midra. On the way back, Hartseed asked him about Prince.

"I didn't know your father too good, boy," Brandon said. "I know him by seeing him, and that don't say much. I didn't see him such a lot. Come to think of it, many people didn't know him too good. He wasn't the kind of fella that mix with a lotta people. He seem to mind his business better than most. And he was always away. On them boats he used to work on and things."

"What about when he get kill?" Hartseed asked.

"Ya mean your mother tell you 'bout that already?" Brandon said, surprised. He took Hartseed's hand. "You too young to understand them kind of things. I don't think your mother should be tellin' you 'bout them things already."

A baby monkey ran from the tall sourgrass at the edge of the road and stopped in front of them. Hartseed bent down to pet the little thing, and she clung to him without fear. When he tried to pass her to Brandon, the mother emerged screeching from the grass, followed by a bunch of angry males. Brandon put the baby on the ground to run to her mother's bosom.

"These little things take to you, eh?" Brandon said.

"Look so," replied Hartseed.

"Funny, people say that you' father was the same way. Had a way with them things. Your mother show me that monkey head you carve out of that piece of mahogany. How you know how to use a knife to do them things at your age, boy?"

The rain began to drizzle.

"Me don't know," Hartseed replied. "Me see the wood and me just feel to do it."

Brandon laughed. Children, he thought to himself, were amazing.

"The rain coming," Brandon said.

"Who get home last is a jackass!" Hartseed laughed and started off running.

Brandon took off behind him, taking care not to catch up to the little legs in front of him toiling as hard as they could. The rain pounded them all the way home.

The wedding feast was held in Mabel's yard. Even Mabel had to admit to herself that the bride was a pretty sight in the cream silk dress Peata had made. Walking with Peata behind Ben's donkey and cart, which carried the married couple from the church, Mabel decided it was time to accept her daughter-in-law. She smiled and commented to Peata that Midra was a lovely bride.

By nightfall Mabel's backyard was filled with noisy, happy village folk. Some had witnessed the union of Brandon Fields and Midra Blackman at the Methodist Church. Most of them, however, came to eat. Forgotten friends, lost enemies, curious onlookers, and gate-crashing well-wishers, on a mission to eat and drink as much as they could, packed into Mabel's tiny backyard, which was bulging beyond capacity by the time the first bottle of rum made its appearance. When the black pudding appeared on the first plate, the large crowd had spilled onto the street.

In one corner the village elders sat under a tarpaulin slung across the yard from the kitchen roof to a post supporting the yard fence. The elders held and fed the babies of those who worked as servers in the hot kitchen, where they tried valiantly to respond to the demands for a variety of drinks and food.

The celebration went on through the night. The guests sprawled on the grass, sat on rocks, and trampled the flowers in Mabel's garden as they gathered in groups to discuss the event, hollering and clapping every time the bride showed her face in a doorway or window.

Someone not even from the village but a guest of his girlfriend's sister—who was a friend of the best man, Kanga—was annoyed that pork chops were in such short supply that he got only one instead of the three for which he had made room in his stomach by not eating for two full days.

"I don't understand," he said to the woman standing next to him in a patch of Mabel's begonias, "ain't the bride father a butcher or somethin' so?"

"The groom father," the woman corrected.

"The groom father? That make it worse! The groom father is a butcher and a man could only get one pork chop? This don't make no kinda sense to me. You would think that he would make sure he got enough pork chops for the guests. After all, he don't have to buy it."

"There's more people here to eat than you alone, ya know," the woman answered.

"But there ain't nobody here hungrier than me. I could eat five or six pork chops now. This minute. And have room for five more." He paused. "These don't taste that good anyway, so I don't really mind."

The woman walked away leaving him mumbling to himself.

By midnight most of the revelers had departed. And except for the occasional belch of a drunken straggler in a corner of the yard and the answering call of frogs beyond the fence, all was quiet.

The family members were still awake. The pork-chop-seeking gate-crasher lay sleeping on the floor in a corner of the house. Brandon roused him and ushered him out the door. As he left he turned to ask for another pork chop. They all laughed. Peata went to the kitchen and, incredibly, found one last pork chop.

Brandon moved in with Midra and her mother that night.

TEN

Hartseed was seven when his sister moved to Monkey Road. Vida, who had left the village carrying Prince Johnson's child in her belly, returned to the man she had run away from; he had spent eight years begging her to come back.

She'd had no thought of getting in touch with Prince when Christine was born. He had shamed her by not coming to visit her in Calvary Hill. And she had too much pride to force herself on a man. Still, she had wept when she heard of his death.

The two children attended the mission school and became fast friends. When Hartseed brought his sister home from school one day Midra saw Prince again. In fact, she almost mistook the girl for Hartseed, except that Hartseed was walking beside her. The resemblance was that striking. One day Vida appeared with Christine at Midra's door, and without a word Midra invited her in. It was clear that brother and sister had already formed an unbreakable bond. However, when the children pressed their mothers for information about their father, there was nothing the women could tell them about Prince. Except for one night, Prince was an enigma to both mothers.

• • •

The two children were born exactly one year apart on the same day of the same month. They both stopped drinking their mothers' milk at exactly eleven months and three days, they liked the same foods: spinach cakes and steamed saltfish. They both liked cornmeal pap before they went to bed, and to fall asleep they took similar positions on their backs. But here is where they were different: Hartseed sucked his thumb while Christine played with her right ear.

Hartseed wanted Christine to live with him. At first Vida would not agree. Christine was dear to her, and though she would not admit it to anyone, dearer than any of her other children. Christine was special. From the moment Christine was born, Vida had felt a renewed sense of purpose, as a mother and as a woman. The spring of her life, which she thought had passed, seemed to have returned with Christine's birth and with it a confidence in her ability to weather any misfortune. During her pregnancy, which seemed to go on forever and was so painful at times that she swore the baby was sent to kill her, she came to the realization that, far from being a mistake, her adventure with Prince was her salvation. She had been taught from the time she was a little girl that obedience to your man was the most important thing next to obeying your mother and God. But slavery was obedience's reward. And she had felt like a slave to her husband, a well-cared-for slave, but still a slave. She had survived that terrible pregnancy and, with her sister's help, had begun working full-time as a maid. On a little spot of land behind her sister's house she grew eddoes and potatoes, which Christine had watered every day. Finally, however, she had consented to return to her husband.

Now Christine pestered her mother daily to let her live with Hartseed. Her persistence finally forced Vida to give in. The fact that they looked so much alike and shared so many of the same characteristics meant that their bond, like that of twins, was preordained by God. There was no point in trying to keep them apart, she reasoned. Besides, it saved her husband the embarrassment of having to gaze every day upon the offspring of her illicit affair. And lastly, Vida rationalized, Midra did not live too far from her; she would still get to see Christine daily. Still, her heart was heavy when she wrapped up her daughter's clothes and took them to Midra's house late one Friday night.

Brother and sister became inseparable. They began playing their own games apart from the other children in the village. Christine won all their games of warri and kept a watchful eye on Hartseed as he made his carvings. Everyone adored Christine and she was always cheerful and helpful. Peata had no misgivings about sending her on errands because Christine could recite an entire shopping list after hearing it once and would remember it for days after, which delighted and amazed Peata. She told Christine things she was afraid of forgetting, and faithfully Christine would commit them to memory, retrievable at Peata's request. Soon, other people in the village began to take advantage of Christine's gift until Midra put a stop to it.

Christine had been living with her brother for two years when one day, as they were walking home from school, she took off running, leaving Hartseed far behind. At the gully she stopped and sat down on the grass laughing. Hartseed was angry.

"What you do that for, Christine?" he said.

"I don't know. I just feel to. To prove I can run faster than you."

"You can't run faster than me."

"Yes, I can," she bragged.

"You cheated."

"You slow like a donkey."

He wrestled her onto her back. But she was stronger than he and soon got the advantage. She locked her legs around his waist and squeezed until he begged for mercy.

"I give up!" he screamed.

Christine released him and stood up. "I want to show you someplace. There's a cave down there."

"Where?"

"Down there," she said, pointing to the path, which was almost hidden because of the overhanging leaves and branches and looked like the opening of a very large bird's nest.

"You lying."

"Would I lie to you, Hartseed?"

"Yes."

She slapped him playfully.

"How you know 'bout it?" Hartseed asked.

"I just know."

"That's what old people does say. 'I just know.' You ain't a old person. How you just know?"

"One evening coming back from my mother house a baby monkey stop in front me. I stoop down to pick her up and she run off. But she stop like she was waiting for me. I went to touch her again and she do the same thing. Run off a few feet and stop. She keep doing this and I realize she was tryin' to take me somewhere. And she take me to the cave."

"I don't believe you."

"I was gonna show you but if you don't believe me . . ."

"Show me."

"No."

"I sorry I say that," Hartseed apologized.

Christine entered the gully and made her way to the stream. Hartseed followed her. They walked along the stream until they came to the point where it fell over a precipice into the deepest part of the gully.

"We going down there?" Hartseed asked timidly.

"That's where the cave is. Come on," Christine asserted.

"Down there? Down there too deep!"

Thick vegetation filled the area. From the bottom rose large mile trees, which reached to where they were standing, their crowns of green leaves completely hiding the gully bottom.

"I can't see nothin' down there," exclaimed Hartseed.

"Of course not! Ya can't see it from up here. That is why nobody don't know it down there."

"I don't think I want to go down there. Suppose we can't get back up?"

"We will. Come on!"

They followed the stream down the precipice as it made a path between the rocks. The going was made slow by the dense undergrowth. Mosquitoes bit them and lazy green lizards smiled, flicking long tongues at them. Halfway down Hartseed wanted to turn back but Christine held him by the ankle until he agreed to continue. Slowly they managed to find a way through the dank underbrush, and after sliding on a sledge of wet leaves for about two hundred feet, they stood at the bottom in a cramped area the size of a large room that was covered by thick green vines.

"Where the cave?" Hartseed asked.

Christine parted the vines to reveal a stony archway that opened up to a large cave. Water ran along its floor and a metallic smell emanated from it. Christine stepped into the cave, scooped some of the water from the floor and anointed Hartseed's head. He did the same to her. Soon they were bathing each other in the ferrous-scented water.

"This is where he used to come," Christine said.

"Who?"

"Our father."

"How you know that?"

"Stop askin' me how I know. Just believe me!"

A baby monkey dropped to the ground outside and sat staring at them. They moved deeper into the dark cave. The odor got stronger. Hartseed followed his sister as she scrambled onto a ledge five feet above the ground. They crawled along the ledge until it expanded to a fifteen-foot-square platform with enough room above their heads to permit them to sit.

No light came from outside, yet Hartseed was surprised at how clearly they could see. Before them were many objects, masks of different sizes and shapes. Some of wood, some brass, some iron, along with carvings of animals.

He gravitated to a heavy, two-part mask made of dark wood. The lower part was the face of a monkey with four thin grooves etched in its face (two on each side) from under the eyes down its cheeks to its chin. The upper part was a woman sitting on the monkey's head with two grooves down her face (one on each side). A child with arms entwined around her neck clung to her back. The woman had only one breast, the right one. It was long and pointed straight at him. Where the left one should have been was a black hole the size of his fist.

"Why she only have one breast?" Hartseed asked.

"I don't know. Maybe she will tell us," replied Christine, taking the mask from his hands.

"How?"

She held it aloft and then solemnly placed it on her face. A thousand images flashed across the void of time, images she would never forget.

"I saw something," she said, taking off the mask. "But it gone now. It gone."

ELEVEN

Peata's parties, which she now gave once a month in the backyard under a tarpaulin that Brandon had rigged up, were as popular as ever. Peata's persistence and success gave Brandon confidence after he lost his job in Calvary Hill when his mentor went out of business. He knew he could find work at the plantation, but working on the plantation, even as a blacksmith, had a depressing and wearing effect. He saw it in his father's eyes; Small Paul had had it; and his friend Kanga was beginning to get it. Their eyes were full of weariness even on Sunday, their day of rest. What he wanted was to open his own business.

Brandon knew that starting a business in Monkey Road would be risky. Pudge's tinsmith business was doing so badly that during the crop season Pudge was forced to sharpen his bill to cut canes on the plantation. His work was good, excellent by some standards, and he worked quickly, but when he asked for prompt payment he would get nothing but curses and rebukes from his customers. He resorted to withholding the tin cups and washbasins he crafted with care until payment was received. This led to the women in the village banding together and refusing to order any utensils from Pudge. Instead, they would walk two miles to Calvary Hill where the tinsmith took a ten percent deposit on all work. When Pudge tried to initiate a similar payment plan, the women complained that his work did not merit payment before completion. This made Pudge angry, for he knew his work was better than that of the tinsmith in the other village. Pudge turned to drinking and cursing his customers, and despite his wife's efforts to calm him, he soon lost most of them. A few loyal customers who swore by the excellence of his banjo playing continued to patronize him.

On the other hand, Kanga worked steadily on the plantation where he had served his apprenticeship, though he complained that the pay was not enough.

Brandon brought the subject up with his wife one day as she was laying clothes out to dry in the backyard where Hartseed and Christine were playing, skipping between Midra's legs as they chased each other in and out of the house. A large piece of mahogany he'd dragged home for Hartseed leaned against the paling he'd put up a few months after the wedding. The back door was wide open; Peata sat in the doorway shelling peas. Hartseed knocked over the bowl of peas as he flew past her into the house, his sister on his heels. Peata just smiled as she picked up the unshelled peas and put them back into the scarred blue enamel bowl. She then held the bowl between her legs safe from the frolicking children.

Sunlight washed the yard, and the wet stones around the washtub glistened as rainbows formed across them. Brandon knelt behind Midra.

"If I build a little shed out back here to work in, I wouldn't have to beg for a job at the plantation," he told her. The glint in Midra's eyes told him she was not going to object to the idea.

"What about the children?" she asked. "That furnace could be dangerous for them."

"Them two?" He laughed. "Them two is God's children self. The Lord got His eye on them children. No fire in the world could touch them unless God send it Himself."

"That's blaspheming, Branny." But Midra knew exactly what he meant.

"I never see two children play so without fighting," Peata said from the doorway. "Them is something special for true. Everybody that come in contact with them say so. Them so polite. That is why the mission school take so much interest in them, you know. I was talkin' to the head teacher at the girls' school yesterday, and she say Christine so bright, she think she could get a scholarship to go on to one of them fancy secondary schools."

"I hope so," Midra said. "It would be good if them both could go."

Midra picked a balled-up red dress from the basin and shook it vigorously. The sudden commotion roused a group of hens sleeping underneath the henhouse, and they scampered around the side of the house cackling loudly. Midra grimaced as she stepped on a sharp stone. Brandon stood behind her quietly feeling the sun bore a hole in his neck. The warmth was invigorating. He nuzzled his hips closer to his wife's buttocks. Peata, seeing this, smiled and got up from the doorway to tend to her pork stew.

"You talk to your father 'bout this?" Midra said.

" 'Bout what?"

"Setting up the shop."

"I don't have to."

"Who go help you with tools and things like that?"

"I got most of the tools I want." He traced the outline of her shoulders with his fingertips, wiping the sweat away from her smooth neck. Her skin was hot. He trailed the wetness down to her bosom before she stopped him.

"You sure you want to do this?" she asked.

"You don't want me to?"

"If it's what you want."

"It's what I want."

She finished laying out the clothes on the stones and wiped the sweat from her bosom. The pale green dress she was wearing clung to her wet skin, and the cloth felt rough and uncomfortable. She wanted to take it off. Leaving the basin in the middle of the yard she passed through the kitchen which was engulfed in the smell of Peata's pork stew and went into her bedroom. She had gotten the dress over her head when Brandon came in, his face wrapped in a wide smile.

"What you grinnin' at, you fool?" she joked.

He collected her in his arms and spread her on the bed. Sweat covered her entire body. They could hear Peata outside in the yard calling to the children.

Brandon struggled to get out of his clothes. Midra found the coarse fabric of his pants exciting between her legs and urged him to keep them on. She moved with him quickly. Too quickly. When he rolled away, she ached for fulfillment. He rose from the bed, buttoning his pants. She grabbed his pants leg, grasping the fabric that had just massaged her, exciting her with its coarseness. She needed it back. He took it as a sign that she was contented.

"Relax 'til I get back," he said.

"Where you off to?"

"Pudge."

"Pudge? For what?"

"Tell him the good news. Ya know he thinkin' 'bout givin' up his business altogether."

"You goin' by Pudge now?" She tried to hide her disappointment, but her frustration rang like the churchbell. He sat down on the corner of the bed away from her.

"What wrong with me goin' by Pudge?"

"Nothin'. Go 'long."

He left her there. The charred smell of sweaty lovemaking followed him out the door.

Midra lay in the bed where he'd left her, rubbing her

hands between her thighs. Slowly at first, then quicker, as Prince broke through her imagination to take her once again on a journey over the mile trees, to that ecstasy she needed so much.

When she opened her eyes, Peata was standing in the doorway of the bedroom surrounded by a haze. The smell of burnt flesh was overpowering, and Midra realized it was smoke that surrounded Peata.

"What happened?" she asked, innocently.

"You ain't smell the stove?" Peata demanded. She looked at her daughter lying half-naked on the bed, her thighs latched tightly together with a look of wonderment in her eyes. She couldn't remember seeing Midra look like this—not since the morning after that Prince-night which had changed their lives so greatly. As she watched her daughter crawl out of her dream, it became painfully clear to her that at this very moment her daughter was thinking of Prince, was making love to him, seconds after she had opened herself to her husband.

The smoke swallowed Peata and drifted into the room. Then it swallowed the room. The sunlight painted a rainbow on the ladder of smoke that stretched from one corner of the room to the ceiling. The look of rapture on her daughter's face reminded Peata that she had not been with a man herself in the longest while. Monkey Road was full of men who still could not wait to get their hands on her, who still defied their wives and girlfriends to spend Friday night in her house. Men still made outrageous offers to her in the street. She had given into the temptation on a few occasions—hidden behind a clump of bushes, or in the secrecy of a cane field—but devoid of any real affection, these excursions of passion proved less and less satisfying, so she stopped them completely. The thrill of the chase was no longer enough.

Peata looked at the dispersed colors of the smoke-fringed rainbow and saw a man sitting at the top of the ladder. It was Prince playing with his gold-tipped locks. His eyes beckoned her, his outstretched arms beseeched her, his smile welcomed her. She walked to the ladder, then he was gone. She felt ashamed: ashamed at her envy of Midra, ashamed that after ten years she still felt this longing for a man that she had not even known. So ashamed that she thought of leaving the house, of running away from this hallucination.

Midra watched her mother retreat and closed her eyes again. She called Prince's name softly as she drifted off to sleep. And she dreamed.

She dreamed that in the middle of the night Brandon had taken her for a long walk through a cotton field. The cotton was ripe, the swollen pods of whiteness fluttered like clouds in the breeze as they walked along. The sky was a hot impenetrable indigo, a color she had seen only at sunset, and then just in flashes. But now, in the middle of the night, without even a token light from the moon, the sky was ablaze with this brilliant darkness. They walked for some time; she was about to ask him where they were going when the cotton field abruptly came to an end, and before them stood a field of sourgrass. A solitary flamboyant tree rose from the middle of the field. Standing under its branches, which were brightly painted with crimson and yellow blossoms, was a man dressed in white. When she got nearer she saw that the man was Brandon's father. In one hand he held a pig by a leash; a long knife was in the other. He beckoned to her to come closer. She watched him wrestle the pig to the ground, tie its four legs together, then deliberately pierce its pink skin with the knife. The steel blade disappeared into the pig's neck until only the wood of the handle was visible. When he withdrew the blade, its tip was ruby rich and blood spurted several feet into the air, reaching the blossoms on the tree. The pig was squealing. The blood flowed to her feet, covering them and the ground all around her. It flowed over the field, hiding the green grass under a red blanket. But the pig would not die. The blood continued to spurt and the pig continued to squeal. A squeal that somehow sounded like laughter. Now the blood was up to her ankles and rising quickly. She tried to run but Brandon's father stopped her, holding her tightly by the waist.

"You have to kill it," he said. "Only you can kill it."

"I don't know how!" she screamed.

"It's easy."

"Why me?"

"Take the knife."

The blood was up to her thighs.

"Brandon!" she screamed. "Brandon!"

And she woke up.

The rainbow was gone and the smoke had cleared. The house smelled of blood. She felt something wet between her legs. Without looking, she knew what it was. She felt underneath the bed where she kept her cotton cloths. Peata came into the room to announce they were ready to eat.

"Brandon back yet?" she asked Peata.

"No. The children hungry though."

"Go 'head. I don't want no food."

"You all right?"

"I all right."

"You look kinda sickly."

"I all right."

"How come you ain't want no food?"

"Leave me 'lone, Ma."

"You sure you all right."

"Ma!"

Peata went to the kitchen door and called to the children.

• • •

Two weeks later that same dream woke her up. This time the blood had reached her waist. She woke up trembling. Her throat was dry, and her skin felt wet and clammy like that of a gecko. Brandon was sleeping on his side with his back to her. She shook him gently by the shoulder but he did not stir. Again she shook him and tried to call his name, but no sound came from her mouth. In a panic she shook him vigorously, screaming his name, but he could not hear her for still no sound came from her throat. Not only had she lost her voice, it seemed, but her husband was in such a trancelike sleep that she could not wake him.

Getting up from the bed, she froze in the middle of the room as she felt something trickling down the hollow of her back. She reached with her fingers as it trickled down to her buttocks and realized it was only sweat. The shirt she slept in was so damp that it stuck to her body. She unbuttoned it, letting it drop at the foot of the bed. Picking a blue dress from the pile of freshly washed clothes on the chair next to the bed, she slipped it over her head and wiped her face with the skirt-tail. The room was buttoned-down hot. The dim light from the kerosene lamp sitting on a tiny table near the head of the bed was on the verge of dying. One side of the lamp shade was soot black because the stubby wick flamed only on that side. The flame seemed to disappear altogether at times, then it would flicker again suddenly, sending a shadow dancing off the wall.

The room had become a cave. A team of geckoes guarded the walls like albino sentinels, their alabaster skins glowing in the half-dark.

She opened a window to let some air in. Brandon hated to sleep with the windows open, but the heat was stifling her. Her throat was still dry and she swallowed several times in quick succession to gather moisture. She spat through the window. What she really wanted was some water. But the water was in the L-chamber, where it was dark. There was nothing to be afraid of, she told herself. Nothing at all. It was just a dream. She was not going to drown in a sea of blood.

The only light in the L-chamber came from a slender beam of moonlight sneaking through one of the cracked boards near the roof. It wasn't enough to illuminate the room, but she knew her way even in the dark. She went directly to the monkey-jar in the corner, took one of the cups hanging from the wall above it, and dipped into the red clay jar. Drinking the cool water quickly, she emptied the cup, then filled it again and retreated to the bedroom with the cup of water.

Brandon had not moved. The geckoes had not moved. There were four of them, one on each wall. By morning they would be gone. She sat on the floor in a corner near the doorway and sipped the water. When she whispered her own name to herself, she was relieved to hear her voice. Had she really lost her voice before, or was it part of her dream? It must have been her imagination. She whispered her name again to be sure. Yes, she must have imagined it. There was no mistaking her slightly hoarse whisper.

Morning came. It caught Midra asleep on the floor. Peata was the first one up, at six, as always, before the sun came up. Peata rose with the crowing of Mabel's fowlcock, and before anyone else in the house woke up she had bathed and had begun mixing cornmeal and sugar to make bakes for breakfast. The sound of the wooden spoon striking the wooden bowl woke Midra. Brandon was still asleep on his side. He must be paralyzed, she thought. How could anyone sleep the entire night in one position? She moved to wake him, but before she could touch him, he sat up like a spring recoiling.

"What you doin'?" he said. He blew out the lamp.

"Why you wake up so?"

"Wake up how?"

"Like that. Like something frighten you."

"What you was doin' leanin' over me?"

"I wasn't leanin' over you."

"What you was doin' then?" he asked. He rolled to the edge of the bed, stretched his arms and legs, and yawned. In the next room Peata began to sing as she created a staccato rhythm with the spoon and the bowl. The sun branching out over the village lit up the room, and as Brandon unfurled his long legs the room felt warm and friendly. "What you doin' outta bed already and all dressed? Where you goin'?" he said, pulling her to him.

"You sleep good last night?" she asked. Finding her naked underneath the dress, he soon found what he was searching for. But she did not feel charitable to his desires. She really wanted to tell him about the dreams, about last night, but she knew if she told him about the dream, it would not stop there. Everything would have to come out. All that had been troubling her of late. And that included Small Paul. Small Paul had been on her mind more and more. Since the dreams had started, he'd begun to materialize every time she closed her eyes, sitting in an orange-red light, curled up like a baby, his arms covering his head in a mock gesture of protection. Laughing at her.

"What's the matter with you?" Brandon's voice jerked her to attention. Her dress was up over her hips, and Brandon's nostrils were flared to their widest to smell her. She pushed her dress down. "What's the matter with you?" he said again, not bothering to hide his exasperation.

"Nothin'."

"Then come here," he ordered.

"I goin' to help Ma."

"Peata don't want no help. What's the matter with you?"

"You go keep asking me that?"

" 'Til I get a reasonable answer."

"Then keep askin'."

She left the room and went to wake Hartseed and Christine, who slept on the floor of Peata's room. They were both up already and outside in the yard. Hartseed was feeding the fowls and Christine was taking a bath. She watched Hartseed place the crushed corn on the ground in front of the five hens and then fill a pan with water.

"Ma," he said.

"Yes, Prince."

"How come we don't have no fowlcock?"

"How come?" She smiled.

"Yes."

"Real good fowlcocks hard to breed."

"What does happen to them?"

"A fowlcock has to be really strong to live. Out of five or six eggs a hen may only hatch one fowlcock, and if he ain't strong, he ain't go make it. When mongoose see a bunch of chicks, the first one he want to eat is the young fowlcock. I don't know why but that's how it is. If he escape the mongoose, is people who go try to steal him to cook him or to put him with them own hens. So to survive, the fowlcock gots to be strong and fast. That is why we don't have none. The mongoose eat them or other people steal them. Now Grandma Fields, she got a fowlcock that older than you. That fowlcock was here when I come to this village and it still goin' strong. That is what you call a strong fowlcock."

"We need a fowlcock around here," Hartseed said.

"Is luck, son. Is luck."

Peata came to the door to indicate that her bakes were done. Hartseed rushed inside. This was the best part of getting up early. Grandma Peata's cornmeal bakes hot from the pan were the only thing worth leaving the warm fire next to his sister for. Sometimes she added currants, which made them even sweeter and moister.

There were already six on a plate waiting for him and Christine. They would save half for the walk to the schoolhouse—one large room attached to the Methodist mission-ary—where girls sat on one side, boys on the other.

Most children their age were already working in the plan-tation fields, picking grass and weeds from among the young canes. But Christine was special, and Hartseed knew that he got treated as special too because he was her brother. Christine spent a lot of time reading and could add and subtract lots of numbers in her head quicker than any of the teachers. He would rather carve things out of ma-hogany. In a few weeks they would be taking a special exam, which the missionaries promised would give them a chance to learn greater things in another school far from home. Christine wanted to go to this new school. He didn't care about the school, he just wanted to go wherever Chris-tine went.

But there was something even more special about Chris-tine. Something no one knew about but him. Something he didn't have to share with anyone.

Once a week, after school, they had taken to sneaking off to the cave. He was glad when Christine made him promise not to tell a soul of their secret place; he wanted it to be theirs alone. At first, he had not believed Christine when she put the mask with the monkey face and the one-breasted woman on her face and said she saw things. "What kind of things?" he asked her. Then she began to tell him stories. He called them stories because he did not know what else to call them. There were funny and incred-ible, but how could he believe Christine saw these things in a mask? It was clear, though, that after she put on the mask she was not herself. She spoke as if she were far away.

The story began a long time ago, she had told him, with men and women and children in bright costumes singing and dancing at a feast. "Who these people?" he had asked her.

"Them is Africans."

"Africans?"

"Yes. And there was a man sitting on a big bench holding a mask like this one. A gift from his brother."

"Like which one?"

"This one we have."

"Of the woman with one breast?"

"Theirs have two."

"Theirs have two?"

"Yes, and she have two children. One is nursing."

"Then how that could be the same mask? Our mask don't have no child nursing."

"I didn't say it's the exact same thing, Hartseed. It similar."

"*Similar* mean the same, ain't it?"

"Ours is broken. That is why we here. We have to find the part that missing from ours."

"You know where it is?"

"Not yet."

Confused and suspecting that Christine was making fun of him, he agreed to put the mask on, becoming angry when nothing happened. He tried it several times in different positions and closed his eyes as she had instructed him, but still he saw nothing. He was now sure she was making everything up. But he listened to her stories anyway because they were better than any he ever read.

The man sitting on the bench was the chief of the village, she told him, and the man who gave him the mask, the chief's brother, was their great-great-grandfather.

"How you know he's our great-great-grandfather?" he asked her.

"Just listen to me, Hartseed. If you want to hear."

He sat and listened.

"Our great-great-grandfather was a master sculptor," Christine said. "He carved things for his brother and the village: benches, bowls, and masks. But this mask was special. He carved it for the spirits of his ancestors. When he was made a slave with hundreds of other Africans from his village, he managed to stay alive crossing the Atlantic Ocean, though many of the others died before they got to these islands. The first thing he think of when he get here was that mask. And he set about carving another one just like it.''

Christine went on to tell him many more things about this man she called their great-great-grandfather, things he was still convinced she had made up. Until one day it happened to him.

A few days before his tenth birthday he put the mask on and began to prance about, making fun of Christine and the way she talked after she had worn the mask. Though he could hear no music, he felt himself settling into a strange rhythm, the rhythm of a drunken man, of a man losing his equilibrium to a trance. And he saw the images, like a dream unfolding. All the stories Christine had been telling him came to life. He saw the man Christine described—their great-great-grandfather. He saw him and was amazed.

He was awe-inspiring. Quiet, stubborn, and fierce. Though his piercing eyes alarmed the first planter who examined him, his powerful-looking body spelled *profit* to the planter who bought him. Fresh off the boat, he began work on the mask, for with it he hoped to call on the spirits of his ancestors to liberate him. Each night, when he returned to the slave quarters after laboring in the fields, he would work on the mask. He hardly slept. In the morning, he would hide it in a hole he'd dug near where he slept. It took him a year and a half to finish.

Working without light, without the proper tools to smooth and polish the wood, his task was difficult. And he was determined to make as fine a mask as the one he had left behind in Africa. Wanting to please his ancestors, he took his time. In the meantime one of the female slaves caught his eye. When he saw the grace with which she moved, he was attracted to her. He was also amazed by her strength. She could lift a load as big as any man, and he had seen her pull a buggy carrying two people by herself. The first time he saw her, she was feeding her three-year-old son in the field under the watchful eye of the driver. A week later she was alone. Her son had been taken from her. And she had changed. Working with the frenzy of a madwoman, she sang all day and worked without eating or resting. That night he found her behind the slave huts trembling violently, her eyes glassy and remote. She had poisoned herself. He knew the poison. Many women used it. He knew what would work against it. He forced her to take the antidote and stayed with her that night; the next day she was well enough to be able to work.

When the mask was finished, he waited for the spirits to tell him the time was right. He waited and waited. One night, as the moon charmed the plantation house to sleep, he decided he could wait no longer. His woman was about to drop their child, and he knew they had to flee before the baby came. He prayed to his ancestors to give the mask the power of darkness and the speed of the wind. When the dogs stopped barking, he unearthed the mask and went to his wife. Together they disappeared in the quicksand of night. His prayers were answered. The mask clothed them in invisibility, carrying them like the wind over the trees and fields of cane.

When they were far enough away from the plantation, they stopped on a mountaintop in a dense, wooded area not far from the sea. The sound of waves crashing against stone galloped up the mountain to greet them. He could taste the salt air in his throat as he breathed. It was sweet, so sweet that it made him laugh. His wife laughed with him.

"We free," he said.

She smiled.

"Don't be frighten. We free."

"We goin' home?" she asked him.

His nod was apprehensive.

"Now?"

"No. First we rest. We sleep."

He drew her close, and her powerful body trembled. He'd felt her tremble like this before. Now she was carrying his child, and no one was going to take away this baby. Her belly was taut against his groin and he felt love stirring its sweet syrup for him. He was proud of himself.

"Can I get my son?" she asked.

He knew what she meant. "Me don't know where he is."

"How can I go home and leave my baby?"

He did not know what to tell her. "We going to sleep now," was all he said. She began to cry. He held her. She was crying for her son, there was nothing he could do. It was the first time he had seen her weep.

Together they lay down to sleep on a bed he had made of dried coconut leaves. She was still crying. He could feel the still, dark flame in the core of her soul that raged for her son. Her suffering was his suffering. He wrapped her in his arms and listened as her quiet sobbing filled the night. The sea below them was singing a song that stung him like salt spray in a fresh wound.

Home. Would they get home?

That was all Hartseed saw before he took off the mask.

TWELVE

"Never fly a kite in the rain." That was the advice his father had always given Brandon around Easter, kite-flying season. For a long time he could not even make a kite that would fly. No matter what design or shape he used, his kites would always flop to the ground. Each year as Easter approached, seeing him struggling to get his contraption off the ground, his father would sit him down and demonstrate the art of kite-making anew.

First his father would spend hours searching for the right kind of bamboo—straight and strong—to make the skeleton. Using a small sharp knife he would cut four sticks from the bamboo stalk and patiently shave them until they were thin and flat, then he would crop them to even lengths. After joining them at the center with a thin nail he would open up the sticks to make a star, keeping the star shape in place by connecting each point to the other with thread or twine. A paper face would then be pasted on with glue from the clammy-cherry. The last and most important step was putting together the right mix of pieces of old cloth that were tied together to make the tail—if the tail was too heavy, the kite had no chance of making it off the ground.

His father had a special knack for finding just the right mix of cloth, taken from his mother's old dresses, to make his kite soar above any other in the village. Brandon used to think it was the color of the cloth that made his kite fly so high. Kanga and Pudge could not hide their envy when they saw his kite dancing toward the sun. Pudge's only comment would be, "If my father was here, he would make a kite that would go higher than that." But Kanga would not rest until he had succeeded in making Brandon's sun-seeking star drop from the sky by snaking the twine until it broke and the kite, like a bird with one wing, fell out of sight. Sometimes Brandon managed to recover his fallen star, but many times it would land atop the mile trees where only the monkeys or the birds could reach it. He would refuse to speak to Kanga for a couple of days afterwards, but by the next time they met in Jessup's pasture to graze the sheep, the whole affair would be forgotten.

His father stopped making him kites when he was twelve, saying he was old enough to make his own kites. That year he managed to make a kite that actually flew for more than thirty seconds. By the next year he had mastered the art.

Now as he sat in his parents' backyard, working on Hartseed's kite a week before Easter, he wondered if subconsciously he had refused to become efficient at making kites—for other than that, he was quite good with his hands—because making kites with his father had been the only time they sat and talked together. And though the thought of blood made him sick, he had endured his father's stories about his exploits as a butcher, related to him as he knelt on his knees in the backyard watching his father slice the bamboo to frame the kite. It was the price he had to pay for his father's attention.

The pride of accomplishment and passion for perfection with which his father pursued everything—whether it was killing pigs or making a kite—left its impression on Brandon. Sometimes it would take his father a whole week to carve one bamboo stick to the right thickness. If after that it still did not appear quite perfect, he would discard it to start all over again. Brandon applied his father's example to his own work as a blacksmith. He could shoe a horse in ten minutes if he had to, but given the choice he would work for an hour or maybe a day to achieve a perfect fit.

Siding with him against his mother in the struggle to bring Midra into the family was the first indication to Brandon that his father had forgiven him for rejecting the notion that slaughtering a helpless pig was the way to prove his manhood. When he graduated from his apprenticeship, his father was the first to congratulate him and he presented him with his first anvil.

Brandon was hoping to keep secret the kite he was making for the children. For a week he had been painstaking in shaping the sticks at his parents' house after work. His march toward perfection was slow but pleasurable. When the sun went down he would return the sticks to their hiding place under his parents' bed to prevent Hartseed, who came there often, from accidentally finding them.

This kite was three feet in diameter, much bigger than the one he had made for Hartseed last Easter. He wondered if it would be too big, but that doubt passed quickly when he remembered that Hartseed was used to dragging around heavy pieces of mahogany. And he and his sister often wrestled. They were strong children.

Though Hartseed called him "Pa," the boy was curious about his biological father, a curiosity Brandon found unsettling at times. Not only was he ignorant of Prince Johnson and his motives for doing the things he had done, but Brandon also hoped that the boy would come to see him as his real father someday. And that might have happened had Christine not entered the picture. It was clear that Christine was driven by a desire to re-create Prince or at least make him a living presence in her life. To what end

Brandon was not sure. Her obsession with her father and the house he had lived in did not bother anyone else. Yet it seemed that every time he passed the empty, boarded-up house he would see Christine entering or leaving through a window, or just standing in front of the house crying. When he pointed this out to Midra, she seemed unconcerned.

"You sure she was crying?"

"I stop and ask her what she was crying for but she just turn and run away."

"Children cry a lot."

"That ain't the first time I see her standing in front that house."

"Well, that is where her father lived. What you expect."

"You ever been inside it?"

"No."

"There's something wrong with that girl, Midra."

"Like what?"

"I don't know. She can't be right in her head."

"Ain't nothin' wrong with Christine."

"This thing with her father is very strange."

"It only strange to you because you grow up with your father."

"What about that day the floor at the mission school collapse and some of the children get hurt bad? One boy break his foot, I believe."

"That's the day Christine and Hart come home early. What about it?"

"She claim she wasn't feeling so good so she come home."

"Yes."

"I don't know what it is. But I get the feeling that somehow she knew that floor would collapse. That she always one step ahead of everybody else."

"That's the foolishest thing I ever hear."

"I really would like to know what goes on inside her

head.'' After a long pause he continued. ''She does act more like she's Hart's mother than you. The poor boy would dig a hole in the ground and bury himself if she tell him to.''

''Why that should bother you? Them is brother and sister.''

''Them does act like them is more than brother and sister if you ask me.''

''You just jealous.''

''Jealous?''

''Since Christine come, Hartseed don't be tripping after you everywhere you go no more. And for me one-one that is fine. I tell you long time I didn't like you having the boy sitting up between you and that loudmouth Kanga whose mouth don't have respect for his own mother. That man can't open his mouth without mentioning the part of his mother that spit him out.''

''You think the boy ain't go ever come in contact with that part of a woman?''

''In time. You and Kanga don't have to rush him.''

''What you really think 'bout Christine?''

''Like what?''

Christine remained an enigma to him. When she had arrived in the village, he was all for her coming to live with them. The truth was he would have welcomed a house full of children. His friends were all part of large families. Kanga had two brothers and five sisters; Pudge had eight sisters.

But Midra had been right about one thing. He had grown jealous of Christine, not only because she had usurped his relationship with Hartseed but also because she kept the mysterious presence of Prince firmly before them. The way she disappeared for hours with Hartseed, with no one questioning her whereabouts, recalled the ease with which Prince baffled the village with his comings and goings, with no one questioning the source of all those gifts he distributed. Midra and Peata treated her almost as an equal—as did every other adult in the village, awed by her prodigious memory and knowledge of books—never questioning where she disappeared to.

Easter Sunday was the peak of kite-flying season, the day every man, woman, or child who loved the sight of colorful man-made stars dancing and singing in the sky turned out to hoist one into the constellation; the day little boys cried and refused to be consoled because their kites would not fly; the day fathers and sons became brothers.

The previous year, he had brought home a kite the night before Easter Sunday. When he woke up and found that Hartseed had left the house early in the morning with his sister, he could hide his resentment no longer. He had to wait until midday before the boy finally came home. He met Hartseed in the backyard.

"I made you a kite. You didn't see it?"

"Yeah."

"Why you ain't fly it?"

"I went somewhere with Chris."

"Where?"

Hartseed looked at Christine for permission to answer.

"Why you looking at she?" demanded Brandon. "Is I ask you the question."

"You don't have to tell him where we went," declared Christine.

"Where you been, Hart?" he said, ignoring what Christine had just said.

"Christine say not to tell you."

"Christine ain't your mother."

"And you ain't his father," said Christine.

"You shut up! I want to know where you went, Hartseed."

Hartseed remained silent. Brandon stood up and unbuck-
led his belt.

"You want to feel this?" He had never struck the boy
before.

"Ma!" Christine began to scream. Midra came running
from the bedroom.

"What happen?"

"He want to beat Prince."

"What's the problem, Brandon?"

Brandon kept his eyes locked to Hartseed, who was
transfixed by the belt.

"Answer me, boy!"

"What's the problem, Brandon?" Midra asked again.

"Stay out of this!"

"What you mean, stay out of this? What you go hit my
son for?"

"This is between me and Hart. Answer me, boy."

"I want to know what going on, Brandon."

"I tell you it's between me and the boy. If that ain't
good enough for you, then I believe I in the wrong house."

The yard fell silent.

"You go answer me, boy, or I go have to use this?"

Hartseed looked at his mother, then at Christine, then
back at the belt.

"I went to the gully," he whispered.

"For what?"

"To pick guava."

"Where the guavas you pick?"

"We eat them."

Brandon put the belt back around his waist. He felt the
boy was lying, but there was nothing he could do.

"The next time you go to the gully to pick guava, make
sure you bring some for your mother and me."

"Yes, sir."

"And the next time you go leave the house so early, let
somebody know where you going, hear me?"

"Yes, Pa."

"Now you wanna go fly the kite or not?"

"Yes, Pa."

That night he made love to Midra determined to get her pregnant.

"I think it 'bout time we have we own children," he said to her after.

"How many?"

"Ten."

"Ten?" Midra laughed. "I don't want no more than five."

"You can have five twins," Brandon joked.

"That would be eleven."

"Oh yeah."

"I had a talk with Christine," Midra said as she stroked his chest. "She sorry she talk to you like that."

"Oh yeah? She ain't say nothin' to me."

"Give her time."

"I think we should send her back to her mother."

"No. Them two children need each other. You can't see it?"

"I suppose you're right."

"Whatever you go do with Hart, you have to include Christine and she won't be no trouble."

Christine never did apologize, but he did not hold it against her. Neither did she interfere with his disciplining of Hartseed after that. Not that Hartseed needed a lot of disciplining. He seldom made the same mistake twice. But with Christine, Brandon was not sure if she was just staying one step ahead of him or if she had genuinely come to respect him.

Brandon was on his second stick for the secret kite when his father joined him in the backyard.

"You think that boy will be able to handle this big thing?" his father asked.

"Between him and his sister, they can handle it."

"Where you go find enough cloth to make a tail for this?"

"Ma don't throw 'way nothin'. I bet she still got some dresses under her bed from when I was a boy."

His father laughed and took the stick and the knife from him. He began to chip away with the same precise, smooth motion Brandon remembered from his youth.

"I used to make you the best kite in Monkey Road, a kite even the birds used to gather 'round and look at in envy," his father said.

"I bet some of them woulda change places with my kite if them coulda," Brandon said. The two men laughed.

"How's Midra, son?"

"Midra? She fine. Why?"

"When the two of you go give your mother a grand-child?"

"What about you? It won't be your grandchild too?"

His father laughed. "I suppose so," he said.

"You sure Ma want a grandchild from Midra?" Brandon joked.

"Don't say that about your mother, Branny. She don't hold nothin' 'gainst you' wife."

"Just jokin', Pa."

"I don't think I mention this to you yet, but this weekend go be my last weekend killing."

"No, you ain't mention it. Why?"

"Believe it or not, I tired of it now. I have to admit I ain't as strong as I used to be and them sharp knives, well, me hands don't hold them as firm as before."

"You' hands still as steady as a rock, Pa."

"A piece of stick don't fight back, son."

"This means that Ma go have to stop making black pudding?"

"No. It just means she go have to buy pig belly from another butcher, that's all."

"You tell her?"

"Yeah."

"What she say?"

"What she could say? Me mind made up."

"So what you go do on weekends?"

"Work the garden. Play with the grandchildren you and Midra go have. You should be happy. You never did take to my killing."

"I just never take to the blood."

"Son, there's one thing you go learn if you ain't learn it already. If you around women, you gotta get used to blood. You know the number of young girls—most of them who didn't even know them was with child—you know how many of them I see drop down in the field, and nobody could do nothing but watch the blood rush outta them womb carrying their unformed babies to fertilize the plantation field? Too many. When your Ma lost our first baby, this is before you, I was there. I helped clean up the blood, even though your grandmother tried to lock me out the room. I wanted to be there. Blood don't scare me."

"Why you and Ma didn't have no more children?"

"She couldn't get no more."

"Why?"

"After you were born, she got pregnant a year later. But she lost that one too. It nearly killed her. After that it was like the Lord take pity on her body and say, 'No more children.' "

"Why that does happen, Pa."

"What? You mean the women losing children like that?"

"Yes."

"I don't know. Is something that just happen to women. It does happen to the white women at the plantation too. Not as much as it does happen to we women, but it does happen to them too. It ain't just we women alone. So is time you stop thinking blood is something to be scared of. You go have to stand up and look at it one of these days, and if you's a man, you can't run away.''

The kite was the biggest one in Jessup's pasture that Easter. They all took turns holding it, Hartseed, Christine, Midra, even Peata. It looked so beautiful in the sky that when the rain came, Christine said it was too beautiful to take down. They tied it to a tree and left it there. The next day the kite was still flying.

THIRTEEN

Thursdays. The dream came only on Thursdays. And each Thursday night the blood rose higher. By the end of the third week the blood was up to her neck. After that night, overcome by the fear of drowning in blood, Midra refused to go to sleep on Thursday nights. She pretended she was asleep until she heard Brandon snoring, then she would get up and retreat to her corner. About that same time she found out she was pregnant.

Fearful of dying in her sleep before she gave birth, she went to Pa Daniel for a remedy, something to make her sleep without the fear of dying in a blood-filled dream. What he told her only made her more confused.

''You with child?'' he asked. It was a question that required no answer. His eyes told her that he already knew. With the grace of a salamander, he slid across the room to where Midra was sitting and held her hand. Their eyes made a steadfast four.

She had heard he was more than a hundred years old. How could anybody be that old? And how could anyone that old move so gracefully? His hand was warm, like the afterglow of a fire. She felt her body begin to radiate, and the urge to laugh came over her. He released her hand before she could laugh but she felt herself smiling. Prince had had that same effect on her, she remembered.

"You go have twins," he said.

"Twins? What I go do with twins?"

He laughed. "Care for them, I hope."

"I mean . . . What that got to do with my dreams?"

"I don't know. You tell your husband yet?"

"No. I can't. Not 'til I . . . I ain't come here 'bout no twins. I come here . . . I come here 'cause I want to stop havin' them bad dreams."

"I can't stop dreams."

"So what should I do?"

"I don't know."

"But you know everything. You must have something to make me sleep without dreaming."

He sat in the shadow of his plants. The room appeared brighter than the last time Midra had been there, and the green glow of the room was also noticeably darker and richer. She looked around to see where the additional light was coming from. Certainly not the solitary kerosene lamp in the corner, which was turned down to its lowest flame. The kerosene flame danced gamely as if to compensate for its limited brightness by being energetic. Looking up, she noticed that the window was open and the moon had come up. A cool draft weaved through the window, replacing the warmth of her body with cold disappointment. She had been counting on Pa Daniel to help her. What was she going to do now? If he couldn't help her, who could? Twins? Goodness gracious! She searched Pa Daniel's face, for some glimmer of hope. His eyes, never faltering, were perfectly blank. It was impossible to tell if he was deep in thought or sleeping with his eyes open. The room was getting brighter and cooler. Midra got up to leave.

"Wait," he said.

She stopped at the doorway, trembling. He had thought of something.

"The girl that live with you."

"What girl?" Midra said, bewildered.

"Prince."

"You mean Christine?"

"That's her name?"

"You talkin' about Christine?"

"Yes. Prince."

"Prince daughter."

"Send her to me."

"Why?"

"Just send her."

"I can't do that. She not mine!"

"She live with you."

"What you want with her?"

The blank look was suddenly gone from his eyes. For the first time he seemed to be really looking at her, staring deeply into her eyes. He spread his long arms like a bird gliding to a stop and smiled.

"What you want with Christine?" Midra asked again.

"She's the one."

"The one for what?"

"Send her to me. I have something for her."

"I can't do that," she cried.

She fled and entered the cold light of the moon. Walking briskly, Midra was still confused. What did he mean by "She's the one"?

Standing in front of Ben's blooming Lady-in-the-Night trees, Midra decided not to go home just yet. Not until she had figured out how she was going to tell her husband about the pregnancy and the dreams. The sweet-smelling flowers made her feel like puking, so she walked on until she was no longer bothered by the scent. She had never had that reaction to Lady-in-the-Night flowers before. Above her, the moon drifted slowly in the wash of tumbling stars. The effect was to give the sky a delicate haze, which made her think of Prince. Prince! The devil himself. It was because of him she was having these dreams, these nightmares. Because of him she could not be happy about the twins and run home to tell her husband so he could be happy too. Brandon would surely want to know how she knew she would be having twins. And why she had gone to see Pa Daniel in the first place. And why she did not tell him before. And . . . And . . .

The sea was not very far away, just beyond the mountains to the west of the village. She had never gone there with Brandon. He went often, sometimes three times a week, with his friends Kanga and Pudge. During their courtship she had begged him repeatedly to take her. She was afraid to go alone because she could not swim. But he always refused. Today, to her surprise, he offered to take her. Though she knew it was because Kanga and Pudge had spent the day drinking and wagering on warri and were too tired to go, she went along gladly.

The scene that greeted them astonished her. Her first impulse was to take her clothes off and run into the water. The sun was bright and the sea was all blue spray and white foam smashing against the rocks. Crabs playing hide-and-seek with the sea foam scurried in and out of holes. She saw the power of the sea resonate in the graceful arc of water rising high against the rocks before falling back to the sea-body, and wanted to feel the impact of the spray on her own body.

There was no one else on the beach. It was as if everything had been swept clean for their coming. Yards of diamond sand stretched out before them, and purple sea-grapes hung ripe, ready for picking.

Acting on impulse she began to shed her clothing, but Brandon stopped her with a long, censuring stare. So, keeping her petticoat on, Midra waded in the water up to her calves while he swam to a fishing boat which was so far away that it was nothing but a dot on the water.

She waited until he was way out in the sea to shed her petticoat and underwear. Then she played in the waves, anointing her head and drinking the sea-water, for it was a wonderful cleanser. Finally tired of splashing and playing, she came out to get half-dressed. Waiting for her husband to return from his adventure, she lay down on the soft sand and fell asleep.

When she woke up, Brandon was lying next to her. The dot on the water had been swallowed up. The sun had made a wide arc and was now a benign red glow in the west. The sea still heaved furiously against the rocks, showering its salt spray onto the sand at their feet.

"How long I been sleeping?" she asked, knowing that it must have been a long time.

"I don't know," he said, smiling.

"How long you been lying here?"

"I don't know." His laugh told her he had done something mischievous while she was asleep. The smell of discarded fish carcass and innards touched her senses for the first time that day, and she wondered if he had collected the stuff and put it somewhere under her nose. She looked around but the beach was as clean as it had been when they got there.

"What you do?" she demanded, not altogether seriously.

"Nothin'. What make you think I do something?" He rolled on top of her. She pushed him off.

Her dress was folded neatly beside her. That she did not remember doing. She remembered taking it off and throwing it in a heap on the sand. It could not be this, the folding of her dress, that was making him smile so. She felt the prickly specks of sand between her legs and started to brush them away. That was when she discovered what he had done. She was naked there. While she was asleep he had removed her underwear. He broke into a cackling laugh. Still laughing, he tried to roll on top of her again but she moved away, filling his mouth with sand as she eluded him. His laughter stopped. It was her turn to laugh.

"What you do that for?" He coughed.

"You too cheeky, that's why."

The sand was in his hair as well as his eyes, and his tongue, capped with ivory specks of sand, was now whiter than his teeth. He looked so funny as he struggled to get the sand out of his mouth.

"Why you didn't do that to Small Paul?" he blurted.

"What?" The weight of his words did not fall on her immediately.

"When he take them off, you didn't do nothin' to him but you go try to kill me for playin' a little joke."

It quickly dawned on her what he was alluding to.

"What the hell you talkin' 'bout, Brandon Fields?"

"You know very well what I talkin' 'bout."

He had tried to keep his suspicions to himself, but he had been unable to forget. He deserved an answer. What was Small Paul doing with her underwear that morning?

"Where my drawers?" she demanded.

"I ain't giving them back. Not 'til you answer me."

"Give me my things!"

"No."

She got up from the sand and brushed her petticoat clean. She pulled her dress over her head and began to button the blouse.

She would walk home without drawers if she had to. That wasn't the problem. What troubled her was finding out he hadn't forgotten about that morning. And that he would wait this long to bring it up again.

For a moment she thought of telling him the truth. But there was no point in doing that now. No way in the world would he ever be able to understand what she'd done. How could he, without understanding what she had felt that night with Prince? And there was simply no way he could listen to her talk about that. What man would want to hear about something another man had done to his wife that he couldn't do?

How could she explain to him that she felt a part of Prince, though she had spent only one night with him? That Prince was at once real and a dream.

Even if Brandon could understand what she had done, what then would he think of her? She looked at him and wondered if he could see the panic in her eyes.

Walking away from him along the beach, she headed in the direction from which they had come.

"Where you goin'?" he demanded. He had no intention of letting her get away without answering his question. She kept walking. He got up to follow her.

"Midra!" he shouted.

She stopped. He caught up with her.

"What was goin' on between you and Small Paul?"

"Nothin'."

"What you mean nothin'?"

"I said nothin'."

"Then how you explain that morning?"

"What morning?"

He slapped her. The blow stunned more than it hurt her. She fell to the sand, and in a rage she dug her teeth into the dense muscle of his calf. She felt the hot skin part as her teeth found flesh, then she heard him scream. She let go of his leg but made no attempt to escape. The outline of her teeth showed on his calf, and blood trickled down his ankle. She expected to feel his foot on her face or against her head, and she braced herself for the pain, but he did not retaliate. Instead, he dropped her underpants in her lap and hobbled into the sea.

He washed the wound in the salt water. After the sting of the salt had abated, he came out. She got up and started walking along the beach. But he wasn't finished with her yet. He grabbed her hand and forced her to the sand.

"What Small Paul was doin' with your drawers?" he insisted.

"Them wasn't mine, Brandon. I swear."

"Tell me the truth, Midra. You was having sex with Small Paul?"

"No, Brandon."

"You swear?"

"I swear."

"Them wasn't yours."

"No. How many times I gotta say that?"

"You swear?"

"I swear."

He walked off, leaving her on the sand. She got up and followed at a safe distance behind. By the time she reached the outskirts of the village, she'd lost sight of him.

She was walking past the gully when the sudden movement of a monkey darting in front of her distracted her momentarily and she slipped on the wet grass, falling heavily on her stomach and rolling a few feet down the incline before she came to a stop. The jolt knocked the wind out of her. Motionless, she lay waiting for her breath to return. When she got up, her hip hurt. She hobbled home.

Brandon was not at home. The children were playing warri. She took off her dress and got into bed.

Pain woke her up. Not the pain in her hip. A pain in her womb. And she was bleeding. Blood was flowing from her womb. It undulated between her thighs. She screamed for Peata. The blood was up to her ankles. Peata came running. The blood was up to her waist. The children came running. The blood was up to her neck. Brandon didn't come. Peata wrapped the dead twins in a sheet to wash.

FOURTEEN

Pa Daniel saw the girl and boy walking slowly up the gap to his house. He had waited most of his life for them. They were the ones, no doubt about it. He was so old now and had been waiting so long, and this feeling was so strong, the blood surged to his temples, making him giddy for a second. He smiled as he watched them. They walked to the same rhythm: the rhythm of blood dripping from splintered bones, the rhythm of the cries of scattered spirits. Their youthful innocence would resurrect the bones and settle the spirits. Finally they had come.

He waited for them at the door and opened it before they knocked. As they entered quietly, he saw that their resemblance to their father was extraordinary. The same flamboyant gold-tipped hair and alert eyes, the flared nostrils that seemed to be quivering, and the long, slender fingers and toes. They sat together opposite him, quiet and absorbed.

"You been to the cave?" Pa Daniel said.

"Yes," said Christine.

"Your mother send you to me?"

"We come by weself," answered Hartseed. "One day

we was in the cave and Christine say, 'We have to go see Pa Daniel. He have something for us.' And we come."

"How you know to come?" Pa Daniel asked. He knew what the answer would be, but he wanted to hear them say it.

"The spirits," Christine replied.

"You not 'fraid the spirits?"

"The spirits living. We feel them. We seen them. But them angry. They cannot rest."

"You know why the spirits send you to me?"

"You have the piece missing from the mask," Christine said.

"Yes. I been keeping it for a long time now."

He reached under the bed for the broken-off piece. Earlier in the day he had dug it up from its grave in his backyard. The children's eyes lit up when they saw it.

"This is yours," Pa Daniel said. "You know what to do with it. My job is over. I been waiting for you to come. Your father before you was searching for it. And your grandmother, but them wasn't the right ones."

"Why?" Christine asked. "Why them wasn't the right ones?"

"Them never come to me, so I know the spirits didn't speak to them. Not the way them speak to you. I feel it the minute you come to the village. When you come to this village, I know it was time."

He looked at their youthful faces: one twelve and one eleven, precocious and unselfish in the love they had for each other. Yes, these were the chosen who would set the past free.

"A long time ago," he said, "it was still slavery times then, I used to groom horses at the fort. The fort wasn't too far from here. Maybe three miles or so. One morning, bright and early, soldiers come riding in from a battle, many of them bleeding so bad, I could tell that them didn't have too long to live. Them had gone out to hunt down Africans

that run away from the plantation, but it seem like them
was the ones that get hunted. This one soldier was cut up
so bad, you could see his innards. Just waiting for death to
get up and open the door to let him in. But even though he
so near death, he was holding onto this piece of dark wood
for dear life.

"When we get him off the horse, I recognize it right
away. You see, before I was put in the fort I worked on a
plantation. Them had a slave there who would hardly sleep
at night. Instead he worked on this mask. He and his
woman disappear from the plantation one night. When I
see the piece of that mask in that soldier hand I figure that
man and his woman had to be dead.

"That soldier died the minute we take him off the horse.
I take the piece of the mask from his hand and I hide it
'cause when I touch it I know it fall into me hands for a
reason.

"After slavery done, I move here and this village spring
up. I been waiting so long now I lost track of the time. But
finally the ancestors find the vessels them want. Finally,
you come."

When it got dark the children took the piece with the
broken-off baby to the cave. It fit securely into the mother-
mask.

A week later Pa Daniel died. Before dusk on that day
the children went to the cave. A band of monkeys were
digging in the damp earth at the entrance. At their approach
the monkeys melted into the trees. When they peered into
the hole they saw that the earth had concealed burnt bones.
Carefully, they gathered the bones, every charred splinter,
every hollow skull, and carried them into the cave and set
them upon the ledge.

The plantation launched an all-out war against the monkeys, a war precipitated by the complete destruction of two

fields of young canes located quite near the gully. Pulled from the ground by their roots, the young canes were laid to ruin one morning in August. Even the villagers arriving for work the next day were surprised by the totality of the destruction.

Traps were set in the gully. Teams of hunters from the plantation patrolled Monkey Road with guns day and night on horseback. But after one full month not one monkey had been trapped or shot. The planters accused the villagers of destroying their traps. The villagers denied this, laughing among themselves at the way the monkeys were making fools of the plantation. "Them smart white men who know everything can't catch a few monkeys." Not only didn't they catch the monkeys, they never even caught a glimpse of one. It seemed as though the monkeys had completely disappeared.

The plantation hired additional watchmen to guard their crops at night. But how could they be certain that the watchmen were not involved in a plot to bankrupt them?

Kenworth Grahame, the overseer of the plantation, had just returned from visiting his son at Oxford University. While in England he had gone to see doctors about the violent stomach pains he'd been having for several months. The doctors told him they were due to the stress of the infernal weather he faced on the island, but despite their warning, he had come back. He had to. He was close to paying off his debts. Another year. That was all it would take.

When his maid woke him up one morning to report that a watchman had an urgent message, the knot in his stomach told him he should have listened to the doctors and stayed in England. Grahame slid on the red robe and red slippers that his wife—who had been smart enough to stay in London—had given him for his fiftieth birthday and entered the kitchen. The look on the waiting watchman's face tightened the knot in his stomach even more.

"Mornin', sir," the watchman began.

"What's the problem?"

The watchman's dark face hid his glee. "Trouble with the nuts, sir. I think it's the monkeys again."

"Westminster?"

"That is the only field of nuts you have, sir."

"I know that. Who's the watchman for Westminster?"

"Baker."

The maid came into the kitchen; the watchman's eyes followed her, and she spun a smile in his direction as she bent over the stove. The smile held promise, the watchman noted.

"Where's Baker now? Why did he send you?"

"Gone home. I send him home. He did shaking like a leaf when I find him, so I send him home."

"Shaking? How many monkeys did he see?"

"None."

"What?"

"He say he ain't see no monkeys."

"What did you just tell me?".

"Baker eyes a little bad. You should think about replacing him."

"I don't need you to tell me what to do."

"Baker say he ain't see no monkeys. But what else could it be? It had to be the monkeys."

"What makes you so sure? It could have been Baker himself."

"If Baker was goin' steal, he would steal potatoes or something his family could use."

This at least made sense to the overseer. "How much of the field was destroyed?"

"The entire field. Westminster get destroy complete."

"The whole field? My God!"

"That ain't all, sir." The watchman glimpsed the maid eyeing him.

"What do you mean, that's not all?"

"The field Ollie Roach was watching, Jamaica Bottom, that whole field of young canes gone. Pull up by the roots. Every last one. And the one next to that, too."

"Is this some kind of joke?"

"No, sir." The watchman switched his gaze to the maid to conceal his desire to laugh.

"Are you telling me the monkeys did that too?"

"You know Ollie Roach is one of the best watchmen you got. Whip and stick always ready. Never drop asleep on the job. Nothin' don't get past Ollie unless it got a pass from God."

"For goodness sake! You can't tell me that monkeys can destroy two entire fields and nobody saw it!"

"I wouldn't put nothin' past them monkeys, sir."

The maid laughed out loud. Grahame scowled at her. She turned quickly to the eggs cooking in the saucepan. Grahame plopped himself down into a chair. He sensed that the watchman was making fun of him.

"And where's this Ollie Roach now?"

"Home."

"So who appointed you spokesman?"

"I appoint meself."

"Tell Ollie Roach and the other one I want to see them right now."

"You ain't go get no more outta them than I tellin' you."

"I believe you heard what I said."

"You want to see them right now."

"That's right." Grahame turned his attention to the maid in abrupt dismissal of the watchman. "Get me some milk," he ordered.

After one last admiring glance at the maid's bamboo-slender neck, the watchman retreated down the steps into the huge yard. At the bottom of the steps he heard a scream from the kitchen. He raced back up the steps. The maid was on her knees, bent over the prone overseer, crying hysterically. The watchman took one look at the man, locked in convulsions, his face white as a sun-bleached sheet, and knew the man was in the grip of death and would succumb if he didn't get help right away. There was a doctor on Hopefield plantation about two miles away. The watchman bounded down the steps to the stable, jumped on a brown mare, and raced out of the compound.

When he returned with the doctor, the sobbing maid was still hunched over Grahame. They were too late. The doctor and the watchman tried to pull her away from the overseer's lifeless body, but she refused to get up. Suspecting she had been much more than a maid to Grahame, the watchman left her with the ginger-chewing doctor.

Exiting the yard, he made a right turn onto the driveway, the only access to the majestic compound that embraced the great house and two smaller yellow brick houses as well as the stables. The watchman avoided the sharp stones by walking on the patches of grass that sprang from the clefts between the gray stones of the road. The damp grass bathed his feet with moisture. He looked up to see if any monkeys were hiding between the green tree branches, but only the sun's sparkle caught his eyes.

At the end of the access road he turned left toward the gully, a shortcut to his house. After a few yards he turned onto a narrow pathway leading to a sugarcane field that sloped precipitously. He made his way through the canes, taking care not to trip or let the sharp cane blades cut his face. The slope flattened into a valley stretching some fifty yards across the cart-road and into the next cane field. This field was somewhat smaller, containing younger canes, and he ran all the way to the other side.

Wiping sweat from his face on his shirtsleeve, he walked across the next field. Strewn on the ground were leaves and crushed petioles. The leaves were still fresh and green, for the destruction of the nuts had happened only a few hours before, and the sun had not yet burned the remaining life out of these vines severed from their roots. He saw that some of the vines were still laden with nuts, and he picked a handful to munch on as he walked.

He continued across the ruined field, examining the destruction more closely. Leaves and stalks were everywhere. The ground had been torn open ruthlessly, leaving large holes, many the size of a man's head. He cracked some of the shells and popped the nuts into his mouth. They were soft and moist with a sugary taste. He fairly skipped across the patched green ground as he chewed. A song that his late father taught him when he was a boy came back to him.

> Listen hard, look good
> Don't let the jumbie catch you
> You don't know where them be
> Them be places you don't see
> The jumbie white, sometimes he black
> But if you see him, don't look back
> Run, run, run; or do like Macak.
> Macak, Macak, them can't see Macak.

This tussle between the monkeys and the plantation had a long history. His father, Small Paul, had told him that for a while the plantation had not cultivated the fields close to the gully because whatever they planted there was destroyed or stolen. Naturally the villagers were thought to be the culprits, but even the plantation had to admit that the pattern of pillage was mystifying. Not only were potatoes and corn being stolen, but before they got a chance to bloom young canes were uprooted and dragged to the edge of the gully, where they were left in a pile. It was then that a watchman reported he saw the monkeys pulling the young canes from the earth. When he approached them, they disappeared. From then on, monkeys were blamed for everything stolen from the plantation, though the watchmen knew that often the villagers were the ones who stole the potatoes and bananas and destroyed the canes.

Over the years the plantation had exacted some measure of revenge for the destruction of the crops. People from the village were accused at random of stealing and hauled before the courts, where, despite the lack of proof, some of them got a whipping. But the destruction of crops continued.

The watchman was now at the mouth of the gully. Having to guard someone else's property from people who were his friends, who were often hungry, was not a job he relished, but it kept him out of the sun. He had, on occasion, had to lash a few of his fellow villagers with his bamboo stick as they tried to make off with bags of potatoes. He understood their predicament, their hunger and desperation, but if he didn't do his job, if it was perceived that he was a lax watchman, he would have a wave of villagers stealing crops on his watch. And before a mongoose could spin around twice, he'd be out of a job.

As he entered the gully, the watchman became aware of a presence, an eerie silence. The mile trees were perfectly still. In front of him the veined tendrils of the bearded-fig tree hung to the ground in massive knots. He felt that someone was watching him.

Suddenly the gully erupted in a rapid fire of piercing screams and howls. Monkeys were everywhere. More than a hundred. More than a thousand. They moved with blinding speed and precision, jumping over his head, flicking their tails in front of his eyes and filling his ears with such noise, it made his whole body shake. He stood still, eyes closed, too afraid to move. The attack was over in a second. Suddenly, it was midnight quiet again. The monkeys had disappeared. He opened his eyes. A young boy was standing in front of him wearing a mask.

The mask stared at him. He stared at the mask. Something about it was disturbingly familiar. It wasn't the monkey face making up the lower portion of the mask, but the woman sitting with her legs open as though inviting him. It made him think of his mother—whom he hadn't seen since he was fifteen—and the way she used to hold him in her lap to comb his hair. The boy turned and walked away. The watchman followed automatically. Along the stream, down the steep, wooded precipice. He was fearful that they were going into some bottomless pit, but he was more afraid to turn back. When they reached the cave, the boy stopped and turned toward him, the mask still covering his face. Then with a precise turn of his heel, the boy disappeared into the cave. The watchman waited a moment to see if the boy would appear again; when he didn't, the watchman peered anxiously into the cave. Blackness. The boy was nowhere to be seen.

The watchman stepped over the threshold and cautiously advanced into the blackness of the cave, into the trap of memory. The darkness encircled him, the stones under his feet were cool and steady. He could hear water trickling somewhere within. He stopped, waiting for his eyes to get accustomed to the darkness, but they seemed unable to adjust. Blindly he threaded himself through the cool blackness, stirred on by the desire to see into this void. To know what the woman on that mask was offering.

He reached out, groping for the walls, trying to feel his way along. Then, overcome by panic, he turned to go back, stumbled, and fell to the ground. His head struck the damp stone of the cave floor. When he regained consciousness, he tried to lift his head but found that he could not move. Someone was standing on his face. Or so it felt. He reached up and touched the sinuous arches of the mask. The mask had become his face, and his eyes saw what the mask had seen.

Through the prism of the mask the watchman saw a man and a woman on a mountain. The woman was sobbing. The man held her in his arms as she wept. A mask lay at their feet. The woman cried and cried. She could not stop. She was crying for her child and for all children born into slavery. She was crying because she was now free.

They lay down together—two who had fled from enslavement—and he covered her with his wide arms. Her sobs filled the night. The sea was singing above everything else. It was a beautiful song: home.

Early the next morning, before the sun had dispersed the last traces of night, the man got up and looked at his sleeping wife. He thought of waking her but changed his mind. They had not eaten since evening, and he knew she'd be hungry when she woke up. In the valley below, the wind was dead. His eyes swept the fields and the green tops of ripe sugarcane. He set off down the mountainside. He would grab a few pieces of cane and be back before his wife woke up, then he would find a place where she could hide during the day while he searched for something more substantial to eat.

Hurtling through the thick grass, he was oblivious to the sharp stones cutting his feet and to the four white men coiled in sleep among the roots of the bearded fig-tree at the foot of the mountain. He passed the four hunters and went into the nearest cane field. The canes were ripe. He broke off four of the biggest and yellowest at the roots and swung them across his broad shoulders. When he turned around, he was face to face with death.

He swung at the men with the canes and missed. One of the four raised his gun and blew a hole in his chest.

The shot echoed throughout the valley and traveled up

the mountain to where the woman was sleeping. It woke her.

Dawn had stretched halfway across the sky. She looked around. A group of tiny yellowbreasts fought over one worm nearby. Another group chirped cheerfully as they hopped smartly from branch to branch in the trees above her. The echo of the shot continued to ring deep within her. Her husband was gone. Not just gone from his place beside her on the bed of dried coconut leaves but gone from her forever. He was dead and she was not safe in that place. She knew she ought to run but she did not want to go on without him, even if he was dead. The child in her belly moved, sending a tremor of pain through her back and down her legs, paralyzing her for a few seconds. She tried to think of what to do. She thought of going down the mountain where the echo of death had come from. The baby moved again. Silence. No silence was ever so pure and final as the silence she heard now.

The peace in the valley was now everlasting. The woman knew she could wait no longer. She tried to get up and felt the first wave of contractions. The pain was numbing. She tried to hold it back but the pain wrenched the cry from her cracked throat. It was the cry of a mortally wounded animal.

She waited for the pain to leave her. The sun chased the dingy dawn-clouds and opened the sky window to reveal its pale sapphire curtain. The warmth revived her and she dragged herself to a nearby stone to rest her head. The mountain was beginning to wake up. Birds flew overhead. Curious brown monkeys kept their eyes on her as they played hide-and-seek nearby. A grass snake peeked out from behind the rock. Another wave of contractions. Her cry sent the monkeys scurrying for the highest branches. She tried to clear her head of the pain to think of a hiding place. If she could only drag herself under a thick bush somewhere, she would feel safer. The contractions were coming faster. Determined to be born where its father had been killed, the child was forcing its way out of her womb and there was nothing she could do to stop it. She tried to hold it back. If only the baby would wait a few more hours, a few more days. She tried to squeeze her legs together, but the child seemed to have superhuman strength. Her legs spread and the baby came.

She heard laughter and crying at the same time. Her son was crying. The laughter came from behind her about a hundred yards down the mountain and drowned out the crying baby.

As soon as that laughter reached the top of the mountain, the eyes of death would see her, shamelessly sprawled on the ground with her legs splayed wide open, her womb stretched to Africa, and would crawl into her the way her baby had just come bawling out. That laughter, clear as a solitary midnight star, was coming for her. She flung her arms to the ground, trying to push herself up onto her elbows. She wanted to look death in the eyes when it came. She was still too weak to get up. Her fingers touched wood. She grabbed it; it was the mask. She managed to drag it to her chest. Hugging her baby boy to her, she put the mask over him. The mask covered his entire body.

The laughter came closer. It reached them, and the woman smelled the blood of her husband. The four hunters passed without noticing them.

The mask was taken from the watchman's face and he opened his eyes. The cave was no longer dark. A fine, rain-like mist made him feel as though he was on a mountaintop that extended into the clouds. He looked into the mist for the woman and her baby, but the face staring back at him was that of a young boy. The same young boy who had led him into the cave.

He knew this boy. He didn't know his name, but he was

Prince Johnson himself. Same red hair. Same bold, articulate nose. Same arched cheekbones. Same playing the fool down here in this gully with these monkeys. Same bloody Prince.

The watchman looked at Young Prince through slitted eyes to make it appear that he had slipped back into unconsciousness. His head hurt and the dream he had just experienced persisted, making him afraid to close his eyes. He thought about the woman in the dream, if indeed it was a dream, for the whole thing was so real that he had his doubts. No dream could be that real, that vivid. So vivid that it was clearer than what was in front of him right now.

The mask hung from Young Prince's right hand. Feet set wide and chest held high, his pugnacious stance made him look bigger than he was. The watchman recognized the mask as the one in the dream. He sat up.

"Who you is, boy?" The watchman did not wait for an answer. "Where you get that mask, boy? And what kinda power it got to make me have them horrible dreams?"

Young Prince took a few seconds to answer. "What the mask show you wasn't no dream."

"That thing take me and spin me round a nightmare, that's what it do to me. And it give me a headache. How you get me to come in here, boy?"

"I ain't bring you in here. Is the spirits."

"The spirits, eh?" The watchman rose to his feet.

"Yes, is the spirits," Young Prince repeated.

"For argument sake," the watchman began, "saying I believe this nonsense that I follow spirits in here, what purpose them bring me in here for?"

"To teach."

"Teach? Who, me?"

"Yes."

"Teach me what?"

"History."

"History? What history?"

"History is a funny thing," said Young Prince. "It like the water running down a hill. It does only change direction when something strong enough stand in the way. You's a watchman at the plantation, right?"

"That ain't no secret. Everybody know that."

"My father would be living today if not for a watchman like you. In fact, more like you than you know."

"What you mean like me?"

"A man who could see things but ain't had no vision."

"Stop playing games with me, boy. You talking 'bout me father, ain't ya? You believe my father had something to do with Prince death?"

"He had everything to do with it."

"Look, boy, 'cause you and that sister of yours get scholarship to go to school with them white children, that don't make you special, hear? I could still whip you and send you home to your mother. You's still a youngster to me. A boy with a big mask. That's all you is. And you don't know nothin' 'bout my father. He find your father's body, that's all." The watchman laughed nervously.

"The spirits bring you here so you don't walk in the wrong footsteps."

"I walk in me own footsteps."

"Before you walk in your own footsteps you ought to know who footsteps in front you."

"Who footsteps in front me?"

"That is what the mask show you."

"What I see in that mask ain't have nothin' to do with me."

Before he finished, the watchman knew it was a foolish thing to say, but he had to say something. He was a man of thirty, and it just wasn't right that a boy so young should be teaching him anything about history. So what if he was Prince's son? So what if he might have the power to change himself into an animal and attack him right now? So what? He was still a boy and ought to show respect to his elder.

The watchman decided he knew as much about history as anyone else. What was their history anyway? One bad story about death and suffering after another. The people in Monkey Road had enough trouble dealing with the present. What good was history to them?

"What the mask show 'bout history is that sufferin' don't stop with death," said Young Prince. "It does only stop when you see the light that connect the past to the future. A light that you know belong to you and only you. The mask bring you in here to teach you that. To teach you that if you see something, then you have to know what is the consequence if you show it to somebody else. Somebody that it don't belong to. Like what your father did."

"My father ain't do nothin' wrong."

"You' father show the wrong eyes what they didn't make to see. And my father dead because of it. That is the light you and me have to walk under. Together. You and me have to make sure that mistake don't happen again. The time will come when the spirits will ask for your help, for you to see them and don't see them. You have to know what the consequence will be if you let your eyes become the eyes of the wrong people."

Young Prince led the watchman to the mouth of the cave and watched as he made his way up the escarpment.

FIFTEEN

What looked like a passing shower on Wednesday took four days to end. The rain stopped Midra from doing her wash on Saturday. She heaped the pile of dirty clothes in a corner of the kitchen till whenever the rain yielded.

On Sunday morning the sun came out. Midra moved the pile of clothes into the backyard where the hens were scratching for worms, flapping their pent-up wings, and cackling for the sheer pleasure of it. The warmth of the sun was so welcome that she felt like cackling too. She stripped down to the waist to do her washing. Hartseed had skipped out of the house as soon as the rain stopped and no doubt was playing in the pond with Christine. Brandon was sleeping late to recuperate from a dawn session of lovemaking with her.

Midra smiled to herself as she set up the bench and washtub in the sun. The memory of a rainbow expanding and exploding inside of her was worth a smile. This morning was one of the few times that Brandon had been able to respond to her passion with the vigor and lasting power that allowed her the fullest enjoyment of their lovemaking.

His stamina caught her by surprise, for she had grown accustomed to his hurried and unbalanced probing—except when they went down to the gully, where he allowed her free rein and did things she could not get him to do in their bedroom. And he had laughed at the end of it, he had actually laughed. A small, soft laugh—small enough to be captured in the shallow basin between her breasts, where it stayed for a while, then spread across her sweating body like gossamer-thin molasses, keeping husband and wife stuck together until the sun broke through the window. It was the laugh and the holding that brought the rainbow bursting inside her.

The melancholy that swallowed her spirit after she'd lost the twins had been slow in releasing it. But it had, eventually. It took all the patience her mother could muster. Brandon tried to be gentle and loving, but he was no match for her fits of gloom and reticence. The dreams had stopped, and she found a welcome solace in sleep, which sometimes lasted for stretches of twelve hours or more at a time. One day Hartseed came home from school with a baby monkey sitting on his shoulder. It was a sprightly little thing, jumping onto the boy's head and then onto his shoulder with a grace that soon distracted her. The little monkey broke through her gloom and made her laugh. It stayed with them for a few weeks. She named it Daisy and took care of it while Hartseed was at school. By the time it abandoned them, the extreme mood swings had left her. Then suddenly, a few days ago, just before the week of rain began, the dream had returned—the dream of blood rising to suffocate her.

She left the sunny yard and went back to the kitchen to get the pile of clothes and the cake of soap. Peata was standing by the stove, stirring cornmeal pap. The perfume of bay leaf permeated the small kitchen. Peata glanced at her daughter's nakedness and shrugged as she brought the spoon to her lips to savor the pap. Her daughter was known for doing strange things.

"It ready yet?" Midra asked.

"In a minute."

Midra looked at the laundry pile and decided to begin with Brandon's work clothes. Those would be the hardest to wash, and if she got them out of the way early, the rest would be easier to handle as the sun got hotter.

"What get into you and Branny this mornin'?" Peata asked, smiling, as she stirred the pap with a smoothness that came from years of practice.

Midra laughed. "I don't know what you talkin' 'bout, Ma."

"I bet you don't. You shouldn't walk around like that, though, Midra. That boy of yours getting big."

"Hartseed and Christine must be down by the pond skipping stones 'cross the water. You know them two. Them ain't go come back here 'til the sun ready to go down."

Peata poured a bowl of pap for Midra and a smaller bowl for herself. "As long as them ain't down in the gully in that cave," she declared. "Ya never know where them caves does lead to. When I was a girl growing up, a group of children went to the marl-hole to get some marl. Them find a cave and begin to explore it. And them get lost. When them families follow the cave, them find that it went all the way to the sea. Them still never find them children yet."

Steam floated into Midra's face as she froze in the motion of blowing cool air on the hot pap in front of her. "What cave?" she said in as perfunctory a voice as she could muster.

"You ain't know 'bout that cave them find down in the gully?"

"No."

Peata glanced at her daughter. Something told her Midra was lying. But why? She had heard Hartseed and his sister whispering about the cave, and though she thought it strange that they wouldn't answer her questions about it, she didn't expect this kind of reaction from Midra. There was something about that cave that bothered Midra. As Peata sat fiddling with her pap, the specter of Prince came before her. That cave was connected to Prince.

Midra stirred her pap absent-mindedly. Before she came into the kitchen she had been very hungry, but she had suddenly lost her appetite.

"What does be going on in that cave, Midra?" Peata asked.

"Ma, I don't know nothin' 'bout no cave."

"Don't lie to me, Midra."

"You know children, too. Them does find the strangest places to play. If the children find a cave, so be," Midra said. The flow of steam from her bowl had lessened. She tasted the pap, then pushed the bowl to the center of the table.

"You not hungry?"

"Yes. I go take it outside with me. It still hot."

"I think wunna hiding something from me."

"Wunna who?"

"You and that boy and his sister."

"You talkin' foolishness, Ma."

"What inside this cave that you can't tell me 'bout it?"

"Ma, you frettin' 'bout nothin'."

"It got anything to do with Prince?"

"Ma, what you worrying 'bout this cave for? It just some thing the children find. And get Prince out your mind. Prince ain't studying you."

"You get him out of yours?"

Midra got up, took her pap, and went into the backyard. The brightness filling the yard could not replenish the enthusiasm she'd just lost for the work in front of her.

Peata left her pap on the table and went to her bedroom. It had been a long time since she and her daughter had really talked, but not since that morning when she found Midra in bed with her hands and feet full of mud had she felt that her daughter was deliberately lying to her. She was sure it had something to do with Prince. Prince Johnson again! What was the power of this man to still affect their lives after all these years?

Peata sat on the bed. "How can I condemn Midra," she said aloud.

Her own fixation on Prince was ludicrous to the point of being tragic, she knew. After years of being pragmatic and sensible where men were concerned, she could not understand how she could have allowed a young pup like Prince to sweep into her life like a storm-wind and disperse all her good sense. Thirteen years of going to bed dreaming about a man who was dead. What a joke! What a fool she was! A man who she'd hardly known. A man who had made her daughter pregnant in one night of primitive passion. Midra claimed there was love involved. Maybe. But what was her own claim to him? Definitely not love. Then what? Something more primal than love?

She looked at her hands. Stronger than most. The fingers still flexible even as they grew thick and knobby from too much fire and water—cooking, cleaning, and washing. But she had seen worse, much worse. She had raised her own daughter, and now she was helping to raise Prince's children. Thirteen years had sped by like a blur. It was time to wake up.

She fingered the little gold figurine of a prancing horse Prince had given to her. She kept it under her pillow and played with it often. Especially when it rained. Somehow she always thought of Prince when it rained. She didn't care if he'd stolen it. If he stole from the plantation, well, they deserved to have things stolen from them. After all, they stole black people, and everything they had in this country they'd gotten because of stolen labor. Peata had never worked on a plantation herself, but she could remem-

ber as a young girl soaking her mother's feet and rubbing
her back with coconut oil after a day of work in the fields.
During crop-time, when the sugarcane was being harvested,
she hardly saw her mother during daylight hours. Her
mother would leave home in the morning before the sun
came up and return at night, long after the sun had gone
down. Together, Peata and her sister took care of everything around the house—the cooking, cleaning, washing—
and with no man around, sometimes fixed things that broke.
And did things break! Their two chairs were always breaking. It was a struggle just to keep the old ottoman in the
corner near the door standing on its rickety legs. If you
looked at the back door too hard, it would fall down. But
she delighted in fixing the balm of hot water and salts for
her mother's feet, then rubbing her back with coconut oil.
After the back rub, her mother would fall asleep on the
floor.

The golden horse looked more alive than Peata ever remembered. She'd never asked Prince where he'd gotten it
and remembered the look of surprise on his face when she
just smiled as he slipped it down her bosom. She would
get rid of the little golden horse today. Take it to the church
and leave it in the pew, that's what she would do.

Her mother would have been a horse if she were not
human; she might have been better off being a horse, Peata
thought, she might have had an easier life. There were days
when she thought her mother would not survive, times
when the chiggers made her mother's feet so raw and painful that she could hardly walk. Still, she would hobble off
to the plantation, leaving her house earlier than usual so
that she would get there on time. Some days she went to
work in the rain only to come home shaking with fever.
And with no man to help out, she could not afford to take
even a day off. Her mother had said it would take death to
keep her home from work. And that is what it took. Death.

Peata was eleven when it happened. Her older sister by

three years had started working with her mother on the plantation, dropping dung. No sooner had she begun than she got pregnant by one of the drivers of the gang. It was a Friday, Peata was sifting flour to make dumplings. The flour was not only very dirty and full of worms, it smelled bad too. She took her time, patiently absorbing the awful smell to get all the worms and bits of dirt out. Her mother loved dumplings—dumplings stewed with yams, eddoes and saltfish—and Friday was dumpling day. When her sister flung the door open and came running through the house, she tore the door completely off the one hinge it hung on. Peata knew something had happened to her mother before her sister even opened her mouth. She dropped the sieve and ran as fast as she could to the plantation. By the time she got to the field where her mother had been dropping dung, a crowd had gathered. Her mother had fallen down in "bad-feels" with the dung basket still on her head and was alive when Peata got there. She clutched Peata's hand so tightly, as if her daughter were bringing her life, that the memory of it always made Peata break out in a cold sweat.

Peata never looked back at the plantation. She went to live with her aunt and grandmother in the city. Her sister later moved to Monkey Road when the man who'd made her pregnant decided to leave his wife to live with her.

She began to undress. She would take one of Midra's clove baths. She had not taken one in years. Maybe thirteen years. She would take a clove bath and go to church. Never much of a regular churchgoer, she had not been inside one since Midra's wedding. But church might be a good place to start to cleanse one's head of musty, unmanageable dreams. Thirteen years! For a man who brought her ecstasy only in the seclusion of her own dreams? How had he managed to capture and imprison her spirit in his dead body? Obeah. It had to be obeah. She swore. It could only be obeah. Why hadn't she thought of that before? That would certainly explain Midra's confusion about that night and her own inability to dispel this man from her dreams. But how did he do it? Those nuts he brought Midra and the wine he brought her? After church she would stop by Brandon's mother's house and buy some day-old black pudding. Nothing like day-old black pudding to clean out the iniquities of obeah.

She never did understand the confusion about Prince's death. It was clear that those men from the plantation had murdered him; it was also clear, at least to her, that the reaction of the village should've been to descend on that big white house hidden behind the mile trees and dismember every man-jack living there. That is what she would've done. But the villagers were content to whisper among themselves: "What happened to Prince was unfair, and something should be done about it." Whispers don't amount to action. After people stayed away from the plantation in protest, the plantation managers threatened to fire them all because Prince was a "no-good thief." The whispers exalting a wronged Prince changed to "maybe he deserve what he get," and that was the end of that. Everybody went back to work.

Peata picked out a dress. It seemed like her life was galloping along too fast, not giving her time to catch up or to catch her breath. One passionate love. One child. One Dove who flew away. One life, and what had she done with it? Prince. Another life. Maybe. Where was Dove now? The churchbells were ringing.

Churchbells and drums.

Brandon woke from his dream and heard churchbells. Was it the bells that woke him or was it the drums in the dream? He did not know. He preferred the drums. He was sweating. The windows in the bedroom were shut, the blinds still drawn. The sun had surrounded the room. In the dream he had been running down a hill that led to the sea. Only, when he got there, the sea became a fire. A man sitting in the middle of the fire was beating a drum. That was when he woke up.

He got up to get some water. Stupid dreams! Why do people dream anyway, he thought, it only stopped you from sleeping properly.

Brandon went into the kitchen. The earth-floor was cool and hard as marble. Something must be done about this kitchen, he muttered to himself. Blacksmithing had not been as lucrative as he had hoped, and Peata's parties were not as popular since Gunny's girlfriend had started giving parties on Friday and Saturday nights. There was very little money left over after buying food nowadays, but the kitchen needed a real floor. He had already been bitten twice by centipedes early in the morning, leaving his foot swollen for days. Twice, on the same foot, in the same spot on his ankle. He had not managed to catch the offenders and knew they must be lurking around somewhere waiting to bite him again. He drank the cool water.

The house was quiet, too quiet for Sunday. No Peata singing at the top of her voice. No Midra screaming for Hartseed to catch a fowl for Sunday dinner. Then he saw Midra in the yard bent over the washboard, her naked back shining as it absorbed the insistent rays. She worked with a quiet intensity, each stroke up and down the rough grooves of the jucking-board as steady as the rhythm of a drum. The irregular splash of water into the air and over the sides of the washtub provided counterpoint to the steady beat of clothes slapping on wood. Brandon watched her from the doorway of the kitchen for a while. What a beautiful woman!

The air in the kitchen was saturated with bay leaf, Peata's trademark spice for her pap. The smell reminded him that it was almost midday, and he had not eaten. His wife looked more appetizing, though. Brandon smiled, remembering the way he had come alive this morning, outdoing himself.

The past six months his wife had not been herself. He had observed her, more than once, waking up in the middle of the night to sit curled up in a corner, crawling back into bed only when the sun rose. When he tried to find out what was troubling her, she stared at him as though he were mad. A look that would have crushed a centipede. The disdain and contempt in her eyes forced him to retreat into silence. He feared that Midra was beginning to grow tired of him.

To make up for the shortfall in his own business, he now spent two days a week at the plantation shoeing horses and doing other chores. A young girl who worked there bringing water to the field-workers had caught his eye, and it didn't take long for him to taste her favors behind the workshop one evening in the soft yellow wash of the setting sun, hidden by the spread-out branches of a huge shack-shack tree. When he got home, he'd found it surprisingly easy to face Midra; the next time he met his sixteen-year-old lover, he'd stayed until darkness surprised them in their bliss.

The affair had ended when he woke up one morning and had difficulty passing water. It did not take him long to figure out what had happened, and Brandon went immediately to find some inflammation bush. In a couple of weeks he was cured of the clap but stayed away from temptation after that.

Unable to endure her abandonment of their bed any longer, he pressed Midra again, to find out what was troubling her. There were no outward signs that she was having an affair. No trips to the shop that took too long; no walks after the sun went down; no surreptitious visits to friends. None of the things that would convince a husband that his wife had another man. Still, the mere thought made him grind his teeth until his jaws hurt, and he decided that he would kill both Midra and any man she might be involved with. That conviction sent him to Kanga's house to get drunk so he could talk about his worry, a blessing in disguise. The rum and Kanga's exhortations to stand up and be the man in the house bolstered his confidence.

He must have been very insistent that night. He did not remember; he was too drunk to remember anything except that she finally broke down and told him that she had been having bad dreams. But that was all Midra would tell him. There was no other man, she swore. And as always, he believed her.

After the miscarriage her strange nocturnal behavior stopped, but the depression that followed made her almost impossible to live with. She would not answer when spoken to and slept most of the time. Day and night. The only persons in the house she paid any attention to were the children. Their lovemaking seemed to have suffered irreparable harm over those bad months.

That was until last night. Last night and this morning. What could he say about last night except that it was heaven? In one night and half of a morning, Midra's lovemaking had wiped away the past six months of torture and reminded him that perfection slept in her arms.

Brandon crossed to the stove. A bowl of Peata's pap would stop the growl in his stomach. Bits of coals were strewn on the ground near the stove, and the table was covered with the residue of pap. Dirty bowls, one half full of pap, sat on the tiny table, and a ferry train of red ants scurried from the bowls down the table leg and across the dirt floor, finally disappearing under a stone that held up one corner of the kitchen. It was unusual for Peata to be this untidy. He opened the bag of cornmeal laying on the table. The sight of little pink worms twisting around in the coarse yellow meal made him close the bag in disgust. When would they ever be able to buy cornmeal without worms?

A few months ago he had heard rumors that Mal Jones,

who had recently returned from a two-year stint on the Panama Canal, was talking about opening a shop in the village to sell quality stuff. He would wait to see it happen before he believed it. That talk wasn't new. He had heard it before.

The first group of men who had come back from the canal a year ago with their pockets lined with gold said the same things. But nothing had come of it. It'd been all talk. Nothing more. Lost in the wave of new friends and hangers-on, they quickly developed a taste for wild parties and expensive whisky. In the short space of six months they were back at the plantation begging for jobs. Because of his craft Brandon was in a slightly better position than most who saw no other way out of hard times but to sign up at the labor recruitment office in the capital and board the steamers heading to Colón. He felt sorry for those men who had to leave their families in order to feed them. He had no intention of leaving Midra to go to Panama. Especially after last night.

Engrossed in following the path of the ants, he didn't hear Midra come into the kitchen. Her wet fingers circled his waist. He turned to face her, pressing his chest against her hot skin. She squeezed him hard, driving her nipples into his cool skin. The firm muscles of his arms and chest aroused her instantly, bringing thoughts of last night and this morning flooding back.

"You eat anything yet?"

He liked the concern in her voice.

"No," he replied.

"Well, get something to eat, eh."

He rubbed his chin on her head. "You ain't 'fraid that young man o' yours come home and see you like this?"

"He ain't comin' home no time soon. Not with that pond full of cockles for he to catch."

He held her tighter. She felt good in his arms. "How you feel?" he asked.

"How I feel?"

"How you feel?"

She smiled. "What you gettin' at?"

"Last night . . ."

"Last night was last night."

"This morning?"

She leaned away from him.

"This morning was like the old days. I glad we back to the old days," he said, pulling her closer. "Them dreams that you was having, whatever them was, I glad them over. I glad you is yourself again."

A long pause followed.

"I ain't really meself. The dreams come back."

He felt her shudder. He looked down at the tiny black mole on her eyelid and wondered why he had never seen it before. It was so small, it looked like a speck of dirt. "I thought you was back to you old self."

"I got a feeling them dreams ain't go stop 'til . . ."

" 'Til what?"

She moved away from him. Water trickled down her forehead and settled in the basin between her breasts.

" 'Til I tell somebody what I do." She stopped breathing. Brandon was silent. Her chest heaved and she inhaled deeply, unable to hold her breath any longer. Her husband remained silent. That moment between them was like fire and rain battling. Water welled in her eyes, his closed in dread. This was it. She was going to tell him about another man.

He sat down. "Who is it?" he demanded in a grieved whisper.

"When I get pregnant with Hartseed," she began slowly, "it was the first time I ever lay down with a man. I was fifteen and I can't begin to tell you how that night change my life. Even now it does still feel like it happen yesterday."

She paused, weighing her thoughts carefully. "I honestly

don't know what woulda happen if Prince didn't get kill, but what I experience that night more than tell me he was a very special man.''

Brandon remained silent. Midra's words exploded past his ears and tumbled together somewhere in his head, but he didn't have time to think about them because Midra was continuing with her story.

''The way Prince die make me sick for weeks. I mean real sick. So sick, my mother thought I was going to die. I couldn't eat. I couldn't sleep. I couldn't talk to nobody. It make my mother so vex. 'For a man you ain't hardly know,' she say every day I refuse the food she cook. But I couldn't help it. I feel like a part of me get cut off. I know it don't make no sense to you but that is how I did feel, Brandon. Deed and faith. It was worse than when I lose the babies. And when I find out who was responsible, I didn't have no feeling for that body no more. It was as if the person that kill Prince was already a dead person and was just waiting for a place to lie down and get bury. I don't mean the white people at the plantation. I mean the body that really kill Prince.''

She paused.

''The white people at the plantation fire the shots, but them couldn't have killed Prince without help. Small Paul is who kill Prince, and then he wasn't even shame to tell me. He wasn't shame to brag to me that he help them catch Prince. If he didn't shame 'bout killing Prince, I didn't shame 'bout killing him neither. That's the truth. I didn't shame to give him the poison. I know he would drink it. He woulda drink anything I give him. I give him the poison and he drink it. He drink it with a smile 'cause he think he was getting something else. He wanted me. But how could he expect to get me when he kill my Prince? He wasn't gettin' me. He was gettin' death. That's what he was gettin'. That's what I give him for killing Prince.''

Brandon did not know what to say. He had braced himself for a confession of an affair. But every word she had uttered was the truth, it was in her eyes. This was no joke. His wife was a murderer. The affair he had braced himself for was with a dead man. There was no way she would ever be his alone. Not while Prince possessed her mind. He could fight any other man—hell, he would kill anyone who touched her—but he didn't have a chance against Prince.

A month later Brandon left for Panama.

SIXTEEN

In January 1911 the Daughters of Zion Universal Revival came to Monkey Road. After a month of open-air meetings, which attracted large boisterous crowds that reveled in the lively music and the chance to "catch the spirit," this unorthodox sect erected a wooden structure in which to hold their meetings and began to baptize villagers into their faith.

Peata was baptized and began going to church every Sunday. The services at the Universal Revival were more to her liking than the dreary services of the Methodists, services she had occasionally attended in the year and a half since Brandon's leaving. One Sunday she saw a monkey peeping into the church. She was the only one to notice the shiny face peering into the window. The rest of the congregation was clapping and dancing with the spirit of the Holy Ghost. Peata saw it cock its ears and listen to the clapping and singing like a messenger anxious to get the information right. When the clapping stopped and the pastor moved to the pulpit to deliver his sermon, the monkey disappeared.

Peata could not remember what Pastor Williams

preached about as she left the churchyard. That little monkey was still in her thoughts. Peata walked past a group of young boys huddled in a heated debate under a clammy-cherry tree. From the excitement in their voices and the exaggerated way they dramatized their arguments, she knew what they were talking about. It had been a hot topic in the village for the last two weeks. From the old women doing the wash by the pond to the old men planting yams in little plots of land behind their houses; from the mothers washing babies' bottoms on a flat rock in the sun to the fathers slapping their sons across their heads to make them husk the corn faster; from young girls pounding mustard in a mortar with a pestle to young boys roasting potatoes for eating—everyone was discussing the latest incident between the plantation and the monkeys.

Peata heard the story from Hartseed. The plantation had devised a plan to build an access road from the plantation to the gully to provide them with a swift, unobstructed approach. They hired the island's best construction team, which brought to the village two machines for crushing rocks, two heavy rollers for smoothing the surface, blacksmiths' furnaces, and scores of picks and shovels.

Every day convicts from the jail, commissioned by the governor of the island (whose brother was part owner of the plantation), crushed rocks, chopped down trees, and cursed their ancestors as they labored in the sun. At night Small Paul's son watched over the equipment. The road was cut, and stones had been brought in from a nearby quarry to cement it when the machines mysteriously disappeared. The police came to question Small Paul's son the next day, but the woman he lived with told them he had disappeared. What the woman knew but did not tell them was that he had left for Panama that morning.

The police searched the village up and down, even attempting to look under people's beds. The inspector in charge of the case declared that he would carry out no further investigations in the matter because it was clear that a force was at work in the village that was beyond their jurisdiction. The villagers had a good laugh. Everyone knew he was talking about obeah. It was talk they lived with day in and day out. Nothing new about obeah talk. What was new was the police admitting in public that obeah was more powerful than them.

Grass began to grow over the road in a matter of days, and without any fanfare the villagers took the largest stones to help prop up their homes. Once more the plantation had been foiled in their war with the monkeys.

Peata entered the gully, holding on to the branches over-hanging the path to keep from slipping on the damp grass. As she took off her shoes and collected her dress-tail, bunching it at the waist, she was struck by a feeling of familiarity, though she'd never been in the gully before. Her every step had the resonance of memory. Brown doves flew ahead of her. A bold-faced monkey stopped to stare at her. A female iguana waited patiently on a bed of ripe cherries while a large male in rustic disguise completed his mating dance nearby. A strong gust of cool air brought her to a momentary standstill as she approached the large stone at the bank of the stream. She waded in the cool water, cleansing her feet of soft mud. Then she stopped at the top of the steep slope, suddenly afraid to go on. But this un-recognizable memory grabbing at her like her mother's hand grasping for life would not let her turn back. She made her way down the deep ravine.

When she reached the bottom she was sweating pro-fusely. And she was tired. Looking up, she could not see the sun. The musty smell of damp leaves surrounded her. Suddenly, the thick vines opened up and Hartseed stood in front of her, at the mouth of a cave, a mask in his right hand.

"You take long to get here, Nana," he said.

"I come when I feel to come," Peata replied.

"We waitin' for you."

He turned and strode into the cave. Peata watched him disappear, then followed him. Deep in the cave she found him sitting with Christine on a huge stone throne shaped like an egg. The only light in the cave came from a lighted oilcloth stuck in a bottle that rested on a ledge a few feet above the stone throne. Blue smoke, hovering on the heavy air, made circles above their heads. The walls shone like marble, and even in the dim light Peata could see her reflection. She felt something drip onto her shoulder and looked up. Clear water percolated from marble-like needles hanging from the ceiling, and Peata opened her mouth to catch the sweet liquid.

Hartseed lifted the mask above his head and stood up. Peata remained still. He moved toward her. The black mask shone in the light, its penumbra dancing on the wall. Hartseed slipped the mask over her head and the light went out.

Peata saw men sitting under a tamarind tree, some playing warri, some eating sugarcane. Two children were feeding a bunch of hogs, taking turns beating them with sticks to hear them squeal. Inside a hut made of wood, mud, and bamboo, a woman was surrounded by a group of children. Their ages ranged between four and twelve. One boy who sat rubbing the woman's ankles was older.

The older boy was the spitting image of Hartseed. Same arched cheekbones and flared nostrils, same penetrating eyes that could see through fire. The woman smiled as the boy—her son, whom she had named Prince—massaged her ankles with a light-as-feather touch.

"Children! Children!" Her voice was soft.

"Yes, Nana!" screamed the children together.

"Wanna hear a story, children?"

"Yes, Nana!"

She laughed.

"Time before time in a distant place, things was so hard that nobody couldn't find nothin' to eat. One day word spread that one buckra grew plenty, plenty corn; and the corn was very near ripe. As the news come pigeon and dem so get ready to fly to the place. Mudfish in the water wake up that morning and swim to the shore and see pigeon and dem flapping them wings to go on their journey. He ask them, 'Bra', where so wunna da go?' Them say, 'Ha Bra'! Buckra corn-piece ripe, nah! We go there!' Mudfish say, 'Bra', wunna carry me wid wunna, no?' Pigeon and dem say, 'Cho, Mudfish! Stay where you is, nah man. What you go do in a corn-piece?' And they fly off after drinkin' water.

"Mudfish wouldn't move from the shore, and when the next group of pigeon and dem come by the waterside to drink, Mudfish say to them, 'Bra', wunna carry me wid wunna, no?' Dem say, 'Mudfish! Why you no stay where you is, nah man?' And them fly off leavin' Mudfish by the river. Mudfish stay there 'til a good-natured pigeon come by, and Mudfish say to him, 'Bra' pigeon, carry me wid you, no?' Him say, 'Bra', what you go do in a corn-piece?' Mudfish say, 'Me too love corn, Bra'.' Him say, 'How you go get there?' Mudfish say, 'Let me lie down 'pon you back.' Him say, 'Bra', suppose you fall off?' Mudfish say, 'Bra', me will hold on tight.' Him say, 'Get on, Bra'. Mek me carry you.' Good-natured pigeon carry him to the corn-piece.

"When dem get to the corn-piece, Mudfish get down on the ground. The pigeon and dem eat the corn on top and Mudfish eat the corn that drop. Mudfish was so busy eatin' that he didn't hear the call, 'Watchman comin'!' Pigeon and dem fly off and leave Mudfish. Mudfish see the pigeon fly off and beg them to take him but them say, 'Cho, we no tell you to come! We no have time to come back to pick you up.'

"When Watchman see Mudfish, him say, 'Why you leave water to come here to t'ief buckra corn?' Him put Mudfish in his sack. 'Me go carry you to buckra.' So Watchman walk to carry Mudfish to buckra, and him start to sing. Mudfish talk to him and say, 'Watchman you love sing?' Watchman say, 'Yes, I love sing.' Mudfish say, 'Ah, Bra' Watchman, if you want to hear man sing, that is me.' Watchman say, 'Is that so?' Mudfish say, 'Is true, me sing sweeter than bird, but me can't sing widout water; put me in one bucket of water and I will sing for you.' Watchman do so. Mudfish shake himself, then he begin to sing.

"He sing so sweet, he mek Watchman dance. Him say, 'Mudfish you sing well, fer true.' Mudfish say, 'Put me in a tub of water and I will sing better, Bra'.' Watchman put him in a big washing tub of water. Mudfish sing again; Watchman dance so 'til the sweat drop off his face. Him say, 'Mudfish, you sing too sweet.' Mudfish say, 'Just put me riverside so I smell river water.' Watchman say, 'No Bra'! You wanna make fool outta me!' Mudfish say, 'No, Bra', you no have to put me whole body in, just put me tail. Let me tail touch river water and me sing so sweet, you will dance like you mad.' Watchman say, 'I will do it, but take care you no make fool outta me.' Watchman put him down. Mudfish begin to sing. Watchman begin to dance. As Mudfish sing, him wiggle him tail. The song was so sweet, Watchman forgot to keep his eyes on Mudfish. Mudfish wiggle and sing. Mudfish wiggle and sing until him get into the water; as him get all the way into the water, him raise him head and him say, 'Bra' Watchman, me gone!' Watchman jump after him but before you could say 'Nan,' Mudfish gone! And that is why you hear dem say 'Never let Mudfish tail touch water.' ''

When the woman finished the story, the youngsters clapped their hands and laughed.

"You like that story, children?"

"It make we for laugh, Nana."

"It more than a story to mek sport, remember that. Don't ever forget, sometimes cunning better than strong. All ya born free. You ain't never been no slave. Them buckra and them bring me and your mothers and fathers from we home across long water to make we slave. Dem beat we all the time 'cause we no like that slavery thing. When we get a chance, we run away from buckra plantation. Don't matter that, them buckra and them still try to catch we to mek we slave again. So 'member, if you wanna stay free, you gotta be smarter than buckra. Now, go and play."

The children left the hut laughing. Only the older boy stayed behind.

"You like the story, too?" she asked her son.

"Me hear that story many times, Ma."

"You never hear a good story too many times," she said, rustling his gold-tipped hair playfully. The woman took a mask from behind the bench she was sitting on. She placed it in her son's lap. "Don't ever part with this, son. It have the spirits of your ancestors. Them help your father and me fly the buckra plantation. Don't be frighten to lean on them spirits when you have to. Them ever strong. Them buckra and them not go stop trying to find us. We t'ief them corn and we help them slaves to run away. As long as we here, as long as we free, them go search for we."

There was a commotion outside, and the woman got up to see what was going on. As she got to the door, it was flung open and a man entered, bracing himself against the door post, his chest heaving in an effort to catch his breath.

"Them coming!" he panted.

"Who?" The woman grabbed an old jacket lying on the floor and quickly slipped into it.

"Buckra. Many horses and them. Soldiers. Guns."

"Where?"

"Over the hill."

"Them see you?"

"No."

"How many?"

"Many, many. Too many for my eyes alone. Thousands. Me never see so much buckra."

Fright streamed from the man's eyes like a silent vapor condensing in the small room. The woman averted her gaze, not wanting to inhale the cloud of panic he brought.

"Buckra never come so far up here before," she said.

Someone must have gone to buckra to tell him where to find them, she thought. Thousands, the scout had said. They had only about two hundred fighting spirits in the settlement. Not enough to dispel that many buckra if they should find them. And it looked as if they might.

The camp had increased a hundredfold since the day the woman accidentally came upon a group of ten runaways like herself after her husband had been killed. By that time she had been wandering for several weeks living on fruit, berries, and nuts. She joined up with the other runaways, and they settled near a stream, never leaving their mountain refuge except at night to steal from the buckra plantation. In the beginning they all went together. All eleven, she being the only woman in a group of men determined never to be slaves again.

The camp grew quickly. Women, men, and a few children managed to find their way into the mountains, and soon the settlement was of a size that made leaving the mountains as one group dangerous and cumbersome. They planted corn and potatoes, while the midnight marauding of the buckra crops was carried out by a small fearless group. The woman continued to be part of that daring group of raiders while her little son stayed in the settlement.

Over the years they had killed many buckra who'd come into the mountains to enslave them again. The treacherous journey up the heavily wooded mountains with their thick, fetid underbrush prevented their settlement from coming under surprise attack, and they discovered that buckra was afraid of the woods at night, so after nightfall they felt safe. On those rare occasions that buckra got within striking distance of the settlement, they were ambushed and driven back down the mountain.

Now something had happened to strike so much fear in buckra that they had gotten the army to move on the settlement. The woman knew what that something was. The rebellion of the slaves in San Domingo had reverberated throughout the slave-holding islands, and all buckra—slave owner or not—were scared. Still, this move by buckra was unexpected. The rebellion in the French island must have really spooked them.

The woman left the bearer of the bad news suspended in his fear in the doorway of the hut and went outside to face the rest of the settlement. By now, the news had spread, and those out farming and cutting wood were hurrying into the compound of huts and holding pens for pigs and some horses. The fifty or so huts were scattered unevenly over an area of about a thousand square yards, with another two thousand square yards outside of the living compound used for cultivation of crops. The men and women gathered quickly, the children came in trickles. The woman spoke to the group of more than two-hundred men, women, and children. Her voice was crisp and unemotional but her eyes spoke urgently.

"Buckra them a come," she began. "And them not far off."

"How many?" a man shouted.

"Plenty," she replied. "Plenty. More than we ever see."

"Too many to kill?" a giant joked.

"I don't know," she replied.

"We can kill all them buckra them!" came another shout.

"That we must decide," the woman said. "We go run or we go fight? We not have a long time to decide."

"We nah run from no more buckra them! We go kill all them!" said the giant, whose name was Hora.

"Them is many buckra coming," said the woman calmly. "Soldiers. Plenty guns. I don't know if we can kill all them."

"We fight 'til we dead!" the giant shouted. "And if I see a man run from buckra, I go kill him myself. Me not born to be no slave and me not go die no slave."

"So we fight," the woman said.

"We fight!"

"We fight!" The group erupted again.

The woman and the giant retired to her hut knowing that the only plan open to them was a surprise attack. Buckra would have to spend the night sleeping in the woods, and that was when they would strike.

Baleful clouds crashed and burst as darkness settled onto the mountain. The warriors gathered outside the hut where the woman warrior distributed weapons. Their arsenal consisted of about a hundred guns seized in previous ambushes and a mélange of cutlasses, knives, and sticks. They set out in the rain.

The woman led the group at a quick pace through the woods. The buckra camp was only three miles away. The woman's son, his mask slung from the neck of his donkey, came with the group, keeping step with the giant.

Moving as one, they splashed water and mud. They tasted the salty freshness of the rain as it rolled off their heads, into their mouths, and onto their backs. Many of them were shirtless, and the warm water, like a blessing from God anointing them, fueled their passion for buckra blood.

The rain was still falling when they approached the buckra camp. The night was mud black. The warriors kept their distance, scouting for the sentinels of the sleeping militia. They located four teams of guards, three men to a team, set at four corners equidistant from the center of the camp. The rest of the militia slept; some braced against tree trunks, others under a huge tarpaulin, others where they lay.

The warriors waited. The woman issued orders. They would strike all the guards simultaneously. Four groups of five warriors each were sent to kill them. The giant, the woman, her son, and two others made up one group. The signal to strike came; in a flash of lightning the throats of the weary guards were slashed.

The camp now lay open to the fury of the warriors, and they struck quickly and mercilessly. Men who could not find their weapons in the dark screamed curses and stumbled over each other in a brave effort to defend themselves. Those who had their weapons fought valiantly against an enemy they could not see. With sleep in their eyes, the only objects they found to shoot at were falling leaves, and their wild shots ricocheted off cascading raindrops while hot knives melted in their hearts. The rout was swift, the victory final. The militia was chased from the mountain.

The warriors collected their dead and wounded. The woman searched for her son to share the moment of victory. She found him bleeding near a pile of buckra soldiers. He was alive but his mask was gone.

The warriors carried their dead and wounded through the rain back to their settlement. When they arrived, tired and sleepy, in the breath of dawn, the rain had stopped. Wounds were washed and salved, and the dead were prepared for burial. The woman took her son to their hut where they slept in each other's arms. She awoke in the middle of the day to bathe and tend his wounds again while he slept. Later that day drums announced the beginning of the ceremony to bury the slain warriors. The giant came to her hut to escort the woman to the ceremony.

SEVENTEEN

Later that night, lying in her bed, Peata could still see that flushed look in the woman warrior's eyes—a white hibiscus opening up at dawn—as she set off to do battle. That same look of hope her mother used to take to the plantation every morning. Peata knew she had somehow experienced the chance occurrence of spirit memory arising, coming alive, superimposed on dream; birth overlapping birth, discrediting and discounting death.

She stared at the ceiling, afraid to close her eyes. Wanting the dream but afraid to lose the memory. Spirit memory coming alive—a journey more fulfilling than any Pastor Williams at the Universal Revival had ever taken her on. That woman was her mother. Her mother was that woman. Hartseed was that boy. That boy was Hartseed. He was Prince. Prince was him. Her feelings for Prince became as clear as water. It wasn't love she felt for Prince. It was passion, yes, hunger—a hunger that burned like sexual love. But in reality it was hunger for the spirit memory that only he could unlock. Through Midra and Vida he had given them the lightning to burst the clouds, to send the rain that would cleanse the memory of their spirit ancestors.

Hartseed and Christine had penetrated those clouds, and soon the whole village would feel the rain.

Midra, who had gone to visit Brandon's mother, returned in the afternoon and found Peata in the same position as when she had left her, staring at the ceiling.

"Ma?"

"Yes."

"You know what time it is?"

"No, what time it is?"

"Two o'clock. You plan to sleep all day?"

"I look like I sleeping to you, Midra?"

"No, but this ain't like you."

"I go get up when I ready."

"You feel alright?"

"I feel good enough to waste my time answering you' stupid questions."

Midra was assured. There was nothing wrong with her mother. Still as acerbic as ever when she didn't want to be bothered. She turned to leave the room.

"Midra?"

"What, Ma?"

"Brandon comin' back?"

"What you mean if he comin' back?"

"Why he leave?"

"To go make money in the canal."

"The real reason, Midra."

"What you gettin' at, Ma?"

"Me just askin' questions."

"What for? Brandon ain't the only man leave his wife and go to the canal. Look how many men gone there and them come back to them wives."

"Is near five years men did leaving to go to the canal. Some went and come back already and near done spend all the money them make. Why Branny wait so long if it ain't something drive him there? You sure it ain't got something to do with Prince and Hartseed and that mask in that cave?"

Midra gazed at her mother in astonishment. "You seen the mask, Ma?"

Peata's eyes watered slightly. "Yes, I seen it. I look inside it. I see all them secrets Prince had inside him. All the pain he had locked away. That is why he used to come here. Them secrets was just too much for one man. He come here looking for a way to let them out."

"Where the cave is, Ma?"

"You don't know?"

"I don't remember."

"What you mean, you don't remember?"

"I tell you from the very beginning, Ma. The whole thing like a dream to me. Like a cloud that set up to rain, then the wind come and blow it away. I can't break it open. I know Hartseed and his sister find the cave. But when I ask them 'bout it, is only stares them give me like I mad. I leave them alone. 'Cause sometimes I wonder meself if I ain't mad. I follow them one day to the gully, but when them get there, them just disappear. I know there is nothing for me to do but wait and endure. Is sixteen years I been walking 'round with this thing, Ma. My husband leave me 'cause of it. I have to find out what it is. If you know where the cave is, tell me."

"So you lied when you say Brandon leaving ain't had nothing to do with all this?"

"Yes. I did something terrible, Ma."

"Midra, I's your mother. I thought I was going to dead when your father leave me. But I bring you. You's mine and I love you. I don't care what you do."

"I poison the man that kill Prince."

Midra related the story to her stunned mother. At the end she broke down in tears.

"I so sorry, Ma."

Peata wiped the tears from her daughter's face.

"You did a terrible thing, girl. I hope God forgive you."

"I need to find the cave, Ma."

"Follow the stream, down into the deepest part of the ravine. It look like there's only trees there, but when you get to the bottom, you'll see it."

"The children down there?"

"I don't know."

When Midra approached the gully, she saw a crowd gathered there. She could make out a number of the village people, but there were also policemen and white men with guns. Fear that something had happened to the children snatched the strength from her legs, and she sat down where she was in the middle of the road. Someone walking behind her helped her up. It was Ben Payne.

"You want me to take you home?"

"No, I'm alright. You know what going on up there?"

"What you think? More confusion between the plantation and them monkeys. Them claim that last night the monkeys not only destroy all the young canes that butt and bound the gully, but them get so bold now, them nearly take over the great house. Mash up all the flowers in them lovely gardens at the great house, mash up all them windows, too."

"Them see any monkeys?"

"What you think?"

"So what them doin' in the gully now?"

"Them say them come a-raiding again. But them nah find a bloody thing. Not a sign. Them start a fire to try and smoke out the monkeys, but the fire just die out so. Every time them try to light another one, it just die out. Lord, I know how them buckra must feel, though. Like them living in a bad dream or something."

She walked with Ben to the mouth of the gully where the crowd was milling around.

"If this monkey business continues," one white man

with a gun was saying, "we will have to shut down the plantation. And where are you people going to work?" This drew no response from the crowd, so he continued. "If you know who's controlling these monkeys, if you know where these monkeys are hiding, you should tell us. It would be to your benefit because you cannot prosper without us prospering. And if we suffer, then you will suffer too."

"But we already suffering!" a woman in the crowd cried out.

"It will get worse if we don't find these monkeys," the man with the gun replied.

"It can't get no worse," the woman hurled back. "All we men gone to Panama. We's a village of women and children. Even we old men gone. How much worse it can get than that? A man harder to come by in this village than a grain of rice. And I's one of them women who can't live by rice alone."

Laughter erupted from the crowd.

The white man with the gun smiled. "You want a man? Come up to the plantation. We have a lot of men up at the plantation. We will give you a man if you can give us the person controlling these bloody monkeys."

The crowd hushed, waiting for the woman's reply.

"What kinda man you got at the plantation for me? Me no want no man from the plantation unless me living in the plantation house proper. Deed and faith! Me would have to be mistress of the house. Have the keys to every door."

This brought more laughter from the crowd. The woman stepped forward for the first time. She was a squat woman with a large radiant face. Her name was Millie. Her husband, Small Paul's son, had left for the Panama Canal along with her sixteen-year-old son right after the disappearance of the road building equipment a few weeks back. Millie flung her thick arms over her head as she approached the white man with the gun.

"I think all ya should just give we this land 'cause them

monkeys ain't go let you rest. Them go make your life hell.
You ain't never go be able to catch them. Them is only a
few people can see them monkeys when them don't want
to be seen. Them monkeys could be watching we right
now." She cleared her throat and observed the hushed
crowd. "You looking at me like I crazy, eh? If you think
I crazy, then good. Don't believe me and see what them
monkeys go do with all ya crops. My husband used to be
a watchman. Was one of the best watchmen all ya had.
Then one day without explanation he quit the job. You
know what make him leave? Them monkeys. He had a run-
in with them monkeys one morning coming home from the
plantation, and it change his life. He never would tell me
what it is exactly that happen between him and them monkeys, but he did say that he know for sure them monkeys
is the spirits of them Africans that get burn up in that gully
a long time ago. Yes, is a story that every man-jack in this
village know, but if you ask them, them go tell you them
never hear 'bout it. All ya here know my husband, Albert,
like his father, Small Paul, could see spirits. He say them
spirits still vex. And them ain't go ever let we forget what
happen to them down in that gully. I think that is what
happen to Albert that mornin' when he butt up 'pon them
monkeys. It change him. So you can bring you' guns and
search up, down, and crossway, and you ain't go find no
trace of them monkeys. You will never catch them. Never!
Never! Like I said before, the best thing is to give us that
land that butt and bound the gully. You and we will be
better partners. Mark my word."

Millie turned and walked away in the direction of the
Daughters of Zion Universal Revival Church. The crowd
waited to see if the white man with the gun would make a
reply to Millie's eloquent speech, but he remained silent.
Then he, the other four white men and the policemen got
on their horses and left.

The crowd lingered for a long time whispering to each

other. As they whispered they became more animated, each murmur breathing more life into them. Their whispers remained that. Whispers. As though they were not talking to each other but to spirits moving among them. Inside them. Slowly, almost reluctantly, they began to disband.

Midra did not move until they had all disappeared. Ben Payne was the last to leave. He asked her again if he could walk her home, but she thanked him and said no.

Then Midra descended into the gully. She had not gone very far into the thick brush when a dark object flashed in front of her and disappeared into the trees. She knew what it was. She had picked up a guide. Light crashed through the spaces between the leaves, giving the stones on the path a faint gleam. She continued, trying her best to be casual and relaxed; she knew the monkeys were around her though she could not see them. Her muscles were poised to embrace them when they made themselves visible. The feeling was different from any of her other visits to the gully. The sensation grew stronger as Midra reached the stream. She stepped in and felt herself pulled along by the unruly current. She slid down the precipice quickly, almost as if the thick brush was liquid, not feeling the sharp stones cutting her feet. And there at the bottom was the cave, as Peata had said.

She entered and saw the mask. She reached for it and put it on. The cave opened up.

It was late in the evening. The giant, Hora, was lying in bed with the woman discussing the recent slave uprisings on the island that had been put down so brutally.

"Them burn a few estates but it was bound to fail," he said. "Them ain't had no weapons and them ain't had no organization."

"Could we have helped them?" the woman asked.

"No. We hear rumors. But we hear rumors 'bout slaves

rising up all the time. Them had soldiers waiting.''

''That musta been why them try to move on our settle-ment. How many African them dead?''

''Near a thousand, I hear.''

''How many get away?''

''We find a group of near fifty last night. I think them buckra soldiers go come up here again.''

''If them go come, let them come,'' she laughed scorn-fully. ''If my boy, Prince, had his way, he won't wait for them to come. It take all my strength to stop that boy from running off and burnin' every buckra plantation he see.''

''We all hate buckra but that boy of yours would kill them and don't even waste his spit on them.''

The woman nestled her head on the warm hearth of the giant's chest and listened to his throbbing heart. She thought of her dead husband. She thought of her other son, who she hoped was not living in slavery. She thought of the promise given to Prince. Prince had grown to a man, and they were still here in this wretched place. The ances-tral spirits had not seen fit to answer their cry for deliver-ance. And since Prince's mask had been taken from him, she'd had to sleep with one eye open, knowing that he was anxious to find it. It was the one thing he could touch that connected him to his father. While his wounds were fresh, he had talked of going off. Now that he was on his feet, it would be impossible to stop him.

A loud banging on the door of her hut drew her. Prince's pregnant young wife, Afa, stood there with a group of women. She was in tears.

''Prince gone!''

''Where?''

''Me don't know. We was walkin' down by the creek when he told me to close my eyes, he had something to show me. Me close them like he said. But he never tell me open them again. So, after a few minutes waitin', me open me eyes and Prince was nowhere in sight. I looked all around. Me hollered his name but he was gone. Me don't even see what direction he gone.''

''Hora!'' the woman cried out. ''Hora!''

The giant woke up.

''Prince gone!'' the woman said, in tears. ''Get fifty of our best men. Prince gone!''

A short time later the group, armed with muskets and machetes, assembled outside their leader's hut.

The woman mounted her mule.

''Where we goin'?'' one of the young men asked.

''To get Prince.''

''Where you think he is?'' Hora asked.

''He can't be very far. There's two estates within a night's ride and a fort in between them. If we ride fast, we bound to catch up with him at one of them three places.''

''Why he take off by himself like that? Me think Prince had more sense,'' the young man said.

''It was a foolish thing to do,'' the woman agreed. ''But everybody act foolish sometimes. Them take a part of him, and he want it back. You don't have to come if you don't want. But if you do, remember this: we just going to bring Prince back; we not going to get into no fight with buckra.''

''We bound to run into buckra. And after them just slaughter hundreds of our brothers and sisters who only want them freedom, you think me could see buckra and not wanna see his blood spout like a spring and feel his bones crack like dirt under my feet?'' the young agitator said. ''If me see buckra, me go kill him dead.''

''Any Africans we can help get them freedom, we help. We never leave them in trouble. That is our way, you know that. But we not going to fight buckra,'' the woman asserted. ''Who wanna go lookin' for blood better stay here.''

Masked by the night they moved nimbly down the mountainside. On reaching the valley below, they increased their pace. Showing amazing stamina, they moved through the valley, over another mountain, through another valley—on and on for hours without slackening. It was close to day-break when the white edifice of the first estate emerged in the distance. They circled it cautiously. Thin black smoke was coming from the house. A dog began to bark. Hora went off with the young agitator to investigate. The dog stopped barking. The two of them came back ten minutes later with about twenty-five Africans—men, women and a few children. But there was no sign of Prince.

They set off again. Dawn was galloping to meet them. They'd be in danger of discovery when the sun came up. Weary as they were, they could not afford to rest. They picked up the pace again until they came to the gully.

Stopping there, the woman contemplated their next step. The next estate was no more than a mile away, but the sky was red. No way they could reach the estate before the sun came up. She would send Hora to look around, the rest of them would stay in the gully until she was sure it was safe to move on.

They walked in single file down the grassy incline. When they reached the stream, the woman felt her mule stiffen. Instinct told her there was trouble ahead. She stopped.

"Wait! Something wrong," she said to Hora. "Take a look."

Hora moved silently to the edge of the trees that surrounded them. He came back quickly, his face deformed by panic and fear.

"Soldiers!"

"Take a look up there where we come in," ordered the woman.

He ran back along the passage that had brought them to that spot. When he returned, he was visibly shaking.

"Them got we surrounded. The only chance we got is to make them come in behind we and use the trees and bush as cover. We can't get out any other way."

The group huddled together around the woman. She was their leader. They would do whatever she said, except give up. They would rather die here, if it came to that, than be slaves again. Life as a slave was worse than death. If they died here, their spirits would remain free.

But the woman had no thought of giving up. They picked the stream to make their stand because it would carry their blood to the sea. They waited for the soldiers to come.

Two hours passed. The sun was out. A wind dispersed the clouds. It was a bright, glorious day.

The animals were first to signal the start of the battle. But it was not the fight the group was expecting. Monkeys appeared from nowhere, flipping through the trees in an effort to escape the coming horror. Wild boars bounded past them squealing in terror. Then Hora saw the smoke.

"Them trying to smoke us out!"

Some of the group panicked. They began to run toward the cordon of soldiers.

"Stop!" the young agitator shouted. "Stop! Where all ya goin'? If we try to run out, them go shoot we like dogs. Me not go give them the satisfaction of seeing the color of my blood."

He struck his machete in a young tree growing behind him.

"All we here know what this tree is," he said.

The woman knew the tree well. She had chewed on its poisonous roots after they had taken her first baby.

Several of the new free Africans decided to take their chances and ran through the smoke. The few that remained chewed on the root, stretched themselves out beside the stream, and waited. When the fire reached them, they were already assembled, a row of cold smiles.

Prince, too, had reached the gully a short time before the group. Drawn to the deepest part that lay beyond the stream, he had made his way down recklessly, and when he reached the bottom, his wounds had reopened. But lying at the bottom of the ravine was his mask. Part of it. Part of it was missing. He had found the mother but the baby had been torn away.

He looked around for a place to rest. His search revealed a cave. He curled up and slept.

He was awakened by the shrieking of the monkeys. Outside the cave he saw the smoke. He put on the mask and rose above the flames. He saw the black bodies burning, huddled in the unity of death. He saw the soldiers laughing.

They did not see the bird circling overhead.

When the smoke cleared and the soldiers had left, the bird alighted. Prince collected the bones and took them to the cave. Heartbroken, he left the mask in the cave and returned to the mountain.

Afa gave birth to a girl. Her name was Eunysthee.

Many years later, after full-free came, the first Prince told his daughter the story of the mask and she left the mountain to search. She found the mask but the bones had disappeared. Then Eunysthee had a son whom she, in turn, named Prince. When Eunysthee fell sick, her father came down from the mountain and after she died he stayed to raise her son, Prince Johnson.

Midra took off the mask. Light as a feather, something settled on her shoulder. She knew what it was. A baby monkey. She knew by its weightlessness she would not be able to see it. Soon, she felt herself being surrounded. Seeing them did not really matter now, for they had come as an endowment of love. Her love for Prince Johnson and his love for his ancestors. By letting her feel their presence, wholly and completely, they were proving that she had overcome the limitations of her senses. That was Prince's gift, she realized now. He had brought her here that night, to this cave, and had set her senses free. Prince had shown her a way to overcome the limitations of time, space, and, yes, even memory. To open herself to feel the vastness of the spirits that had brought her life. And with that freedom an obligation to free the spirits of her ancestors, to give these spirits a voice. A voice that would resound in triumph. Not a lonely voice crying in the wilderness, but a chorus of African spirits walking through time with their heads held high. Held high because they had not been forgotten. Held high because each generation would resurrect them and remember them.

These spirits, now surrounding her with their silence, had endured in the silent memory of the village. It was time to acknowledge their presence wherever slavery had committed Africans to a prolonged muteness about their past. Anywhere that slavery had mutilated and obliterated the memory of Africans and replaced it with indecipherable muttering. Now that her own memory had been freed from the silence of history, this obligation to free the memory of the village, locked away in collective silence, scared and scarred by history, surged in her. By freeing the village of the fear of its own memory she would be able to free the spirits locked away in burnt bones. The effects of slavery must be talked about openly: around the kitchen table, in the bedrooms, in the plantation fields, the anger and pain must be confronted. By reclaiming the bones of their ancestors, the village, for the first time, would mourn together and that communal loyalty that traveled with them from Africa would endure. The mystery of that one night with Prince had taken her many years to grasp, but she had finally walked into the light.

EIGHTEEN

Midra told her mother, "We have to take possession of the gully. We gots to own it outright. We gotta make that place, that cave that hold them bones, we gotta make it a shrine. And we gotta make sure that every man-jack in this village go and see the fire we pass through."

"All that land belong to the plantation," Peata said. "How you go get it from them?"

"I don't know. But a way will come. Christine and Hart-seed will make it possible."

"If anybody can, God knows it's them two."

Midra began to braid her mother's hair.

"Ma?"

"What?"

"You think my father go come back from Africa?"

"It'd be a miracle if he reach."

Peata looked like a little girl. Midra laughed and went to her own room.

Her room still smelled of Brandon. His scent was so strong that she momentarily expected him to rise up from the bed and, as he often did when her back was turned to him, flip her dress over her head and make love to her.

Though he did not write often, he sent a money order for two pounds, fifteen shillings, every six weeks. Most of the money she'd hidden away. When Brandon came back, he wouldn't have to return to the plantation like so many who had wasted the money they made in the canal.

As she undressed, she let her hands roam across her belly. She wished she'd been able to give him a child, but after the miscarriage she never got pregnant again. She knew he wanted children, but he was the kind of man who wouldn't fight things beyond his control. Fortunately there was Hartseed. And Christine. If Hartseed and Christine were endowed with the same gifts as their father, maybe together they would find a way to wrest the gully from the plantation, restore the legacy of courage and fearlessness to their ancestors and in doing so chart a future of respect and honor for them all.

She wondered if Brandon would ever return to their marriage. The money he sent her was no guarantee. From his brief letters she did not know what to expect; they revealed nothing of his world in the canal, not even what he did there. He wrote only of their marriage and Prince Johnson, wanting to know if she still thought of him.

After her confession to him the dreams had stopped. She wished he were with her now. She could explain to him the kind of spirit memory that Prince had given to her, to the children. To them all. But to give him this gift, this gift of memory, she would first have to cleanse him of his jealousy of Prince. Prince the man.

Hartseed and Christine got out of school early. It was the last day before summer vacation and, perhaps, possibly the last day of school on the island for Christine. She would find out during the summer if she had won a scholarship to study in England. She had mastered every subject taught beyond the level reached by any other student of the school.

Putting up with the jealousy and resentment from the other girls had been difficult. Most of them, children of merchants, felt insulted that they had to sit in class with this wide-eyed girl from a plantation tenantry who came to school on many occasions without shoes. The other girls seized every opportunity to mock and make fun of her: pulling and threatening to cut off her "red knotty" hair, and taunting her with names like "Yam-foot" and "Mongoose." Christine never acted as though their behavior offended her. To retaliate might make her lose her scholarship. Eventually, she won them over.

During the years Christine had kept her promise to her mother, Vida, visiting every day, sometimes sleeping over on weekends. They would play warri or Hiddy-Biddy-Shut-Ya-Lap together with the other children or Riddle-a-Riddle until it was time to go to bed but while the rest of the house slept, mother and daughter would rise and wander outside onto the limestone steps at the kitchen door to watch the night fly by on watery wings as they talked and joked with one another. However, it was a worried Christine who arrived at her mother's house on the last day of school. Vida had been sick for four weeks now. After coming home in the rain, she had awakened the next morning with the right side of her face dead. She also developed pneumonia, which put her flat on her back with chills and thunder in her chest when she coughed. During the third night of her illness Vida coughed up blood, which sent her frightened husband scurrying to get Mabel Fields. Mabel brought with her some eucalyptus bush, which eased the thunder in Vida's chest, but nothing worked for the paralysis. The muscles on the right side of Vida's face began to atrophy, and her speech became grotesquely slurred. Still, incredibly, Vida managed to keep in high spirits, mostly because Christine moved in to take care of her.

Christine did not expect to find anyone else in the house when she came home. But her older sister, Marcelle, who now worked for a white couple as a maid, was there. Her other two brothers, Cecil and Samuel, worked on the plantation. Marcelle was sitting in the back door, her six-month-old son clinging to her neck as she peeled yams.

"You ain't work today?" Christine asked.

"I get half-day."

"How Ma?"

"She go be a lot better now you here."

"Why?"

"She been askin' all day if you get home yet. She ain't want nobody do nothin' for she but you. I give her food, she won't eat. Maybe she would eat it if you give her."

"She probably wasn't hungry."

"She was hungry. She just playin' the fool. She must be feel that you can cure she or something." Marcelle nicked herself with the knife. "Bloody hell!"

"Let me see." Christine bent down to help her sister. Blood began to drip from Marcelle's finger.

"Leave me alone."

"Look, Marcelle, I know why you gettin' on so. Stop worrying. Ma go be all right. She go get better. Believe me."

"How you know?" She began to suck her bloody finger.

"A feeling. Faith. Whatever you want to call it. But believe me."

Christine stepped over the bowl in the doorway and went to the bedroom.

She found her mother sitting up in bed, her face thin and misshapen. But Vida smiled when she saw Christine.

Christine sat next to her mother. The castor oil anointing her mother's head dribbled down her forehead and down the dead side of her face.

"How you feelin' today?"

"Be-be-t-ter."

"You sure? Marcelle say you won't eat."

"I-I not hungry."

"You have to eat." Pause. "Ma, I want to show you something."

Christine wiped the trickle of castor oil from the corner of her mother's eyes as Vida stared at her.

"You feel strong enough to walk?" Christine continued.

"W-a-lk? W-a-lk where?"

"The gully."

"The gu-gu-lly?"

"Yes."

Vida had not been into the gully since that night with Prince seventeen years ago. She remembered that night, and shame flooded in.

"No gu-gu-lly. No gul-ly. Not th-there."

"It's a special place I have to show you, Ma. A place Hartseed and me go. A place you need to see."

"What th-this p-place is?"

"Come along."

"No."

"Please, Ma."

"Tell m-me or m-me not g-g-goin'."

"A place that will speak to you. A place that will help you."

"—How?"

"Ma, you got to come."

"W-why?"

" 'Cause it will help!"

"H-how?"

"Ma, please! Just do it 'cause I tell you to. Please, Ma. Even if you don't think I know what I sayin', just do it. Please."

Vida gave in. Rising from the bed, she faltered momentarily, then steadied herself with Christine's help. Christine found her broad-brimmed hat under the bed. Vida squeezed the hat over the head-cloth holding the castor-oil-soaked pawpaw leaves. They set off slowly under a hazy sky.

It took them about fifteen minutes to get to the gully.

The heat, like lead, weighed them down, and Vida had to stop every couple of minutes to catch her breath. She was sweating by the time they entered the gully, but her chest felt better. When they reached the steepest incline, the treacherous gateway to the cave, Vida stopped and leaned against a tree.

"D-down th-there?"

"It ain't so bad, Ma. Once you start goin' down, it a lot easier than it look."

"G-girl, I must be be-be-witch."

Holding on to Christine's hand as tightly as she could, Vida made her way down the precipice. When they reached the bottom Vida was again out of breath, and Christine waited patiently for her mother to regain her strength before they entered the cave.

The air in the cave had a bitter taste, and Vida tried not to swallow as she followed Christine along the ledge. She was about to tell Christine that she wanted to turn back when a shard of light from the gleaming bones stiffened her legs. The cave suddenly felt warm and the radiance emanating from them drew her hypnotically. She was no more that a yard away from them when she stopped. She felt her eyes sucking in the vision of those black bones until she was so full she wanted to explode.

"What this, girl? Yo-you do-in' o-be-ah?"

"No, Ma."

"Lo-Lord, girl! Is what you in-vol-volve in?"

"These is the bones of our ancestors. You know the story about the Africans that get burn to death?"

Her mother nodded.

"This is the proof," said Christine. "This is the living proof. Touch them."

"T-t-touch?"

"Yes."

"Them l-l-ook like them would burn."

"Touch them."

Vida kneeled and reached out both hands. With her fingertips she grazed the bones as if trying to wipe away the gleam. First her fingers, then the palms of her hands settled on the bones. They were hot. The heat of a hundred years of tears locked away in silence; the heat of faith being transformed into memory. Vida felt the gleam. Felt the repossessing of time. Felt the repossessing of her spirit. Felt the blood flowing to her face. Felt the muscles waking up. Felt the joy.

Vida danced all the way home, her speech clear, her face no longer deformed.

Everyone was amazed at her sudden recovery. Mabel knew for sure it was her eucalyptus syrup that did it. Gunny's girlfriend asked Vida what obeah woman helped her. Vida just smiled and said, "Faith."

The next day Christine and Hartseed went to the cave to prepare for the future.

Hartseed entered first and sat on the stone throne. She sat next to him. His woolly red hair seemed to illuminate the dark cave. Six years had passed since the first day they had put on the mask. Midra and Peata and now Vida had been embraced by the spirits. It was time for the village to understand. Soon, in the middle of the day when the sun was most savage, people would gather in the shade of shack-shack trees to talk about the spirits that inhabited the gully and why they would not rest. In backyards, as they stoked fires to roast corn, women would discuss openly the whispers they had absorbed since they were children, no longer biting their tongues when the children asked how many of their ancestors had burned to death in the gully.

Christine knew there was only one way to make the whispers an everlasting shout.

She nudged Hartseed, who had closed his eyes.

"You sleeping?"

"No."

"You been quiet all day. Something wrong?"

"No." He paused. His sleepy eyes opened. He looked at her. When his nostrils flared like this, she knew he was troubled.

"Tell me what's wrong," she said.

"You go take the scholarship?"

"Them not give it yet."

"Them go give it. You know that."

"You don't want me to take it?"

"No."

"I have to take it, Prince. You know that."

"But you go leave me here."

"Not for long. I go come back."

"I don't want you to go away."

"I don't wanna leave you, Prince, but if them give me the scholarship, I have to go. I have so many things to learn. I know you understand that."

"Why everybody have to go away?"

"What you mean?"

"My father and now you."

She paused a moment, slowly understanding who he meant.

"He not your father."

"Almost. And yours too."

"Don't say that, Prince. He not your father."

Hartseed turned away from his sister, fixing his eyes on a shadow on the wall. Why was she talking like that? Like she didn't like Brandon. As he watched a white lizard struggle to escape a spider's web, he suddenly wished this whole thing with their father's life and their ancestors' memory was over. Despite all the things they had experienced and seen, Brandon was still the one who took them to the beach and made them kites to fly at Easter. Brandon was the one who helped him cut down mahogany to carve, the one he

woke up to every morning and said good night to before
he went to sleep.

"I'm sorry," she apologized.

"Never mind."

"You know better than to think that I want to go away
and leave you," she said, reading his mind. "Please understand."

"Suppose you don't come back?"

"That's nonsense!"

"Suppose you meet somebody in England and get married and stay there and have children, and I don't see you
again."

"I ain't go do nothin' like that."

"But suppose . . ."

"Have I ever lied to you?"

"You don't know what could happen if you go away."

"I ain't go let it happen."

"You promise?"

"I swear. No matter what, I go come back. I bet when
I come back, you be the one with children," she laughed.

"Not me."

"Oh, yeah. I see you helping Malcolm's granddaughter
carry home water two days straight. And you see how fast
them girls in that house does get pregnant."

"That ain't nothin'. I just happen to be walking by her
house when I see her with the bucket and I offer to help."

"If you don't be careful, you go soon be walking into
her house with a baby in your arms."

"She's only fourteen," he laughed, slapping her playfully. She pushed him down. He got up and wrestled her
to the ground. They rolled around on the damp floor, neither gaining an advantage over the other. His hands under
her dress did not alarm her at first, because often when they
wrestled, her clothes got mangled and his hands touched
just about every part of her body. But this was different.
This was no accidental touching. And the feelings that

flooded her brain surprised her. She knew she should attempt to push him away but couldn't bring herself to do it. He had her pinned to the ground and her body became supple and wanting, unable to resist his inquisitive hands. She closed her eyes and suddenly saw the soldiers laughing as they lit the fire. The woman warrior came before her as the fire surrounded them.

"Stop, Prince! Stop!"

He slackened his grip and she got up. He remained on the ground. She straightened her dress.

She climbed onto the ledge where the bones lay. He followed and found her crying.

"I'm sorry," he said.

"If I get the scholarship, I have to take it, Prince. You have to accept that."

He looked at her. "How much longer we have to keep this a secret?" he asked.

"Now that Ma and Grandma know and understand, it not go be long. The rest of the village will soon know."

"Why we don't just bring everybody down to the cave and show them the bones. When them see the bones, them blood bound to crack open. How they could forget what them eyes see?"

"That is true, but we can't move the bones. As them lay, so them stay. And before we bring people here, we have to make this place a shrine."

"But it already a shrine."

"No. The land ain't ours. Can't be our shrine 'til we own the land."

"You saying we have to buy the land?"

"Yes."

"Where the money go come from?"

"It will come."

"Maybe the plantation will give up the gully if we ask them nice."

"This ain't no joke, Prince. Besides, it ain't just the

gully. There's the land that butt and bound the gully. If the plantation don't know by now that fallow land is worthless, something go have to be done to hasten their decision.''

"I know you promised, but something keep telling me you ain't go ever come back here when you go away.''

"What more can I do?''

"Take me with you.''

There was a long pause.

"I can't stop you from coming if you want to.''

He put his head in her lap and closed his eyes. She rocked his head back and forth the way she rocked her sister's baby. He fell asleep.

Now that the time had come for them to pursue different paths, she realized that it would not be easy to leave him. She eased his head onto the ground and descended the ledge, then left the cave and climbed up the precipice. A languorous breeze greeted her near the stream, where a short man with long silver locks was kneeling. The man ducked his head into the stream and kept it there for a long time before sliding his entire body into the water. She watched, half-expecting him to not emerge again. But he did, shaking his locks and jumping up and down as if participating in some dance ritual. He was walking toward her now with his head down. He was almost on top of her before he stopped, raised his head, and spoke directly to her in a soft voice.

"You know who I is?''

Christine nodded. "And I know how you come to be here.''

"Yes. I suppose you do.''

"We have suffered for what you did, and Midra has suffered for what she did.''

"I know you have suffered and I am sorry. I beg your forgiveness. I cannot rest in peace until you forgive me.''

"We forgive you.''

The short man with long silver locks bowed his head and

walked past her. When she turned around, he had disappeared.

When Hartseed awoke, he found he was alone. As he left the cave he noticed that the shadow on the wall was still. The alabaster lizard had given up its struggle. Hartseed turned to see what the spider would do. The web had disappeared.

NINETEEN

At the Daughters of Zion Universal Revival Church, Ben Payne was joined by two men at the back of the church after the Sunday service. Horace and Julius, Ben's nephews, had recently returned from the Panama Canal and were excited about the prospect of becoming land owners. Midra sat listening.

The news that the plantation was inviting offers from anyone interested in buying the four lots of arable land that butt and bound the gully, with the gully and its hated inhabitants thrown in for good measure, was greeted with exultation in the village. Never mind that most of them could not afford a row of potatoes, far less half an acre of land. The Panama men had returned with money to burn, and those who hadn't spent it all on women and jewelry were already beginning to organize themselves into little groups to invest in the land.

Ben Payne was one of the few men who owned land in Monkey Road, and no one could remember seeing Ben working on a plantation. Horace, a nimble giant with a distilled, earnest voice, was the first of the triumvirate to speak.

"I have quite a bit of money," he started, "and I know there's a few people come back from the canal feel like me. We don't want to end up back in the situation we was in before we leave. I think we should get everybody in the village with money and buy all the land together. Form a little group to work the land and make the land work for all of us just like them people at the plantation do."

"But look how much land them people got," Julius interrupted.

"Ben," Horace continued, "you think we could raise enough money in this village to buy up all that land?"

"Me don't think so, son," replied Ben.

"I think we should take our money and buy what we can afford," said Julius.

"What you think we should do, Ben?" Horace asked.

Ben folded his hands into the pockets of his gray suit. He looked at the young men before him and saw himself multiplied by two. He looked first at Horace, a colossus who looked even bigger since his canal experience. Ben remembered him as being a quiet, moody boy. The canal had changed him. It must have something to do with the two fingers now missing from his right hand, Ben thought to himself. Ben cocked his head and looked into Horace's eyes. Nothing in the world would stop this one. He asked Horace whether he was prepared to fall in line if he could get a group of people together interested in buying land.

"What you mean by that?" Horace asked.

"You won't be the big man in the group," Ben replied.

"I don't have no problem with that," said Horace. "But you just say them ain't enough people in this village with that kinda money."

"I didn't say the people would come from Monkey Road."

"I don't get you, Ben."

"Monkey Road ain't the only place in this country that got people who want land, you know."

Horace laughed. "I know that."

"And there's been people here with money before you went to Panama," Ben continued. "You just happen to come back at a very strange time. A lucky time for you. Lately the plantation been getting attack left and right. I don't just mean the crops, I mean the great house too. All the horses get scare off the plantation. All the animals. The dogs. The cats. Everything. All the maids. Seems every night the monkeys turn up and create so much noise, not a soul can go to sleep, though nobody can't say for sure them see a single monkey. And now the whole village all excited 'bout that old story of them Africans who get burn to death down there in that gully."

"What you gettin' at, Ben?" Julius asked.

"I ain't sure meself, boy," Ben said. "I mean, you hear that story, as a boy, didn't you? I hear it when I was a boy, and I born long before you, so we know it is a old story. And nobody never make no big to-do 'bout it. But now everybody seem convince that them monkeys is the spirits of them Africans and is them terrorizing the plantation.

"And I suppose it catch the plantation at the right time. Things bad all over. All the plantations all over the country sufferin'. The people in the village catch onto that. Them never see white people make to look so foolish and them enjoy it. Whether the plantation believe them monkeys is really spirits, I don't know, but the result is they want to get rid of that gully and all the land surrounding it. If we can raise the money, we got weself some land *cheap*."

Julius stroked his beard. "But what you think, though, Ben? You think that story really true, or is just obeah somebody working 'pon the plantation? True, I hear 'bout them Africans getting burn up in that gully but it always sound like a joke-joke story to me."

"People make up all kinda stories, boy," Ben said. "All kinds. I ain't sayin' the story ain't true. I don't know. I wasn't there. But some terrible things get done to we people in them slave times. So ya can't blame people for wanting to forget 'bout them. But we also know that some things in life does have a reasoning behind them that ordinary thinking can't explain. So, if them monkeys is them African spirits come back for some kind of revenge, I certainly ain't go get in them way.''

"What is you true-true feeling, Ben?'' Julius insisted. "You believe them monkeys is really spirits?''

"Stranger things have happened in this village. Things that you and I ain't smart enough to ever figure out.''

"Like that time when all the Lady-in-the-Night trees just die out,'' Julius said. "And then spring up again without explanation. For all we know that was the work of them African spirits, too.''

"It so happened it was about that same time that them monkeys start to come into the village proper,'' Ben said. Julius had opened the door to his favorite memory: his wife. "Before that, them never used to leave that gully. All of a sudden them monkeys was all over the place. Coming all over people house like them ain't had no fear of nobody. It all started with my wife's death, if you remember.''

The church was empty except for Midra, who was sitting in the corner by the window. Horace could tell she was listening to their conversation. He started to walk to her but changed his mind as he heard Ben begin to evoke memories of his wife. He had to bring the conversation back to the land before Ben got carried away. When he got started, there was no stopping him. Right now all he wanted Ben to talk about was land. Nothing but land. And how they were going to get it.

"What about these people you know, Ben?'' he asked.

"I would have to talk to them,'' Ben said.

"Talk to them,'' Julius urged. "And soon. We have to get this done before them half-white merchants from town come up here and gobble everything up.''

"I have to tell ya the truth, Julius," Ben said. "Is them kinda people I talkin' 'bout."

"Who?"

"Them same people you just mention."

"Merchants?"

"Them is the only people with money to buy this much land."

"I thought you say is people you know who come back from the canal!" Horace exclaimed.

"Don't holler so hard in the church, boy," Ben said. "I know one or two of them kinds, too. You think the word ain't already get out that this land up for sale? Ya gotta move fast. And finding enough people with Panama money go take too long."

"I don't think I want to deal with them kinda people," Julius said.

"Don't worry, eh. You want to get land, right? You will get your land," Ben said.

"Why would them people wanna join with me?"

" 'Cause I tell them to."

"How you so close to them merchant people, Ben?" Julius asked with a laugh.

"Look, I know some people 'bout here think that the sun does rise and set in this village, but you two went outside and get a different view of things. Sooner or later this village go get open up. Split apart. People with different ideas and plans go come into it. You have to know how to walk amongst all kinds of people. Not just the people you grow up with. But in the long run you go find that everybody is the same. Them want the same things. Them half-whites from town ain't no different. Them is the same as you or me. I does go to them, and them does pay the same money for my goods. Them does eat plantain and potatoes just like you."

"Them don't cook them the same way, though," Julius laughed.

"Who does cook for them? Not people from little villages like ours?" Ben pointed out. "Them does try to live like white people that is true, but you would too if you was them."

"I don't think this is a good idea, Ben," Horace said.

"Don't worry," Ben said. "Leave it to me."

Midra got up from her seat by the church window. She had heard enough. Outside on the steps she took off her hat to let the sunlight warm and enrich her face. A sudden breeze touched her lightly, flowing swiftly under her dress when she arched her back seductively as if in worship of the eternal power of the sun.

She descended the steps and leaned against the trunk of the flamboyant tree in front of the church. The tree was in full bloom. Red and white blossoms crashed together in a seething tide of color. A regiment of black ants struggling up the tree trunk with a cockroach's leg caught her attention. Her eyes followed them, observing their patience and persistence with an object ten times their size until they reached the zenith of their ascent and disappeared into the rainbow of blossoms.

The three men emerged from the church still absorbed in their discussion. Midra caught Horace's eye and smiled. He acknowledged the invitation and moved away from the other two men. In a matter of strides he was standing next to her. The other two men stopped.

"I go catch up with you two later," he said.

Ben and Julius moved on.

Keeping his right hand in his pocket, Horace reached up and plucked a blossom most people would have had to climb the tree to reach. He put the blossom in his mouth, smiling as he chewed; his eyes fixed on Midra's bosom.

"You ever eat these blossoms?" he asked.

"A long time ago. When I was a child."

"I think them sweet, don't you?"

"I suppose."

"You don't like them?" he asked.

"I too big to eat blossoms."

He laughed. "You never too big for blossoms, girl." He picked another one and offered it to her. She refused it, and he put it in his mouth.

"I think you just eat an ant," she laughed.

"That's all right. Them always eating me up," he joked. He leaned against the tree trunk, swinging his large hand to lightly touch her dress at the waist. She moved away and began walking. He locked step with her.

"You was listening to we conversation," he said bluntly.

"Yes."

"Why?"

"What you decide?" she asked.

"Decide? About what?"

"The land."

"Why?"

"I want the gully."

"The what?"

"The gully."

He stopped, eyes darkening. "You want the gully? What you mean?"

"I want to own it," she said without stopping.

"Wait a minute!"

She continued walking. He caught up and stood in front of her, blocking her path.

"What's in the gully?" he asked.

"Nothin'."

"What you mean nothin'? Then why you want it?"

"I just want it. I like trees and monkeys."

"Who money you go use? Your husband?"

"Not your business."

"Aha!"

They walked on in mock silence. Midra could hear the

wheels turning in his head. She knew the giant was a generous man, but he was also a seducer and she would have to be careful dealing with him, at least until she was sure she would get what she wanted. He gripped her by the elbow, bringing her to a stop. She broke into a nervous sweat. She tried to avoid his eyes and looked directly ahead instead, putting her eyes in line with his massive chest. He was wearing a blue suit that hung loosely. It was too big for him. The thought made her want to laugh. Anything too big for this man was indeed too big for anybody. She found herself wondering what it would be like to be wrapped in one of his suits. She pulled away from him but he moved to block her way again.

"When he coming home?"

She made no reply, still trying to get around him. He blocked her at every turn. Trying to walk around him was like trying to walk around a moving shack-shack tree. She stood still and broke out laughing.

"You' husband know you want to use his money to buy worthless land?" he asked.

"Who tell you it worthless?"

"What's it good for? A few guava and cherry trees."

"If you open your ears, you would know what it good for."

"What you talkin' 'bout?"

"I talkin' 'bout honoring and respecting our spirit fathers."

"Them monkeys is really the spirits of them Africans?" he asked in a hushed voice as if he was afraid to utter the words.

"I need that land," she said.

He opened his mouth to say something but stopped. There was determination in her eyes that reminded him of the look in the eyes of many of the men he had met in the Panama Canal.

"You was there when the plantation people try to burn it a few months back?" he asked.

"Yes."

"It true what them say?"

"What them say?"

"You know, that the fire wouldn't burn. That as them light it the fire went out like God blow it out."

"If that is what them say, then that is what musta happen."

She stepped away from him to survey his massive frame. He was a beautiful man. A man like him, not married at his age and still living with his mother, would be a hard man for any woman to tame. She felt a tremor in her belly as she looked at him. It lingered there briefly, then it slid down to the apex of her thighs. Behind him the church stood, a dull white, glazed by the blistering sun.

"You know the story 'bout the slaves and that gully?" he asked.

"Everybody in this village know the story."

"You think it true?"

"You don't?" she replied.

"I always wonder 'bout it."

"Believe it. It true," she whispered.

He did not speak. His eyes dimmed, then closed and opened rapidly as if for a moment he was blinded by a bright light.

"How you know?" he asked.

"It true," she whispered again, lavishing the word *true* as if it put her in a state of ecstasy.

His eyes were fixed on hers, and his mouth opened and closed but no sound came. She trembled. A breeze came and lifted her dress-tail, playing with her ankles. Her ecstasy passed, and the dress once again settled in a heavy knot around her ankles.

They walked on, this time the silence between them deep as a shadow. When they came to his mother's house they stopped. His eyes searched hers, offering an invitation that she refused. Then he turned and walked through the open front door without a word.

In November, Midra got a letter from Brandon telling her that he would be coming home in a month. The next day the land put up for sale by the plantation was bought by a consortium of merchants from the city and a small group from Monkey Road including Horace and his brother, Julius. After the sale the new landowners got together in the Daughters of Zion Universal Revival Church to divide the land as agreed and to arrange the filing of the proper deeds. Horace and his brother got two acres of land next to the gully and, at Horace's insistence, the gully. One of the merchants wanted the gully so he could redirect the stream flowing there to irrigate his land, but in the end he gave in to Horace. The merchants, a group of three brothers, got most of the land, about fifteen acres; the rest was divided into quarter-acre lots that went to ten people from the village.

Midra agreed to meet Horace the next day. She left her house prepared to accept any offer he made, including the one she had refused before.

The gully was humid that morning, more humid than usual. The smell of ripe cherries hung on the damp air, and as she descended into the gully, she opened her nostrils wide to suck in more of the intimate scent. Reaching the stream, she sat on the dew-covered stone under the cherry tree to wait for Horace.

She did not hear him come up behind her. Feeling something brush her neck she turned and saw him there looking polished in a green shirt trimmed with gold, his eyes shining like brand-new pennies.

"Something tell me you'd be here first." He grinned.

"Something tell you right."

His laugh was happy. "This is yours, you know."

"How much?" she asked.

"How much what?"

"How much I have to pay?" she asked.

He picked a cherry and crushed the piquant fruit in his mouth, making noises like a little boy as he ate. He took off his shirt and pirouetted around her before settling smoothly onto the damp grass at her feet. She stared at his right hand with the two missing fingers. He tickled her toes with the three that remained. She laughed and drew her foot away.

"A woman like you shouldn't walk barefoot, you know," he said.

"And why not? You don't walk barefoot?"

"I's a man."

"And I's a woman."

"Let me wash your foot in the stream."

He took hold of her feet. She felt his strength and relaxed as he drew her feet to the warm water. While her feet soaked in the stream, he found a blackened dirt-stained stone on the bank that looked like it had been seared by fire. He washed the stone very carefully. She watched him and marveled at how dexterous he was with his right hand, though it was missing the thumb and index finger. Smiling, he painstakingly rubbed the stone with his hands, intermittently swishing it around in the water trying to dissolve the blackness. The stone still looked charred.

Horace set the stone on the grass next to him, then took her right foot in his hands and gently rubbed the sole, lingering to massage the tightly hooded calluses on her heel and big toe. Her toes tingled with the warmth that had traveled all the way up her calves to her thighs. She closed her eyes. When he applied the stone to her feet for the first time, she opened her eyes but drifted away again as he launched his assault on the hardened flesh, vigorously massaging her feet in quick stabbing strokes.

When she opened her eyes, he was lying next to her on the grass. Her whole body was now tingling. She sat up and stared at his supine body. His eyes were clear as the sky.

"Did I fall asleep?" she asked.

"I don't know. Did you?"

She looked at the bottom of her feet. The calluses were all gone and the flesh was soft and pliant. She caressed them for a long time in amazement.

"Thank you," she said.

"For what?"

"Why did you do it?"

"Wash your feet?"

"Yes."

"I had often dreamed of it."

"Washing my feet!" She laughed.

"It may sound funny to you but that is what I have dreamed."

"What else you dream?"

"Nothin'."

"And what else you want to do with me?"

"I done everything I dream I would do." He lowered his voice to a whisper as if reluctant to reveal a long-held secret.

She looked at his eyes again and wanted to kiss them. With moistened lips she leaned over and placed her mouth on his eyelid. Eyes closed, he did not flinch. She rolled on top of him. He could not budge her. Finally he gave in, and she locked him deep inside her, bracing her hands on his shoulders.

It was abundant and powerful. She stayed on top, waiting for him to swell inside her again. While she waited she licked the teeth marks she had left in his neck. That seemed to hasten his arousal because she could feel him swelling quickly. His renewal was a miraculous sensation, one she had never experienced before. This time she let him pin her to the ground, her legs locking around his neck as he gently fitted himself snugly between her thighs. His eyes were soft and smiling and she found this pleasurable. She locked her eyes to his with a passion that continued to stretch and grow as he surged to overwhelm her with his uncompromising power. She loved the strength, the quietness, the tautness of his movements. She had never felt so open. He took his time but with a sudden, quick burst of energy like a light bursting, it ended and he was quiet. She let her legs relax and cradled him in her lap.

The sun broke through the leaves and focused on them. They were already lathered in sweat. He sat up. She stayed on the ground, waiting for the sun to give her new life.

"You go stay like that all day?" he laughed.

"You still ain't tell me how much," she said, sitting up finally.

"How much for what?"

"I have to pay you."

"I told you. It's yours."

"This is something you see in a dream too?"

"What?" he asked.

"That you should give me this land."

"No. That money you have belong to your husband. What he go do when he come back and find that you spend his money buying land that is just bush and trees?"

"That is my business," she said.

He threw his shirt over his shoulders and fumbled with the buttons, muttering under his breath. He folded his arms across his chest. A look of pain flickered briefly in his eyes.

"If you know what it take for a man to go to that place and get back . . ." He paused. "One day, I was working my drill and them light a hole next to me. I was so intent on what I was doing, I didn't hear when them give the signal to clear the area. I look up and see somebody waving. Is then I realize what was happening. I see the fuse and I know I couldn't get away. I fall down on that thing fast, but not fast enough. The cap exploded in my hands. I was lucky. It coulda been worse.'' He paused again. ''You can't take the man money and use it like if he find it on the street.''

''I doing what I have to do,'' she said.

''I not sure I understand what it is you doing, but I telling you that the land is yours. You don't have to pay for it. It done pay for.''

''This is not a joke, Horace. Too much shame done lock away down here. I have to buy the land. Outright. The proper way. I would be shaming myself and my children if I accept the land like this. After what we just do. Them Africans that get burn to death down here dead without shame. And owning this land is one way to show them we ain't shame to be their offspring.''

''I think you making a mistake anyway. Trying to get these people to respect them dead Africans. Most people would rather not think about them days. And a hundred years from now, how many people you think go believe them had Africans who woulda rather burn than become slaves?''

She stood up. She thought for a minute of taking him inside the cave. She could understand why it would be hard for him to believe. Prince, a spirit messenger, had tossed her into that tiny space where spirit memory and dream overlapped, where there was no place to hide. It had taken sixteen years, but her memory had finally surfaced. This memory, dark as it was, illuminated their very presence on this island. It was their truth.

Horace watched her straighten her dress. The desire to make love to her again bubbled inside him. He was not surprised that she would not accept the land as a gift. She wasn't the kind of woman a man could buy with favors. There were plenty of women like that in the village, and since he had returned from the canal he had taken many of them to bed. His good fortune, he knew, came at the distress of other men. Some would come back and find their wives pregnant, bearing other men's children. The lucky ones would return to a stronger relationship than they had left. He suspected that Brandon was in the latter group, that despite her affair with him, Midra would welcome her husband back with a celebration befitting the prodigal son. But he would give anything to have her again, and again. He would give anything to have her forever.

"You still need to tell me how much you want for the land," she said.

"I tell you before, my portion of the deal would probably have come to the same with or without the gully. The plantation people just wanted to be rid of it."

She looked at him quizzically, smiling. There was no way he was going to convince her to take the land without paying for it.

"What you smiling at?" he asked.

"I ain't make love with you to get this land, you know," she said quietly.

"I know that. What if I tell you that I believe in what you tryin' to do, and this is my way of showing it," he said.

"If you ain't believe now, one day you will."

"I'm serious," he said.

After a long pause he continued, "I think it's funny that it take somebody who ain't even born in this village to come here and do something 'bout resurrecting the spirits that sleeping in this gully."

"I don't think them sleeping," she said. "Them been working in their own special way to get all we 'bout here to recognize them. I doin' what it fall on me to do. It don't have nothin' to do with me being born in this village or not."

"What you go do with this land?" he asked. "After you get it?"

"Show the people what really in here. What nobody ever

see before. Show them what really happen. Show them in a way that will leave no doubt in their minds. In a way them will never forget.''

"How is that?"

"Show them the burnt bones. People will come from all over the country to see these black bones that burned but did not crumble to dust. That survived fire and rain. And still as strong as if them was living bones.''

He looked stunned.

"So tell me how much," she said quietly.

"Where these bones?''

"In the cave.''

"How come nobody never see them before?''

"God have a time for everything," she replied.

"I want to see them," he said.

"Tell me how much.''

"Whatever you can pay me, I will take," he said. "I will not set a price for you. It's up to you. Whatever you give me, I will take it.''

"I have twenty pounds.''

"I will take it.''

For days talk swirled around the village about Midra's reasons for buying the gully. A rumor got started that she was looking for bones to make duppy-dust to work obeah. The village was ready to believe that somehow they had not noticed all along that Midra and her mother were obeah women. That is, until they saw the sign posted at the entrance of the gully. Christine wrote the words and Hartseed painted them on a piece of bleached board in black letters.

It read:

THIS GULLY, FROM NOW, SHALL BE CALLED
"THE SHRINE AT MONKEY ROAD"
THIS SHRINE IS DEDICATED TO THE AFRICANS WHO

WERE BURNED TO DEATH IN IT FOR THE LOVE OF
FREEDOM.
IN THIS SHRINE REST THEIR BONES.
TO VIEW THE BONES, SEE MIDRA.

The villagers floated around the sign like butterflies around a flower. A small group came to Midra and asked to see the bones. Midra sent Christine as their guide. Christine led them, with flambeaus aloft in single file down the dangerous incline.

From that day, there was a trail of villagers anxious to view the bones. Those who were skeptical before they entered the gully were miraculously convinced when they saw the blackened bones. People from nearby villages heard about the bones, came to see them, and believed.

TWENTY

Two days before Brandon was to come home, Mabel's fowlcock blew his trumpet four times at six o'clock. It was a Saturday morning and Mabel was making love to her husband. Mabel threw him off of her with such force that he fell off the bed. She ran naked to the kitchen window to find the fowlcock. He was nowhere in sight. She flew back to the bedroom.

"I don't see the fowlcock, Darnlee."

That was it, Darnlee thought to himself. That fowlcock had gone too far.

Darnlee got up from the floor, struggling with his rage and his khaki pants.

"Darnlee, today is Saturday. Where you goin'?"

Without a word he went out into the yard. He knew where the fowlcock was hiding. A brown hen he had just brought into the yard was setting behind the pigpen. The fowlcock would be there drawing up next to her. Darnlee went directly to the spot, grabbed the fowlcock by its neck, and with one quick flick of his wrist the body of the fowlcock flew into the center of the yard while the head remained in his hand.

Mabel was at the kitchen door when she saw the fowl-cock's body fly across the yard. She screamed and fainted.

Brandon's return was a day away. In his letter he had asked Midra to meet him at the wharf.

She had thought of writing to him when she bought the land but changed her mind. She decided it would be better to explain in person.

She was very excited about going to meet him, but she knew the trip home from the wharf would be critical. To let him come back to the village and be surprised by some-one else telling him what she had done would be unforgiv-able.

Christine had come up with the idea of a day at the beach. Midra liked the idea. Why not? Brandon loved the beach, and he deserved a surprise befitting his sacrifice for them. Many people had gone to the canal and not made it back; they were grateful that he was not one of them.

The family was just as excited about the day at the beach as the homecoming; they pitched themselves wholeheart-edly into preparing food for the occasion. For a while Ma-bel and Darnlee were not on good terms after his slaying of her fowlcock, but it didn't prevent them from working together on a special batch of black pudding. Peata dressed a leg of pork in fiery spices, leaving it to season overnight for roasting next day. Christine's scholarship to study med-icine in England had come through, upsetting Hartseed to tears, but together they grated coconut for Midra to make cassava pone. Sorrel was boiled, brewed, and sweetened with spices and sugar. The smell of nutmeg and cinnamon filled the house that night, mingling with their hopeful laughter.

. . .

During the time he had been in Panama, Brandon had not written as often as his mother had expected. The embarrassment of relying on Midra's haphazard reports to find out how her son was getting along in the canal was tempered somewhat by the money Midra gave her as coming from Brandon. For a while, though, she had refused to speak to Midra after it became clear that she had used Brandon's money to pay for that useless piece of land. Maybe there were African spirits in that gully that needed to be soothed, but did it have to be her son's money that soothed them? Mabel had finally given in to her curiosity and gone to see the bones, and yes, there was a certain feeling she got when she saw them. A feeling of fear more than anything else. But strangely, after that day, she began to remember her grandmother's stories of slavery. How the plantation didn't want to pay them for working after full-free came, and how, when they did get their money, it was always short because the plantation did not think they could count. She remembered her grandmother laughing as she told this story. What the plantation didn't know was that a few of the slaves had secretly learned to read, write, and count numbers too. So, these ex-slaves went to the great house, with a whole parcel of workers, demanding the rest of their money. The police were called in and the workers were arrested, but the plantation never short-paid them after that. Still, was it necessary to buy all that useless land to show people that Africans' spirits were strong and everlasting?

She was also aware that the canal had a way of changing many of those who went there. Precious few returned as nice and as uncomplicated as when they'd left the village. Young men she had seen grow up to be decent and respectful came back from the canal with an impatient stare and a new reticence. It was their aggressive stance, however, which caused the most concern in the village. These young men were quick to fight, sometimes about little things, and their anger was not easily charmed away by the good sense and persuasiveness of their elders. As Mabel worked side by side with her husband cleaning the pig's belly to make black pudding, she could not help but wonder what kind of man her son had become. The fowlcock's crowing worried her. What if Brandon brought with him the same anger and aggression that followed some of the other young men home? How would he react to Midra's doings? As she left Peata's house that night, Mabel was uneasy.

Brandon was to arrive at the harbor at seven in the morning. Midra stayed up all night baking, finishing just before four o'clock, which was the time she had planned to leave for the wharf. After wrapping a large piece of saltfish and some biscuits in a piece of white cloth, she dressed carefully in a yellow cotton dress, a white hat, and a pair of white shoes given to her by Pastor Williams' wife. Shortly after four she set off in solid darkness to meet her husband.

Hartseed, who had stayed up with her, offered to accompany her to make sure nothing happened along the way, but she refused.

She walked briskly through the sleeping village. Then, flanked by twisting blades of canes, she settled into a leisurely gait that would take her to the city in three and a half hours. The cane blades swept her along for two miles. The silence of the fading stars and the singing of the cane blades in the vigorous wind were her only company as she sucked the salt from the fish while she walked. She had forgotten how cool it got in the early morning hours, and the chilly wind nipping her neck spurred her to walk faster. One of Brandon's wool jackets would do nicely now, she thought, as she pulled her hat tighter on her head. Brandon had taken his two jackets to Panama. He had taken all of his clothes, actually, leaving nothing behind. Many times, during those nearly three years, she had found herself wishing he had left her something. Anything. Even an old hat. Something she could touch occasionally to remind her that even though he was far away he was still close to her.

When he told her of his decision to go to the canal, she'd cried and begged him to stay. But he quietly made his arrangements and, when the time came, packed his borrowed suitcase and left. There was nothing she could do. His leaving was an indication of the depth of his pain and anger, made more so by her inability to offer any explanation for her actions other than revenge.

Whatever drove her to poison Small Paul was the same force that compelled her to buy the gully with her husband's money. And now, as she stepped over a large stone in the road, kicking up the loose gravel with the tip of her shoes, she knew that if she wanted to win him back she must find a way to explain what that force was.

Her brisk walking was beginning to warm her, but the shoes had started to pinch her toes. After a few more painful steps she decided to take them off. Though a size small, they were pretty, and she had wanted to meet him looking her best. She walked on barefooted.

She had traveled about three miles through the villages of Mount Pelle and All Saints before she met two women who were also on their way to the capital to sell their load of yams, potatoes, and pumpkins. The women proffered a friendly greeting to Midra as they passed her. Midra smiled, offered an equally warm greeting, and settled in behind them. In spite of the load on their heads the two women walked very quickly, but she had no trouble keeping up with them. They kept this formation for a while—the two women in front of her chatting with each other, Midra a few steps behind them—before Midra realized one of them was limping. She was about forty years old, a rather tall woman with a thick neck and sloping but sturdy shoulders. The problem seemed to stem from an impairment in her

right hip, which caused such a pronounced limp that Midra
was surprised she had not noticed it right away.

Midra quickened her pace and drew alongside the
women. She offered them some of the saltfish and biscuits.
The one with the limp took a chunk of the saltfish and
began chewing vigorously. The other woman declined but
offered Midra a piece of ham skin. Midra found it pungent
and spicy, just the way she liked.

"You goin' to town?" Midra asked.

"Where else would we be goin' so early in the mornin'?" the other woman answered. She was also tall—
younger and more slender, with a supple-looking back but
a large, grim face. Her face seemed to be slightly out of
proportion to her body, as though it were swollen. She did
not smile as much as the woman with the limp, who
laughed constantly; sometimes, Midra thought, she seemed
to be laughing just to hear herself. It was a lively laugh,
however, that spun a web of cheerfulness around them as
they walked. As soon as one web would evaporate, the
woman with the limp would laugh again, spinning another.
And she did not laugh at anything in particular, at least
nothing that was said, because sometimes the laughter came
at moments of silence. The other woman was obviously
used to this and neither commented nor turned her head in
surprise.

"I goin' to meet my husband," Midra said. "He comin'
home from the canal today."

The woman with the limp laughed. Midra heard a trill
of pain in her laughter this time.

"What you' name, honey?"

"Midra."

"I's Dorian. And my friend here is Janetha. Where you
from?"

"Monkey Road."

Dorian laughed. "Oh, that village with them crazy monkeys? It true what they say 'bout that village?"

"What they say?" Midra asked.

"That them monkeys make the plantation sell the land to the people in the village."

"I don't know who make them sell the land, but it true. They sell us some of the land."

"What about them bones them say them find in a cave? That true too?"

"That's true."

"We been meaning to come up there and see them bones, ain't that right, Janetha? I hear them bones black as night."

"You been meaning to go, not me," Janetha said. "The only bone I want to look at is a cooked ham bone." Janetha and Dorian laughed together.

"Them say them is bones of slaves that get burn up. You ain't want to see what slave bones look like?" Dorian laughed.

"Slaves bones look any different to bones from anybody else?" Janetha asked.

"I don't know. That's why we should see them bones," Dorian said.

"I don't believe them is bones from no slaves," Janetha said.

"Tell her, Midra. You seen them bones, ain't ya?"

"I seen them, yes."

"Them is slave bones, right?"

"No," replied Midra.

"Who them is then?" Dorian asked, looking confused.

"Them is bones of people that burn, all right. But them wasn't no slaves. Them was Africans but them was free."

"Well, looka here. You was right, Janetha," Dorian laughed. "Them ain't no slave bones after all. Them is free bones."

"I still don't believe that story," Janetha said.

"Janetha is a very skeptical woman," Dorian said. "One time I get a nail-juck, and before she would believe that a nail juck me, I had to bring the nail and show her my blood on it. But she's still the best friend I have 'cause without her I wouldn't be here today. Right, Janetha?'' Dorian put an arm around Janetha, who hugged her back.

"Yes," Dorian continued, "this woman here is responsible for me being alive today. You husband a nice man, Midra?"

"I think so," Midra answered.

"You lucky. I had a bitch for a husband. He dead now, thank God. In that same canal you husband coming from. He went there about three years ago, and I pray to the Lord to keep he there. And when I get the news he get kill I ain't shed a tear for the wretch, I tell ya. My eyes did dry as you see them now. That man would not leave me in peace. See this hip here? He's the body do this. He break my hip, and had not for Janetha he woulda kill me, I swear. I always feel I get married too young. Too young, yes. When we get married he had a decent job as a shoemaker, but no sooner than we get married he start losing customers because he won't do the people work on time. He would spend so much time peeping behind me, he couldn't work. Everywhere I go the man would be behind me. Even if I say I goin' by my mother, the man would find a reason to follow me. If I go to pass water, he want to see what color it is.

"I get so fed up with it that I threaten to leave him. And that is the first time he hit me. From then it was one beating after another. One day he even beat me right here, between my legs. The thing did swell for days. He did sorry after 'cause I use that as a excuse not to let him touch it for a fortnight. I wanted to kill that man, ya hear, but in truth I didn't have the gumption. Instead I do something that I don't know how I do it up to this day. There was this white man at the plantation who I know had his eyes on me. He was always brushing next to me and telling me fresh things that I always used to ignore. To tell the truth he wasn't a bad-looking man. He was young and slim with real curly hair. I liked him, but you know that them only want one thing from we. But this one evening I decide to stay after the gang get knock off, and it didn't take the white man long to figure out why. Anyway, after we finish, I didn't even feel shame. I feel kinda relieve, ya know, 'cause I decide there and then I wasn't goin' home to me husband. I went back to me mother. Ya shoulda seen my husband, the way he come begging me to come back, but I refuse. But something happen to me that I didn't expect. The white man get me with child. My husband did trying so hard to get me with child, and it take one juck from a white man in a field of canes and I get with child.

"Life is something, eh, Midra? Midra, girl you sure got a pretty name. When my husband find out that I was with child, he think the child was his, and you should see the way he get on. Like he get a present from God self. And he begging me more and more to come home. And like a fool I decide to go back 'cause in my heart I hoping that maybe this baby is really me husband own. But it wasn't to be. When the baby born, my husband take one look at it and nearly dead. He went crazy. He take up the first thing he hand land on and he hit me. It was a iron stake. The blow land right on my hip and break it. I fall down and start screaming bloody murder, and Janetha and she husband hear me and come running. They drag my husband off me and take me and the baby to their house.

"But that wasn't the end. The man keep hounding me every day is God send. He threaten to kill me and the baby. Luckily the white man see the little girl, fall in love with her, and take her to live with him. I was so scared, I never leave the house without somebody with me. And most of the time it was Janetha. She was my protection. Thank God for that Panama Canal. When he left for the canal, I pray that he wouldn't come back. And the Lord answer my prayer."

Midra offered Dorian the cloth with the saltfish and biscuits and she accepted it. After stuffing a chunk of saltfish into her wide mouth, Dorian passed the bag to Janetha. This time Janetha took a small piece of saltfish from the bag. She rolled it in the palm of her hand to dust off the salt, and then she sucked it slowly into her mouth, spitting occasionally to get rid of the remaining salt. She passed the cloth back to Dorian, who took another nugget of saltfish before passing the cloth back to Midra.

"You must be happy you' husband coming home, eh?" Dorian said.

"I think so."

"You think so?" Dorian laughed. "I really hope that husband of yours keep on treating you nice. You never know what you in for with some of these men. Some of them just don't know how to treat a woman. That is why I have to thank God I have a friend like Janetha, you understand what I mean? I would be in the madhouse had not for she." Dorian hugged Janetha and the women laughed together.

Midra found Dorian's laughter liberating. She felt Dorian's fingers searching for hers, and she clasped the woman's hand instinctively. The three women walked on confidently.

By the time they reached the capital the women were sweating and their faces shone. The town was still half-asleep. Only a few men on bicycles gave a hint of life. Low pink buildings huddled together around the river like women doing their wash. A huge manchineel tree sat in the middle of a square, giving shade to a fountain set a few feet away. The fountain was dry. Behind the fountain was a bridge where the women stopped to say good-bye.

"If you ever come to Monkey Road, ask for Midra. The woman who own the bones," Midra said.

"You! Them bones belong to you?" Dorian exclaimed.

"Them don't really belong to me, but people say so. So

I don't argue. Them on my land, that's all."

"Is them real African bones?" Janetha asked.

"Them is real African bones," Midra replied.

"How you so sure?" Janetha persisted.

"If you see them, you would know."

Janetha shrugged noncommittally.

"We go definitely come. Right, Janetha?" Dorian laughed out loud. The two women left Midra standing in the street and walked away toward the square where the hawkers were gathering to display their harvest.

A crowd of people was standing around the wharf when Midra got there. It seemed as though the boat had already docked. Men with dirty faces and little suitcases were hugging women. Women in Sunday dresses and pretty bonnets were crying.

Midra put on her shoes when she spotted someone who looked like Brandon standing by the edge of the loading dock. The man was puffing hard on a pipe. She had not known him to smoke; this was something new. He looked gaunt and his shoulders drooped slightly.

She was upon him before he saw her. "Brandon."

He turned to greet her. His smile warmed her immediately, and she threw her arms around him. He held her gently at first, then as tenaciously as he had been smoking. She clung to him. Hand in hand they left the city behind them.

Brandon took off his jacket and unbuttoned his shirt as he began to sweat. Midra likewise took off her hat to let the wind flood her hair.

They had walked about two miles when Brandon suggested they stop to rest. A cluster of flamboyant trees with large roots spread out above the ground offered them shelter from the sun. Brandon sat down on a root-bench and pulled Midra to sit in his lap. She giggled and playfully pulled away, making him chase her around the tree for a while before she gave in. She leaned against his heaving chest and felt the sweat running down his shirt. Midra could smell the sea. Brandon's arms circled her waist as he drew her closer to him. His arms felt stronger than she remembered; his body was a thin slab of iron.

"Why you start smoking?" she asked.

"Loneliness," he replied. His eyes hardened. "Loneliness and fear. I missed you."

"I bet you miss the sea too," she laughed.

"You bet!"

"Want to go?"

"You know what I want," he said, tickling her.

She lost her balance and fell off his lap to the ground, still laughing. He fell on top of her.

"Brandon! It's broad daylight!"

"Since when that bother you?" He grinned.

"Since them have all these houses 'round here, and I don't know who watching us."

"Nobody can't see us from here. Not with all these trees blocking the view."

Her struggle was unconvincing. Using his strength to pin her arms at her side he mashed his mouth to hers. The force and the power of his attack amazed and stimulated her. She soon realized that his hunger was of a temper that could have come only from months and months of abstinence, and she wanted to give herself to him in every way.

He rolled off her when he had finished, and she lay there looking up at the red flowers hiding the sun, feeling the last gasping winds of the storm that had just teased her. He smoothed her dress down over her thighs and leaned against the tree to catch his breath.

He lit his pipe.

"Brandon?"

"Yes."

"I have something to tell you."

"I have something to tell you, too," he replied.

She was still lying on the ground. Beneath her the grass was cool and a blade tickled her ear. She shifted her head to get away from the unruly strand of grass.

"Something very strange happened to me this morning on the way home," he said. He took a huge drag on the pipe. "Very strange."

She turned to look at him. "Strange? How?"

"A couple miles before we reach the harbor, the schooner hit a little boat. It was night. I look over the side of the schooner and see a man in the water. I jump overboard to help him but he refused. He was hurt but wouldn't come aboard the schooner. The captain didn't want to leave him out there, but the man insisted that he wasn't leaving his boat. I felt bad about leaving him. I don't think he go make it to shore. But the strange thing was I felt he looked familiar. Like I seen him somewhere." He paused.

"You couldn't force him to come aboard?"

"He was like a mad man. Said he would jump overboard if we made him leave his boat."

"Where you seen him before?"

"I don't know." A long pause. "You say you have something to tell me?"

"Yes."

"What?"

"It's about the money."

"What money?"

"That you send."

"What about it?"

"I use it."

"I send it for you to use."

"I know, but I use it all."

He was silent. A man escorting a horse strolled past the tree, and the animal stopped to pluck at a hairy green shrub. The man nudged the horse on.

"You spend all that money?" There was no anger in his voice, only bewilderment.

"Yes. I know it was a lot of money."

"Yes. And I work hard as hell for it. I never work so hard in me damn life, ya hear me. Them people make you work even when ya sick. Them ain't have no feelin' for ya at all. What you buy with all that money?"

"Land."

"Land? Where you get land to buy?"

"The plantation."

"Wait, you tellin' me you buy a plantation?" He began to laugh.

"No, I ain't buy a plantation. It's a long story. But the plantation started sellin' off some of the land that butt and bound the gully, and some people who had money get together and buy some."

"How much land you buy?"

"I buy the gully."

"You do what?" He jumped up. "You do what?"

Midra sat up.

"Sit down, let me tell you the whole story."

"You buy the gully? Is this a joke?"

"Sit down, let me explain."

"Explain what? You have to be jokin'!"

"Sit down."

"No, I ain't sitting down. This is a joke, right? Just tell me this is a joke."

"It ain't no joke. Sit down and I will explain."

He sat down.

"I ain't even sure I know where to begin. I guess everything start with Prince."

"Prince! Prince been dead for sixteen years. Ya mean this man go always haunt me, Midra? My God! I left to go to the canal 'cause I was tired of this man ghost coming into our bedroom. I wanted some peace from this man. After three years I come back and find out that this man

GLENVILLE LOVELL

ain't really dead at all. He been spending my money to buy worthless land!''

Brandon was close to tears. The last name he wanted to hear was that of Prince.

"We go settle this once and for all, Midra. I ain't running from this man ghost no more. I spend three years in hell; I was dead and come back to life so there ain't nothin' Prince have on me." He broke a branch from the flamboyant tree, and Midra thought he was going to hit her, but he flung it across the field, then retrieved it and broke it into many little pieces.

He returned to the shade of the flamboyant tree with tears streaming down his cheeks, his face sweating and distorted from the exertion and distress. He sat in silence.

"I will tell you the whole story," Midra began, "but you have to promise not to interrupt me."

"I don't have to promise you one blasted thing."

"Please, listen to me, Branny, and when I finish you can do whatever you feel like doing."

"I don't know what I feel like doin'."

Midra began slowly. "There's some things that just can't stay hidden no matter how proud you is or how hurtful them may be. That is what I realize from all this. You know part of the story already, but there is part I couldn't explain to you before that I can explain now. Prince do something to me that no other man coulda do at the time but he. And it take all these years for me to know what it all mean. In that one night that I spend with Prince he make me soar like a dream. He lift me out of myself. I didn't know until lately meself what it was I had experienced that night. But he opened me up in a way that no matter how I try to I couldn't close up again. He plant seeds of wonder, and I couldn't ignore the questions them bear. Am I who I think I am? Are we who we think we are? If you don't really know who you is and you accept what everybody say you is, what does happen when you come face-to-face with another picture of yourself? So now you confuse. The confusion bring you to tears, but you can't shake the confusion. You have to deal with it. That is what Prince do to me that night. He plant questions and he leave a story. Prince show me the middle part, and it take me this long to find the beginning. Now I know the beginning. And it beautiful. Ugly but still beautiful. We only know the ugliness. Prince help me find the beauty of the beginning. And now the children know. And the rest of the village. And when you get home you will see what I mean. From now on the people of Monkey Road will walk with them head higher than the mile trees.''

She glanced at him. His eyes were closed and his face had tightened even more. As she began to chronicle the events leading up to buying the land, the buoyant confidence she felt walking to the capital with Dorian and Janetha returned. She told him everything that had happened since he left for the canal, including her affair with the giant.

His silence continued for a long time after she had finished. Finally, he stood up. She searched his eyes once more for a sign of understanding. A look of forgiveness.

''You go ever get this man outta your head?''

''He ain't in my head, that's the point. He's part of my spirit. Of all of us. That's what I tryin' to tell you. I loved Prince. I still do. But in a different way to the way I love you. You're here. I need you. Look at the children. Look at the village. Take a look at the bones. That is what Prince mean to me. I waited a long time for you. Them years you was in the canal was the loneliest I ever spend.''

''I need a drink,'' he said and walked off toward the road.

They came to a brightly painted shop at the side of the road and Brandon went inside. Midra remained outside leaning against the door. An old woman sat on a rickety bench in the corner. A thin girl with saucy eyes in a faded blue dress waited behind the counter. Brandon ordered a shot of rum and gulped it down. Before the fire could engulf his throat he swallowed another one and waited for the explosion in his blood. It came suddenly and the shock made him gasp for air. He took a deep breath and ordered another one. The old woman was rocking back and forth in the corner. He saw her throat move in unison with his as he swallowed. He bought her a drink and she panned a toothless smile of gratitude. He left the shop feeling an inch taller.

When he stepped outside, Midra was crying. He sat on the steps. The old woman came to the door and looked out.

"What you crying so for, dearie?" she quivered. "You got too nice a husband to be crying, honey."

Midra burst out laughing. She leaned into him as they walked off, and he made no attempt to push her away.

TWENTY-ONE

They arrived in Monkey Road after eleven o'clock. The rest of the family was waiting outside the house. Hartseed and Christine could not hold back their excitement when they saw them turn onto the little walkway. They ran to Brandon and flung themselves on him with such force that he almost toppled over. He righted himself and hugged them fervently. His mother and father, as well as Peata, greeted him with hugs and they all moved inside.

The house smelled like always. Just like he remembered it. Pork and spices.

"I just finished making the pudding. Good timing, eh?"

"I ain't hungry right now, Ma," Brandon said.

"You ain't what? Boy, don't make me laugh! You think I work all morning on this pig belly for you to tell me you ain't hungry? You go have some of the pudding right now, you hear me? And then it's off to the beach."

Happiness filled the house.

At the beach Brandon wandered off by himself. He needed some time to think about what Midra had told him. He had thought of buying land, but the land he wanted was to grow sugarcane and vegetables, not to raise monkeys.

He settled about a hundred yards or so from the others. Sitting on the beach he watched the lazy waves roll up to his toes, soaking them in fresh sea-wine. The sun battled surging gray clouds of rain. During his years in the canal he had often thought of this day. He had endured the suffering, the bouts with malaria, the days when it rained nonstop until he was no longer sure what day of the week it was. Had he endured all that to come back to this? Prince again? No! He had worked through the blasted wind and rain, through storms that threatened to swallow him; he had worked on with thoughts of his wife and the promise of a new beginning. A beginning without Prince.

He cast a long glance at Hartseed and Christine playing in the water. "As much Prince's children as mine," he muttered to himself. But then he smiled, just as he had smiled walking through the village on his way to the beach. Brandon had felt a difference in the posture of the people he met, a miraculous boldness in their eyes and a graceful confidence in their stride that wasn't there before.

By mid-afternoon the sun had grown in brilliance, and the threatening rain clouds finally fled, leaving nothing but an azure sky holding court with blue salt-tipped waves. Brandon felt his skin relax as it got hotter. It was as though he had been tightly wrapped in a blanket that was now slowly unraveling. He stayed another hour in the sun, then moved to a cooler spot under the shade of an almond tree and spread himself out on the sandy grass. The sound of the waves crashing against the rocky cliff that rose twenty feet to his left was soothing, drowning out the sound of train whistles and power drills still reverberating in his head. He suddenly wanted nothing more than to follow his wife into the water and make love to her.

He remembered the night that really changed their relationship, the night she took him down to the gully, where he experienced for the first time the liberating magic of submission—the wonderful feeling of giving himself over to her pleasure. Outdoors she was the sexual aggressor, he the willing purveyor, her supple instrument, doing what it took to pleasure her. Indoors Brandon became the aggressor and she acquiesced to his needs. He enjoyed this dual role, and on humid, shapeless nights in the canal he had dreamed about it even as he'd wrestled to understand how she could have killed a man.

But he had almost left all his dreams in the canal—where the sun had been no match for the rain, where the rain re-created everything in its own image, where his friend Kanga had died one Monday evening—in the very place he had gone after swearing that nothing could make him leave his wife.

Kanga had helped him get one of the better-paying jobs in the canal, driving rivets into the massive steel locks that would control the gates. It was dangerous work. Like the other West Indians who had made the odyssey from Jamaica, Trinidad, Barbados, Saint Vincent, Martinique, from cities, towns, and little villages—bouncing to Panama on the ripple of their own laughter and the trill of pregnant women they'd left behind in search of money—he found that the canal held out money in one hand and death in the other. He had seen two people fall to their deaths in one day. One of them was Kanga, who landed on a spike that pierced his neck. When he scrambled down to his friend's side, Kanga was still alive. Blood was spurting from his neck like a fountain. He had screamed for help and could think of nothing to do but clamp his mouth on his friend's neck to stop the blood from flowing. But Kanga had died before help could come.

His own story almost became a postscript one Friday morning about six weeks later. Standing on the scaffold some seventy feet above the canal floor, waiting for his partner to arrive with more rivets, he suddenly felt himself floating through space. The fall was so quiet and quick that he had no time to think. But there was enough time to see the angel that grabbed him. Dark and beautiful, she had grabbed him by the foot and placed her body between his and the cart filled with soft wet earth. Emerging from the cart, half his body dyed earthbrown but miraculously unhurt, his first thought was of his wife. After that incident it took him only a few days to decide to come home.

He could run from Prince no more. Prince was dead and he was alive. Prince's nature was strong, evident in his children, and his spirit was enduring, evident in the effect it had on his wife and the village; but maybe Prince's spirit made him stronger too. He had returned from Panama, where many men had left their dreams, their smiles, and their restlessness. Here he was, watching his wife play with the youngsters in the water. When he considered the many men who must have tried to steal his wife while he was away, he knew it was a miracle that she was there to meet him at the harbor when he arrived. She was still his. Yes, maybe Prince's spirit made him stronger too. He smiled and went to sleep.

It was late when he woke up. The wind that nudged him was cool and insistent. It rustled the leaves of the almond tree and raised the tiny hairs on his arms erect. The blue sky had given way to a sheet of purple and yellow as the sun slid toward night. The sea was calm. Dark plumed birds circled overhead, occasionally flying close to the water in uneven formation, then dipping their beaks into the gentle waves in search of food before climbing quickly into the air. He watched the birds play hide-and-seek with the waves, half-mesmerized, half-asleep. He got up and stretched, then ran headlong into the sea, bracing himself for the shock. The salt water stung his eyes. Closing them, he dove as deep as he could go, staying under until his lungs felt like they were about to burst. He surfaced, mouth open, grabbing the air—heart pounding and arms flailing, sending a school of sprats scattering in a thousand different directions. He took a deep breath, filled his lungs to capacity, and made another dive, this time keeping his eyes open, trying to reach the bottom. He saw the dull ivory of the seabed before him and touched it with his tongue, scooping a mouthful of sand before surfacing triumphantly. He washed his mouth with seawater and then swallowed three gulps and waded back to the shore.

On reaching the grassy bank he turned around. A familiar-looking boat drifted off-shore. It was about two hundred yards away but he was certain it was the same one. He ran back into the water and swam furiously toward it. When he reached it he found the man lying, barely conscious, in the bottom of the boat.

As quickly as he could, he navigated the boat to the shore where his father and Hartseed helped him push it onto the sand.

When Peata saw the man, she screamed.

"Dove! Oh, my God! Dove! Dove!"

"You know him?"

"Dove! Midra, it's Dove!"

Brandon looked at the man and then at Midra and saw the resemblance.

"Dove? It's Peata. You've come back!"

The man struggled to get up but he was too weak. He spoke in a faint voice.

"Peata? It really you?"

"Yes, Dove. It's me."

"The baby?"

"Why you take so long to come back, Dove? Where you went?"

"The baby. I want to see the baby."

"The baby? What baby? The baby is a woman."

"I came back to see the baby."

"Look, she here. Come Midra."

Midra knelt beside the man. His tree arms had withered

away but his eyes still smiled. He held her hand.

"Where you been, Dove? Why you now come back?"

"Africa. I made it there and back. And I seen my baby."

He squeezed Midra's hand, then dropped it.

"He's dead," Brandon said.

Midra led Brandon into the gully. "I go bury my father down here," she said.

"Yes, I think that's good." Pause. "You never tell me your father went to Africa."

"You believe him?"

"Why not?"

"If he really went to Africa, why he come back?"

"To see you. Ain't that what he said? You ain't glad he come back?"

"He shoulda stayed there."

"You don't mean that."

Pause. "No."

"Ain't you glad?"

"I suppose. But now he's really dead. Before, even though I didn't know him, had never seen him, he was always living. Now he's dead."

"No, he ain't. What I mean is it's up to you. You kept him alive before. Why you go let him die now?"

As they were leaving the gully something darted in front of them and clambered up a mile tree.

"Look!" Midra shouted. "There! In the trees. A baby monkey!"

Midra waited to see if the mother would appear to join the baby sitting quietly on the branch not far above their heads. But the mother did not appear.

"I think it by itself," Midra said without surprise.

Inside the cave the bones continued to glisten.